PROTECTED

JACOBS FAMILY SERIES
BOOK 2

VANNETTA CHAPMAN

Cover design: Ken Raney
Interior design: Caitlin Greer
Printed in the United States of America
First printing, 2015

ISBN-13: *978-1511883993
ISBN-10: *1511883995

Praise for *HIDDEN* (Book 1)
Jacobs Family Series

"*Hidden* is a great addition to the world of romantic suspense! ~ Brittany, Suspense Sisters Reviews

"Superb imagery and intricate details pulled me right into the story and gripping suspense kept me on the edge of my seat" ~Buzzing About Books

"Poignant, composed with sensitivity, compassion and artistic expression, this is a compelling book you won't soon forget!" ~Nancy, BookFun

"The pace of *Hidden* is constant and fast." ~Chat with Vera

"The spiritual themes woven throughout really brought everything home for me." ~Books, Music and Life

"Vannetta Chapman ramps up the intensity and delivers it to the nerve endings of readers. Combined with an overlapping romantic plot, it becomes a compelling roller coaster read to the end." ~Harold Wolf, top 50 Amazon reviewer

Dedicated to

All employees,
The Department of Family and Protective Services

Employees and volunteers
for animal shelters across the country

I will not leave you as orphans; I will come to you.
—John 14:18

"May the perfect grace and eternal love of Christ our Lord be our never-failing protection and help."
—Saint Ignatius

One

Erin Jacobs recognized the note of desperation in the woman's voice.

Desperation like she'd heard in past calls.

Desperation like she'd seen etched on her sister's face.

Desperation like she'd experienced, echoing through her own nightmares.

Switching her cell phone to her left hand, she stole a peek at the clock beside her bed—twelve minutes after four in the morning. Since opening her ARK animal shelter, she averaged three middle-of-the-night calls a month.

Canine rescues. Gator rescues. Even one equine rescue. None of them had turned out well.

Darkness seemed to frustrate all her attempts of bringing any animal safe and whole back to the ARK.

With a sigh she held the phone away from her and squinted at the screen. Confirming the caller ID read ANONYMOUS, she fell back against her pillow.

"I need you to repeat what you just said." She struggled to sound more awake than she felt.

At first silence filled the other end of the line, but then she heard the hoot of an owl—a great horned owl if she wasn't mistaken. Even through the line she could make out its five-syllable call, sounding strangely like "Who's awake, me too." The owl reminded Erin of her childhood, of that terrible night, and instantly, all vestiges of sleep were gone.

Heart tripping, she sat up in bed, pushing away the old patchwork quilt. "Hello?"

"I said I need you to come now. This is Erin?" The woman's soft, ragged voice drifted through the line. She'd either been crying or was suffering from acute allergy problems. In Livingston, Texas, on September 18 it could easily be the latter.

"Yes, I'm Erin Jacobs. Who is this?"

"You save…" The rest of her sentence fell away into the unfinished hours of the morning.

"I rescue everything, Miss. But most things can wait until daylight. Tell me what you have and an address, and I'll be out at first light."

"This can't wait." The woman's plea took on an urgency Erin had heard few times before, when someone called about an animal that had only hours or minutes left to live.

She snapped on the lamp beside her bed and reached for her jeans. Some folks panicked when a litter came in the middle of the night. More than once she'd arrived too late. In abusive households, the woman would sometimes smother the animals before her husband could find them, claiming it was kinder than what he would do.

"I can come now if it's a true emergency. Tell me your location."

"Promise you'll be alone."

Erin hesitated as she pulled on her right boot. "Say again."

"Just you. No one else." The woman's voice quivered, nearly broke. "Give me your word."

"Tell me what you have and where you are, Miss. I'll come and get whatever it is. You need to stay calm. I'll bring it here to the ARK and find it a good home."

"I know you will. That's why I called *you*. An Ark, Moses, it has to mean something…" Her words melted into the sobs she'd obviously been holding back.

Erin pulled a sweater over her nightshirt, unwilling to put the phone down for even a minute, afraid to break the connection. Grabbing her keys off the front entry table she hurried out toward her Chevy.

"I'm in my truck now. What side of town are you on?"

The woman hesitated and drew in a deep, shaky breath. "Go south on Highway 59, then enter the forest."

A shiver danced down Erin's spine as she realized the woman was giving her directions from the ARK to her location. Few people had ever actually been to her animal rescue facility. She was located on the remote outskirts of Livingston.

Doc England's warning rang in her ears. "Do not go alone in the middle of the night, Erin. Always call someone first."

But there wasn't time to call anyone else, and if she broke the connection now—

3

"I'm not far from there. I'll be at Shepherd in fifteen minutes."

"And you're alone?" Desperation filled the woman's voice again, causing it to rise above a whisper.

When would she have had time to pick up someone? Erin fought the urge to lash out at the woman, focused instead on the rescue.

"I'm alone like you asked. Talk to me, Miss. Tell me what I'm going to be dealing with when I reach your location."

"You'll know what to do. You're good at taking care of little fellas." Her next words were barely a whisper in the night. "He's not yet two months, not until this weekend…"

Alarm bells rang in Erin's head, but the woman sounded calmer now, although she still offered no further directions.

"I'm almost to the forest." Erin increased her speed.

"There's one more thing." The woman hesitated, stumbling over her words. "Promise me *you* will keep him."

"I can't adopt every—"

"Erin, this is different."

Again the familiarity. Erin wanted to question her about it. Before she could, the woman rushed on, the words pouring from her like water from a long dammed-up stream.

"I wouldn't ask this if I didn't have to, don't you realize that? If there were any other way. But there's not, and if you don't hurry… we'll be too late."

The plural pronoun clinched the deal for Erin. Most people tossed her their responsibilities as they drove by and never glanced back. Everything indicated this woman was taking some responsibility and possibly risk as well.

"Give me the directions," she said quietly.

"When you enter the forest, take the third road to the right. A mile down you'll see a logging trail. Turn right again. A bit down the trail is a hunter's cabin. Go around to the back porch." She paused in her directions, stumbling on a sob. "Hurry."

Something about the woman's voice suddenly struck a memory nerve in Erin's mind. She searched for it but failed to find the association. Gripping the cell phone tightly, she nudged the old truck to the speed limit.

She struggled over which question to ask first, but then an eerie silence filled the line. She glanced at her display. The words there caused her stomach to spasm—CALL ENDED.

Pulling over to the side of the road, she punched the number two and held it.

Doc picked up on the second ring.

"What's wrong, Erin?"

"I'm on an emergency rescue." Her breathing slowed and evened as she repeated the directions to him. By the time she'd summarized the situation, her hands were no longer shaking.

"Where are you now?"

"About to turn into the forest."

"Wait for me. I'm twenty minutes out—"

Erin pulled her truck back onto the road, her stubbornness returning as quickly as her panic had fled.

"Bad idea. There's an animal in a critical situation, and it's my job to go out there and rescue it. That's what the people of Livingston depend on me to do. It's certainly what this woman is depending on me to do. You should have heard her voice, Doc. She sounded practically hysterical. I'm sure you'd agree with me, if…" Erin suddenly realized her mentor and best friend wasn't arguing with her. "Doc? Are you there?"

Pressing the phone more closely to her ear, she heard a soft beeping. Glancing down at the display, she saw SEARCHING FOR SERVICE. Somewhere under the canopy of the trees, her phone had dropped the connection.

—

Confident she'd done the sensible thing by calling Doc, she pressed on through the forest. He would be no more than twenty minutes behind her, fifteen if she knew Doc's driving habits.

Still, the forest stirred Erin's emotions about things she'd rather not confront this night. That combined with the woman's desperation and Doc's warning set her nerves on edge. The wheel became slick with the sweat from her palms. As Erin turned onto the logging road, she did something she hadn't done in quite a while—she prayed.

Prayed for the safety of whatever lay waiting for her.

Prayed for wisdom that this time, this night, she'd be successful.

Prayed for the woman, whose name she didn't even know.

And lastly, she prayed Doc would find her—and quickly.

She might have felt like a hypocrite doing so, but Nina's quiet assurance and soft words settled into the old truck. "The Lord is near when you need him, Hon. He doesn't hold your absence against you. He misses you, same as any parent misses a child."

Erin rubbed her eyes, pushing back the tears. Now was not the time to have an emotional moment over her dead foster mother. Must be the forest unsettling her. Peering through her windshield, she suppressed a shudder. Tonight the tree canopy pressed down, deepening the darkness and blocking out all starlight.

She loved hiking through this area by day, even camping in it, but driving down an unknown logging trail in the dead of night? No thanks. She slowed as a rut in the road caused the axle in her truck to groan. Repairs would only further strain her budget.

There was little to fear here, and the sensible part of her brain knew it. The tall pines towered to beautiful heights by day, but in the solitary beam of her headlights they seemed to crowd her truck, practically hiding the road in places. She gripped the steering wheel, determined to fight for her space if necessary.

The fact that the state penitentiary was situated forty miles to the northwest crossed her mind. *He* was less than an hour away. She wrestled the thought into the box she kept locked in her mind, refusing to confront the memory.

Drawing a deep breath, she reminded herself she was comfortable in the midst of the forest. The walks here with Nina and Jules had first created in her a love for nature and animals.

No, it wasn't the vegetation making her uneasy. What had the woman said? *If you don't hurry, we'll be too late.*

She had no desire to confront a controlling spouse who didn't want to give up some pup, especially in this isolated setting. Memories of *him* tugged again at the corner of her consciousness, but she pushed them safely away as the hunter's cabin came into view.

She slowed a good fifty feet from the front door. Where was the woman's car? No one had driven out past her. A few yards beyond the cabin, the road plainly hit a dead end.

Erin stepped out of the truck, careful to leave her lights trained on the front of the small wooden structure. There was no sign of movement at the two front windows or the door. Other than her headlights, the cabin lay in complete darkness.

Taking a deep breath, Erin's senses were nearly overwhelmed with the forest smells—loblolly pine and water oak. Even the sweet odor of a magnolia carried across the warm summer night. She reached behind her seat and grabbed her emergency pack.

I'll check the back porch and leave.

As soon as she stepped away from the truck, the night enfolded her. She resisted the urge to turn on the forty-thousand candle power light she carried. It would steal her night vision and make her a clear target if anyone meant her harm.

Waiting, her eyes finally adjusted.

At first she could make out the limbs of the pine tree closest to her, then the outline of a stack of wood next to a chopping block, and finally the trail which led around to the back of the cabin.

She shouldered her pack and picked her way down the path and around to the back porch. Years of pine needles carpeted the trail, muffling the sound of her approach.

Though her footsteps made no noise, her heart beat like a drum, pounding its rhythm more loudly and more quickly with each step she took toward the cabin's porch.

This, too, lay in darkness, except for one small light in the southeast corner.

Erin wondered if it could be a heat lamp the woman had set up. Of course, it could also be a trap. By this point every horror film she'd seen as a teenager played merrily in her head. She pushed the images away and crept closer to the porch.

Placing her foot on the bottom step, a sudden shadow and flurry of wings caused her to gasp and fall back to the ground. The free-tailed bat swooped off into the darkness.

Erin uttered her second prayer for the night—this one for longevity—as she envisioned herself dead of a heart attack at the ripe old age of twenty-two.

Turning back toward the porch she noted the layer of dirt covering the wooden floor. She could see the neglect even in the near darkness, along with a single set of footprints—small ones about her size. Deer-feed sacks, a pair of work gloves, and a bucket someone had turned upside down to sit on were scattered across the porch.

Her eyes barely registered those things though. The old washtub had claimed all of her attention. With the light positioned over it, plainly what she had been sent to rescue waited there.

Erin hesitated.

Nothing moved inside the cabin.

Leaves rustled around her as a slight breeze stirred the night air. An owl called out again, reminding her of the phone call, of the woman, and of her promise.

Then she heard it—a slight mewling from the washtub.

From the second the sound registered, she never had a choice.

She snapped on her light and walked back toward the porch.

Her work boots echoed as she climbed the three steps.

The stench of dust and something rotting overpowered the forest smells as she covered the remaining distance— bolder now, intent on her mission.

She didn't stop until her fingers grasped the sides of the washtub.

Erin peered into the bucket. First she saw the blanket— tattered and old, but surprisingly clean. The camo design nearly hid what lay inside.

Erin stared down, blinking, trying to comprehend.

Peering up at her quietly, expectantly—blue eyes.

Peeking out of a camo-colored cap—blond, curly hair.

Finally, struggling free from the confines of the blanket—two small hands.

Two

Derrick woke with the taste of alcohol stale on his breath. Why was he sleeping in his car? He must have passed out again. He quickly checked for his wallet and his car keys. Finding them both, he pushed the door open and stepped out into a day half gone.

A forest? Where was he? And why?

He shook his head, but no answers jostled loose. Staggering around to the trunk of his car, he opened it and pulled out a bottle of water. Good thing he kept supplies there for just such emergencies. He downed the first bottle in one long pull, threw it into the trunk, and fetched another. Slamming the trunk lid, he leaned against the sedan and looked around.

Most of the night before was a complete blank.

But he did remember Tara and that squalling baby.

That was it.

Shrugging, he returned to the driver's seat, started the car, and drove down the logging road. He had no idea if he was going the right direction, but it had to lead somewhere.

Find civilization—he couldn't see any further than the need for a sandwich and coffee.

It was when he'd made a left off the road—he always turned left when he was lost and that strategy hadn't failed him yet—that he remembered chasing her through the woods.

Find civilization and then find Tara.

She had some explaining to do.

Three

Travis Williams sank into his office chair late Tuesday afternoon, spied the note on his desk, and grimaced.

He liked his new boss well enough. Tabitha Moring acted tough but fair and seemed to be leading the department in the right direction. No, that wasn't the problem.

He took one more gulp of the bitter coffee leftover from breakfast—cold, stale, but still caffeinated—and walked toward her office.

The problem was he'd been with The Department of Family and Protective Services long enough to know a call into the boss's office could only mean one more case added to his already bulging work bag. And not just any case, or she'd have left it on his desk.

Knocking, he rolled his eyes when James walked by and slid his finger across his throat, mimicking a quick and merciful beheading.

"Enter," Tabitha barked.

Travis stepped cautiously into the director's office for Polk County, Texas. It never failed to surprise him how she had tamed the previous clutter. Every social worker he knew, himself included, stacked folders on any flat surface. Not Moring.

She was an imposing figure at five foot eleven, nearly reaching Travis's height. His mother had seen her at a city function and declared if there was one tall woman in Texas, there were more. Laughing at his expense, she said perhaps it wasn't hopeless and Travis would one day find a wife. She'd playfully suggested it was the reason he remained single—that he didn't like looking down from his six-foot-one vantage point.

Travis wished the explanation was so simple.

He never would have guessed Moring's age, but the department had celebrated her fiftieth birthday last summer. As he entered her office, she stood like a professor, preparing to address a class. She looked ageless—perfect posture, ebony skin, rail thin. Everything about her affirmed she tolerated no nonsense. Even her straight black hair, cut at the jaw line, proclaimed as much.

"Travis, thank you for coming in so promptly." Her composed expression gave away nothing. "Have a seat. I wanted you to start on this right away."

Two chairs were arranged in front of her desk. Travis chose the closest and resisted the urge to sigh. Four thirty in the afternoon, and he had started work before seven that morning.

"As you know, my caseload stands at 120 percent currently." He offered the fact without returning her greeting. Maybe she could still catch James in the hall if she hurried.

Director Moring had been reaching for the single file on her desk. Returning his gaze, she stopped, sat in the leather chair she had inherited, and studied him for a moment.

"Every social worker in our office has a heavy caseload. I imagine you're aware your coworkers are all overburdened."

Travis nodded, but didn't blink. "Of course, though not every worker travels to the far side of the county."

Moring steepled her fingers and seemed to consider his comment seriously. He suddenly remembered James's beheading antic in the hall and felt his palms begin to sweat. Something in her eyes told him she was merely deciding how to vanquish him.

Instead, she sat up straighter and tossed him the folder. "You're going to want this one."

"That's what you always say."

"And I'm always right."

Travis checked the name on the folder: BABY JOSHUA. It wasn't unheard of to list no last name, but it was unusual.

"I could stop by tomorrow morning," he muttered.

"That is a Baby Moses case. I want you to go out there tonight."

Intrigued, he opened the file and scanned the single page.

"Jacobs is listed as a vet tech, not your usual emergency infant care provider." Travis continued to stare at the single page. "I'm not convinced this qualifies under the Safe Haven Code."

"Which is why I want you out there within the hour." A finality in her tone caused Travis to shift uncomfortably in his chair. He allowed his gaze to wander past the plate glass windows a moment, then finally settle on his boss.

"Who took the preliminary notes on this? What's so special about—" he glanced back down, "Erin Jacobs? Why didn't we assume custody of this child early this morning?"

"Good questions." Moring leaned back in her chair, a smile tugging at the corner of her mouth. "I knew I could count on you to ask good questions."

Travis tapped the folder against his leg and waited.

"I took the prelim notes when I received a call today from Commissioner Ray. You may not realize it, but Ray is responsible for pushing through the budget requests for this department last month. He was a foster child himself. In the four months I've been here, I've developed an abiding respect for Commissioner Ray, even if I don't always agree with his political stands."

Travis waited and watched, resisting the urge to comment.

"I saved Baby Joshua for you, Travis. I wanted my most experienced caseworker on this one." Moring picked up a pen, turned it end over end, then laid it down perpendicular to her calendar. "Ray had an early morning visit from a Dr. England. Apparently, they are old buddies. Dr. England runs a local veterinary clinic."

"I know him," Travis said. "Not well, but I know him."

"Dr. England is the supervising vet for Erin Jacobs, who runs Noah's ARK—an animal rescue facility. You can get the full story from her tonight on your site visit. The abbreviated version is England vouches for the woman, and Ray vouches for England."

Heat flooded Travis's face. "Since we owe Ray—"

"We don't owe anyone." Moring placed both palms flat against her desk, fingers splayed. "What we do, we do by the standards set in this department before I arrived, upheld since I've been here, and laid out in the Texas Family Code. I expect nothing less in this situation."

Her expression softened as she waved at the folder. "Take it. Go out there and get the specifics from Jacobs. She was the one who found the child. See what makes her different while you're at it. I trust Ray's intuition, but I told him I back my people. Your decision is final."

"Police report?"

"I'm sending it to your e-mail now."

Travis nodded, stood, and walked toward the door. Moring immediately turned her attention to her computer and was tapping on her keyboard before he left the office.

As he carried the file toward his cubicle, it seemed to gain weight. Stuffing it into his leather shoulder bag, he wondered how he could manage the responsibility for one more child.

"What did she give you?" James asked. He was three inches shorter, with what would have been black hair if he ever let his crew cut grow out, which he didn't. They'd been friends since baseball days in high school.

"Baby Joshua." Travis pulled the file back out and tossed it to him as he checked his e-mail and hit the PRINT button. Then he repacked his bag and grabbed his keys from his desk.

James studied the one page, shook his head, and handed the folder back. "Haven't had an abandoned baby case this year. This one will make the news. Who named the kid? And is Moring going to allow Jacobs to serve as an EMS provider?" He asked his questions while frowning as he sailed the Nerf ball into the basketball hoop positioned over their two cubicles.

"I've no idea. On top of it all, what makes this Jacobs woman think she should care for him until he can be properly placed?"

"You told me once that you chose Child Welfare because you enjoy solving puzzles." James leaned back in his chair until it groaned. "This has all the markings of a good one."

In spite of his long day, Travis felt his energy level return as he hiked to his Chevy Blazer. Baby Joshua did have the markings of a good puzzle, and the police report he'd printed had raised more questions than it had answered.

Checking the address, he turned left onto the loop and accelerated. He could be at Noah's ARK in twenty minutes.

Noah's ARK. He hoped the woman had a better 'knack for running a business than she did for picking names. Otherwise, she wouldn't make enough money to support herself, let alone Baby Joshua.

—

Thirty minutes later he pulled up in front of what looked like an old ranch on the outskirts of Livingston. From the road he could barely make out the main house, some stock buildings, and a pond. It had taken him ten minutes longer than expected because it wasn't exactly located in the business part of town.

How did Miss Jacobs hope to attract customers when she was so far down a county road?

He shifted the Blazer into park, hopped out, and opened what he hoped was the final cattle gate, then maneuvered the Chevy through it. After closing the gate, he continued up the hill toward the ranch house.

The place appeared clean and orderly enough, but it also looked dated. A main house sat to the east of the property, while the corral and barn buildings were located to the west. Everything looked as if it needed a new coat of paint.

He parked in front of the sign proclaiming he'd arrived at Noah's ARK parking, which basically consisted of a fence in front of the buildings. It separated the house and barns from the grass parking area. At one time gravel had been spread there, but that had apparently been done long ago and needed replenishing.

Stepping out of his car, he was met by familiar farm smells—hay, manure, and livestock. He did a slow three-sixty and noted with surprise how close the main county road actually was. The route to Jacobs's place had circled back around it. The ARK sat in an alcove—tucked back quietly by itself.

A screen door banged shut and the sound of work boots clomping across the back porch indicated which way he needed to go. Grabbing his site evaluation tablet and case folder, he took off in that direction.

He hurried through the small gate encircling the house's yard, which did not squeak, up the three steps of the wraparound porch, and hesitated at the front door. Plainly, he'd heard someone at the back. Knocking at the front would be useless, and already it was nearing six. Probably she was out back with her husband settling the animals for the evening.

Turning, he nearly smacked his head on a planter of yellow, purple, and pink flowers. Why couldn't women leave plants in the ground? Pushing his irritation down, he continued around the porch, his rubber-soled dress shoes silent on the wooden floor.

It never occurred to him to call out.

Rounding the first corner he was surprised to see old wicker furniture—a couch, chair, and table. Again it was clean, but in need of paint. The scene was homey—cozy in a way he couldn't have defined—and it stirred something inside of him. Raised a bittersweet feeling he thought he'd buried long ago. He ignored the emotion and gave the woman points for trying.

Winding through the furniture, he gained speed as he rounded the last corner, hoping to catch the Jacobs family before they took off to the barns.

He didn't actually see Erin Jacobs or the baby before he practically knocked them off the porch.

He did look down into auburn hair—curly, thick, and smelling of something floral. She'd cut it about two inches all over, so the curls swirled like the icing on his mother's red-velvet cakes, tapering off at the base of her neck. He didn't have time to think about anything else as he attempted to stop his forward momentum, tried to keep from lobbing her and the infant she carried in a front baby pouch off the porch and into the yard.

Travis's heart rate shot up as he dropped everything in his hands and grasped her shoulders, desperately trying to steady them. A gasp escaped from her lips, but she never looked up, didn't even spare him a glance.

They tottered, locked in some asynchronous dance, and then the world seemed to right itself—teeter back from the brink.

"I am so sorry." He didn't let go, worried she would still fall over, terrified he had trampled her like some tackle crossing the twenty-yard line headed into the end zone. Sweat trickled down his back as adrenaline pumped through his system.

Jacobs stepped back, barely looking at him, and focused on the baby in her pouch. Concern masked her features as she bent her head over the child.

"Are you all right, sweetie?"

The infant had started to cry, so she turned and without even a backward glance fled around the corner and into the house.

Four

Travis made his way into the yard, retrieved his materials, then climbed the steps leading to the back porch. He hesitated, hand raised, before knocking at the door. Baby Joshua's cries had subsided from outright yowls to occasional whimpers. The kid sounded healthy enough. Whatever Jacobs had done to calm him seemed to work.

Perhaps he should proceed to the barn and introduce himself to Mr. Jacobs. Either way he'd have to interview both adults. He could knock or he could give the woman time to cool off. The one glance she'd given him had been none too welcoming.

Then again, he was here, and he would need to question her.

He raised his hand to knock when Erin pushed the screen door open and walked out.

"Perhaps we should try this again." Having discarded the baby pouch, she now cradled Baby Joshua in the crook of her left arm. Based on size, the child looked under two months. A doctor's opinion would be required to confirm approximate age. At the moment he had his face pressed into her blouse, rooting around.

Jacobs extended her right hand. "Erin Jacobs."

Belatedly, Travis realized he needed to juggle the pad into his left hand in order to shake hands with her. The entire process took longer than it should have. He could feel her watching him curiously.

"Williams. Travis Williams."

"Nice to meet you." She shifted the baby to a more comfortable position.

He noted she seemed a bit awkward with the child, as if she couldn't find the exact way to hold a two-month-old infant. Finally, she slung Joshua to her shoulder like a small feed sack.

"I assume you're here with Child Welfare." She studied him in the waning light.

"Correct. Director Moring asked me to come out tonight. Actually, we're required, in cases of child abandonment, to assume care of the child by the close of the first business day."

Jacobs stepped closer, and Travis stepped back.

"I don't want you to assume care of *the child*, who has a name by the way." She turned and started away from him, then turned back. "His name is Joshua—Josh. I call him Josh sometimes, but his name—it's Joshua."

She drew her bottom lip in, worried it with her teeth, and he wondered what she was trying not to say.

With a start, it occurred to him *she* made *him* nervous. As a social worker he'd grown used to having that effect on other people, but this made no sense at all. He was here to interview her.

Everything about Erin Jacobs had caught him off guard. For one thing she seemed incredibly young. What was the minimum age to marry these days? Had she even graduated from high school? For another, she was small—barely reaching his chest.

He eyed her carefully, checking to see if he'd broken her in some way. "We started off badly. Are you sure you're all right? I'm sorry about before."

Jacobs took a deep breath, closed her eyes for a moment, then smiled up at him, brown eyes narrowing as if she hadn't decided whether to trust him. "You don't always bowl over your clients?"

He shook his head, feeling the heat rise up his neck, and continued to stare. She wore work boots, old jeans, and an oversized, men's flannel shirt. She reminded him of a sparrow wrapped in a crow's outfit. Her face was exquisite—slightly pronounced cheek bones, a button nose with slightly more character, remarkable lips the lightest shade of pink—the color of the flowers he'd nearly creamed near her front door. It was her eyes he wanted more of though—round, expressive, and the same brown as his morning coffee. They seemed to hold nothing back.

Mr. Jacobs was one lucky man, and no doubt he relished the fact every morning.

Travis finally found his tongue. "I need to do an intake interview, and no, I don't normally knock my clients off their feet. I thought I heard you headed to the barns, and I was trying to catch you."

She cocked her head to the side, considered him, and accepted his explanation, then shrugged. "No harm done. Why don't we sit on the side porch?"

"Sure. I'll need to ask a thousand questions." Travis followed her around to the wicker furniture, aware he towered like a redwood tree beside her. She had to be under five and a half feet tall.

Tossing a look at him as she sat in the chair, she refocused on the baby, gently lowered him to her lap, and murmured, "Best get started then."

Baby Joshua appeared to be under eight weeks old, with the beginnings of blond, curly hair. His color was good as far as Travis could tell. He seemed a little on the thin side, but otherwise healthy—at least from three feet away.

"It might save some time if Mr. Jacobs could be here from the beginning." Travis sat carefully on the wicker couch, hoping it would hold his weight. "Then I wouldn't have to ask the same questions twice."

Erin shook her head and repositioned the baby with his head on her knees and his feet pressed against her flat abdomen. He bet she didn't weigh a buck fifteen—though there was no blank for weight on his report. She did seem obviously healthy, which he'd need to check once she filled out the health form questions—if she insisted on petitioning for custody. A piece of the puzzle which still made no sense to him.

"That won't be necessary, Mr. Williams. Next question."

Travis looked up from his pad. "Pardon?"

"There is no Mr. Jacobs. You were assuming I'm married. I'm not. I'm only twenty-two."

"Twenty-two?"

"Correct."

Travis dropped his pen, picked it up, then knocked a pillow off the wicker couch to the floor. Leaning to pick up the pillow he felt her curious stare, knew his face was turning beet red like when he'd been chewed out by his baseball coach for missing a catch. Pulling a handkerchief from his back pocket, he mopped the sweat from his brow and tried to think how to begin again.

The pen was the clue. He grasped it and the pad and focused doggedly on the interview questions before him. "You were saying—"

"I was saying, twenty-two is a bit young to be married. Especially given the fact I'm trying to launch this business off the ground."

Travis looked down at his form, checked unmarried, and worked to collect his thoughts. The entire interview had spun out of his control from the moment he'd stepped on her porch.

"Is something wrong, Mr. Williams?"

"Call me Travis."

"Is something wrong, Travis?"

"This obviously isn't a normal situation." He looked up as Erin glanced down at the baby and watched her face soften.

"No, I suppose it isn't."

"Why don't you tell me what happened."

The night fell around them as he listened to her story. He was at first mesmerized, then alarmed by what he heard.

"You went into the forest alone?"

"Yes."

Joshua fussed in her lap, his face wrinkling as his cries split the night. Erin reached into a feed bucket beside the wicker chair and pulled out a clean disposable diaper. She began changing him as she continued her explanation.

"Some rescues occur in remote locations. As an animal rescuer—"

"Which is another problem—you are not an EMS provider. I'm not convinced this is a Baby Moses situation."

"What did you say?" Erin stopped mid-task, still holding one of Baby Joshua's legs straight in the air.

"I said I'm not sure this qualifies as a Baby Moses case. Under the Safe Haven provision a baby must be surrendered to an EMS provider before the child turns sixty days old."

Erin finished haphazardly tabbing the diaper. Travis felt sure it would fall off the minute she picked Joshua up to hold him. Focusing on something past the porch, she again hefted the baby to her shoulder, walked to the railing, and stared out into the darkness.

"She mentioned Moses."

"Who did?"

"His mother—Joshua's mother." Erin turned and looked at him. When she did, the intensity of her gaze, the yearning, hit Travis like a punch to his gut. "I thought she'd mixed up the name of my business. She said, 'An ark, Moses, it has to mean something.' Those were her exact words."

Shaking her head, she sat back down across from him.

"Tell me what that means. What is a Baby Moses?"

"Texas enacted Safe Haven laws in 1999—basically saying a parent, usually a mother, wouldn't be prosecuted if they left an infant under sixty days old—"

Erin's hand flew to her neck. Her slender fingers wrapped around her throat as if to protect herself.

"What's wrong?"

"There was something else. At the time I thought I was on an animal rescue." Her eyes widened as she stared again at the babe in her arms. "She said he wasn't two months old, not until this weekend."

Travis pulled out the copy of the police report. "You didn't mention this to the officers who came here this morning."

"I... I didn't even think of it until you said sixty days."

Making a notation on his form, Travis tried to pick up the thread of their conversation.

"So is he? Is Joshua a Baby Moses?" she asked.

"That's what I'm here to determine, Miss Jacobs."

"Erin, please."

"Erin. Normally with a Baby Moses case the child is surrendered at a hospital or fire station. The law states the child must be unharmed and left in the care of EMS personnel. In such a case, there is no criminal offense, and a court will usually agree to terminate the parent-child relationship. Since this child was not taken to a proper facility and no EMS personnel were present, a court could find cause to prosecute the mother for—"

"And what if she couldn't get to a proper facility?" Erin rocketed off the chair, placing the baby on her shoulder again, bouncing him up and down as she paced back and forth in front of where he sat. "What if she... what if she lived in the woods? What if she didn't have a car? What if the only way she could surrender her child was to leave him, carefully wrapped, on the back porch of a cabin?"

"Then why didn't she call an ambulance or the police?"

Travis stood as well, tired of containing his own agitation.

"Have you ever been in an abusive household, Mr. Williams?"

"I work for Child Welfare, Erin. Do you really need to ask me that question?" Travis stood frozen, waiting for her to back down.

"But have you ever *lived* in one? Because when you live in one you can't always pick up a phone and call the police. Sometimes the best you can do is sneak down the road a bit."

She turned then, and he knew from the slump of her shoulders they weren't talking about Baby Joshua anymore.

"Sometimes the best you can do is run out into the woods." The words were spoken into the night, carried away so quickly he might have imagined them.

"Miss Jacobs, Erin, I'm sorry. I really am, but even if the court agreed this mother couldn't reach a safe location, calling you—and I don't mean this in a derogatory way—was putting the baby at risk. You work with animals, not children."

Erin turned, took a deep breath, and drew herself up to her full height. "I'm Red Cross certified in several areas, including CPR, First Aid, and Disaster Response. All of which are listed under my qualifications on my website. Maybe Joshua's mother knew I was a safe person to call."

Travis ran his hand over the top of his head and reminded himself they had the same goal—the health of a baby.

"All right. Say she knew your qualifications, and say she couldn't get to a baby Safe Haven, so she called you. If I declared this a Baby Moses case, which would still be subject to review by the court, I would need to take possession of the child and place him with a temporary foster family."

"Why can't he stay with me?"

"You've never applied with our office, never shown any desire to provide a home for a child. If you did, as a caseworker, I would still consider it reckless for you to take off in the middle of the night into the forest on rescue calls."

Erin's eyes widened, and Travis knew he'd stepped into the middle of the ant bed. Instead of picking up the feed bucket and chunking it at his head, she perched on the edge of her chair. "Sometimes my job necessitates going out alone in the middle of the night."

"But…" Travis stumbled on the words, then plunged ahead. "But it could have been some maniac trying to lure you into the woods."

"Mr. Williams. Don't you think I can tell the difference between a maniac and a woman who needs my help?" Brown eyes flashed at him, and even though her tone remained quiet, her words flew at him like darts. "I wouldn't have gone if I didn't believe her, and I did call for backup. Dr. England was there within twenty minutes."

"You could have called the police if you thought someone was in danger," he insisted.

"Call the police? Usually I rescue cats, dogs, calves, colts, and occasionally iguanas or pet snakes. The police call me!" Erin placed Joshua to her shoulder, stood, and resumed her pacing up and down the side porch.

"I know it might seem like I'm going off on a tangent, but what you do, your profession, is an important component of Joshua's temporary placement." Travis shifted on the couch and heard it groan under his weight. "By the way, why are we calling him Joshua?"

Instead of answering, Erin walked over to a bag and retrieved a baby blanket. As she placed it in his lap, her fingers traced the letters hand-stitched along the bottom border—Joshua.

Travis looked up into her eyes, continuing in a gentler tone than before. "It's very unusual for us to place a child of any age, let alone an infant, in a home not previously registered with foster care."

She angled away from him and stared into her home where a single light shone over the kitchen sink.

"I'm trying to ascertain if this is a safe place for Joshua. That's part of *my* job. I need to know if it's customary for you to take off in the middle of the night when you receive calls from strangers."

Erin turned on him like a tornado changing its path. "Don't you dare judge my career because it's not neat and set out with guidelines like yours. I provide a service to this community, and I do it within the standards of my profession. Perhaps you should take the time to check those out. I'm not a nut out collecting animals, Mr. Williams. My business is a member of the Animal Humane Association and I lead the county Disaster Animal Rescue Team."

"But—"

She paused to draw in a breath, then plowed on as if she hadn't heard him, as if he wasn't the one conducting the interview. "I'm approved by the Livingston City Council, and I operate under the supervision of Dr. England. So how about you stop judging what I do? Because you don't understand what I do, don't have a clue when it's appropriate for me to conduct a rescue alone and when it's not."

Travis mentally marked through the adjective fragile and held up both hands, palms out. "Truce. I apologize if I've offended you, which I obviously have. I'll admit I'm not familiar with your profession, and if we determine this is a good temporary placement for Baby Joshua I will do my research."

Erin drew in another steadying breath and turned away from him. When she turned back he saw the tears in her eyes. Travis had seen many clients cry before. Sometimes it was sincere, often it wasn't. Seeing tears in Erin Jacobs's eyes felt like a knife slicing down his palms, filleting them open.

"Joshua has to stay with me—permanently," she whispered. "I promised his mother."

Five

Erin forced herself to return Travis's stare. He watched her as if she'd lost her mind, and honestly she couldn't blame him. Twelve hours ago, she'd been pretty clueless herself. Amazing what a difference one night could make in a person's life—two people's lives.

Truthfully, he grated on her nerves. The man looked too perfect, sporting his khaki pants, pressed shirt, and paisley tie—not to mention his blond hair and GQ tan. She couldn't help wondering if he'd ever cleaned a hog pen or pulled a calf. Six feet of muscle wasted on interrogating people when it could be put to good use making an honest living instead of pushing paper.

"Back up a minute. You promised the mother you'd keep Joshua?" He opened his folder again as if he might find the conversation transcribed there.

"I haven't told anyone yet." Erin forced herself to sit back down across from him. She knew she resembled a yo-yo the way she'd popped up and down, even paced back and forth like her sister used to walk the dog. Right this minute she longed to take Joshua and go finish her chores. Already he felt natural in the papoose harness Doc England had given her. Instead, she cradled him in her arms and stared at Travis Williams, pushing down her impatience.

How much more time would she have to spend with this man? She should be in the barn.

"While you were making these promises, I don't suppose you asked for Joshua's medical history as you're required by law to do." Travis frowned and made a notation on his tablet.

"You might want to wait until I explain what happened before you start writing."

His head snapped up, and his eyes bored into hers. "All right," he said softly.

"She never admitted to being his mother. She didn't even tell me what I was rescuing, but now as I replay the conversation in my head it's obvious to me."

"How so?"

"She used the word *we*. Some folks are detached, like they're leaving out their garbage for me to pick up. She was obviously emotionally involved, practically begging me to come quickly and come alone. I could hear the terror in her voice—for herself, but more for Joshua." Erin reached out and touched the baby's face, grateful beyond words that she had reached him in time. "I've witnessed many abusive relationships, Mr. Williams—"

"Travis."

"Travis. I suppose you have as well." She paused and pulled her eyes away from the baby to look up at this man who had the power to remove Joshua from her care.

"Yes," he admitted.

"She was panicked, worried I wouldn't get there in time. Said she wouldn't have called me if there was any other way, if she didn't have to."

"Those were her exact words?" His voice had taken on a hard edge. She peered at him and realized he was clenching his jaw. No doubt he would defend the families in his caseload well. Despite the fact he would go by the book, he would also be their advocate to the very end. She could hear it in the anger behind his question, see it in the glint in his eyes.

Erin felt the beginnings of respect for him. She didn't want to know him so well, didn't want to see the man beneath the preppy clothes. What she wanted was for him to sign the paper and let her and Joshua be. To leave.

"It's important, Erin. Were those her exact words?"

"Yes." She brought Joshua to her shoulder and rubbed his back in soft circles. "Then she said if I didn't hurry *we* would be too late. That's what did it for me, the way she said we—as if both of us were taking a big risk."

"No sign of her when you reached the cabin?"

"None."

"You're sure you didn't pass her on the road?"

"I'm sure. She must have hiked back out through the woods. There are so many roads through there, I suspect she had a car parked less than a mile away."

Travis massaged his forehead, disturbing his too perfect blond hair. "You should have left the baby there until you contacted the proper authorities."

"There was no cell service, no phone or electricity going to the cabin. It seemed Joshua might be in danger, and I

35

couldn't very well leave him there alone." Erin fought to keep the anger out of her voice. She'd asked herself the same questions a dozen times. "Do you honestly believe I should have left him so I could call 911?"

"No." Travis stared at the baby, then raised his eyes to hers. "I suppose not. By law, Joshua should have been transferred to a hospital as soon as possible. Why didn't you drive straight to Memorial Medical Center?"

Erin continued rubbing Joshua's back. She'd known this question was coming, had anticipated it would be the hardest thing to explain. When the police had been here earlier, Doc had said something to the older lieutenant to soften his questions.

Now she had to justify her actions, and there was no one to stand beside her.

She again wished the interview could be over. The cows in the barn would be growing restless. She needed to get back to work.

She couldn't resist the urge to glance out into the gathering darkness.

"Do you need to be somewhere?"

"I need to be in the barn. My animals are waiting to be settled down for the night."

He held her gaze, didn't check his watch though she bet he wanted to. "I suppose we could continue over there then."

She gave his clothes a once over before raising an eyebrow.

"We're not done here. If you have work to do…"

Erin considered her options, but before she could come up with another plan, Kizmit's bawl interrupted them.

"Cow?" Travis asked.

"Kizmit. She needs milking, and she isn't known for her patience."

"Your cow is named Kizmit?"

"She's been good luck. She sort of came with this place." As they walked toward the back steps, Erin stopped near the door. "Let me get the papoose harness for Joshua."

"I can hold him," Travis offered.

"You sure?" She again took in his clothes.

"Absolutely. Not a problem at all."

Erin realized he was only being polite, but at the same time she needed to take care of Kizmit and Bells. If he insisted on staying, she might as well take him up on the offer.

—

As they turned toward the barn, Travis wondered why he was breaking all his own rules. He generally tried to sit back and observe, keep a professional distance between his clients and himself. He believed it helped him to serve them better. By not becoming emotionally involved, he could better ascertain what they needed.

But he had to decide whether to take this infant with him or leave the baby here in Erin's care, and he needed to decide in the next half hour.

As he accepted Joshua from her, the baby's softness overwhelmed his senses. The child reminded him of holding his mother's china—a breakable, priceless treasure. Erin peered at him as he juggled his case folder, work pad, and pen.

"You could leave your things on the porch. Pick them up when we get back."

Travis let her take the items from his hands, afraid he might drop the baby if he tried to set them down himself. He'd forgotten how fragile infants seemed—like holding a dozen cartons of eggs. How long had it been since he'd cradled one? His niece had turned eight years old last month, so he supposed it had been awhile. Given that he didn't actually hold his clients' children...

"You asked why I didn't take Joshua to the hospital."

"Why didn't you?"

They walked toward the barn in the darkness. Soft solar lights shone around the out buildings. Stepping into the barn, Erin picked up a pail by the door. A yellow barn cat and two striped kittens followed in her wake. She turned on a light in a tack room, then walked over to a large white-and-brown cow.

"Kizmit?"

"Yeah." She patted the cow's side, rubbed her hands up and down its flanks, then dropped some fresh hay in front of it. "You can sit on the bench there."

Travis sat and watched as she pulled up a stool and began milking Kizmit. The first time he'd tried milking his grandfather's dairy cow he'd been fourteen. He still remembered the old man holding his sides and laughing when he'd barely managed to coax a trickle from the stubborn cow. Then Granddad had sat beside him and patiently shown him how to use his hands to bring the milk down. It had shocked him how difficult the work was. He'd been young and cocky and considered such things women's work.

Looking at her small hands, he thought of that summer and his grandfather's patience. He remembered the way his hands had ached for weeks before he'd grown accustomed to the labor.

Erin effortlessly squirted milk into the pail. She only paused to aim a stream at an old saucer, which she nudged out of the way with the toe of her work boot. The cats immediately began lapping at it. Travis could hear their purring from where he sat.

"I thought about taking Joshua straight to the hospital, several times." She glanced at him, then turned her attention back to Kizmit. Her milking had taken on a rhythm. In the dim lighting, he almost didn't see her tears. Then she brought up the back of her hand and brushed them away. "He was wrapped in the camo blanket when I found him in the washtub. Doc had a baby seat in his truck—for his grandkids. He let me borrow it. When I put Joshua in the car he suddenly seemed cold and tired. He started crying, and I could tell he was hungry."

Travis looked down at the baby, sucking on his closed fist and staring up at him. He tried to envision him abandoned on a porch, alone in the woods, cold and hungry. Tried to imagine what he would do. He didn't realize he was clenching the bench until the splinters from the wood began to dig into his palm.

"Didn't Dr. England tell you to go to the hospital, Erin?"

"Yes, but I couldn't do it. I couldn't take him where they would poke and prod him. He's just a baby. He only wants to be loved."

She stopped milking, and Kizmit turned her head and stared at her as the cow chewed the hay.

"When we reached the highway, I called Doc, asked him to go by the store and pick up some formula, a bottle, some diapers..." Her voice trailed off. "Why would she throw him away? He's so perfect."

Her words barely reached him across the stall. "As I drove back toward town, I couldn't understand how this priceless gift could land in my lap."

Travis didn't know what to say, so he stared into her eyes.

"The woman seemed to know me," Erin continued. "She used my name several times."

"Isn't your name on your business listing?" Travis carefully moved the baby to the crook of his left arm. Joshua's light weight had somehow caused his right arm to fall asleep, maybe because neither of them had moved while listening to her story.

"No. I list under E. Jacobs. Joshua's mom called me Erin several times." She resumed her milking. "I told myself I'd bring him here, feed him, then call the authorities—and we did. But before they arrived I remembered the article in the paper."

"What article?"

She stood, moved the stool to the next stall, and repeated the earlier process of patting the heifer and giving her a bit of hay. This time the cats sat on their haunches and watched her while they cleaned their paws and faces.

Travis could still see her from where he sat, still make out her expression in the shadows. Worry lines had formed between her eyes, but she didn't look at him.

"What article, Erin?"

"The one about the shortage of foster and adoptive parents, about how there are never enough and sometimes kids have to wait years without permanent parents."

"Erin, that article applied to children with special needs or older children. A child like Joshua would have no trouble—"

"But don't you see what such a thing implies?" She turned on him then, the urgency in her words alarming the cow, causing it to moan softly. Erin put a hand out to calm her, then continued. "Some families want a perfect child."

"Yes, but—"

"Some couples won't take a child that is older."

"That's true."

"Many families don't want a child with the smallest of handicaps."

"Erin—"

"Or a child that is ethnically mixed. Because Joshua's blond doesn't mean he couldn't have some minority heritage. What if the adopting family decided they didn't want an interracial child?"

Travis searched his mind for how to argue with her, but before he could line up his defense she'd plowed forward.

"What if they found out something about him and changed their mind? Then would they throw him away?"

"No. Erin, it doesn't work that way."

"But I promised her. You didn't. I'm the one who gave my word." The tears shone in her eyes, but this time they didn't spill. "Don't you see? I don't care about what problems might crop up. When I give my word, I keep it. It matters to me that I honor my promises."

It was Travis's turn to look away.

How could he retain any objectivity when he stared into those beautiful brown eyes? When he heard the ache in her voice and saw the evidence of it still drying on her cheeks?

He needed to ignore the warmth of Joshua in his arms. What did the manual say he should do next? He knew this process, had been through it several times before, though admittedly never in a barn with a woman like Erin Jacobs.

When she stood and carried the buckets of milk to the tack room, he stood too.

She stopped to feed an iguana and three rabbits. Apparently, the dogs in the kennel running adjacent to the house had already enjoyed dinner. They trotted along companionably, but didn't raise a ruckus. How many animals did the ARK house? What percentage eventually found homes?

Travis walked in silence, considering the list of emergency contacts in his phone. The night had settled around them. He wondered what time it was, then realized he didn't care. He knew what his gut instinct was telling him—what he should do in this situation.

Pausing at the porch, he reached out his hand to slow Erin. When she turned and met his gaze, worry clouding her expression, he wanted to touch her face—smooth it away. Instead he gently transferred Joshua to her arms.

"I'll be in touch tomorrow. I need to talk to my director."

She nodded, but made no move to walk up the steps.

After he'd driven all the way down the lane, closing cattle gates behind him, he realized his folder with his case notes still lay on her porch—forgotten.

Six

Travis wanted to go home and forget the Baby Joshua case for a few hours. Better yet, he could take a left on the loop and head out to the marina. A few hours on his boat, even docked, would sooth his nerves.

At the intersection, he looked left and could just picture Lake Livingston and his 2005 Skeeter.

Tightening his grip on the wheel, he turned right—back toward the office.

Minimal lights glowed downstairs, but one office at the second floor level blazed like a lighthouse in a dark ocean. He knew who else would be working after hours. As usual, he took the stairs, hoping to burn off some of his frustration.

Instead of heading straight for Moring's office, he stopped by his cubicle to check his e-mail.

She found him there thirty minutes later playing with Newton's Bracket, a game James had given him for Christmas.

"Where did you get that?" She frowned at the seven metal balls clicking into one another with the precision of a well-designed robot. They hung from V-shaped swings in a perfect line. "I thought mutant mice had invaded the office from all the noise. Sounded like tiny claws scampering across the floor."

They both stared at the mechanism as the law of physics slowed it to a stop. Travis reached for the end ball to start it over, but Moring cleared her throat and he thought better of it.

Instead he sat back in his chair and stretched, nearly touching wall to wall of his cubicle. "James bought it, of course."

"So did you stop by just to irritate me with that noise?"

"Nope. Wanted to check my e-mail."

Moring stared pointedly at his computer, still dark and powered off.

Travis shrugged. "Haven't gotten around to it yet."

She stepped into his cubicle, moved a stack of folders off his lone extra chair, and sat down. "Tell me about the baby."

Travis started to answer her, stopped, then reached out for the silver ball of the game. Surely if Newton could understand physics, he could make sense of one child custody case.

"Don't do it." Without raising her voice, she'd issued a command—even managed to insert the edge of a growl into it.

He sighed and sank into his chair.

"Joshua appears to be a healthy six- to eight-week-old infant. Looks to be Caucasian. No obvious signs of abuse."

"How long did you spend with Joshua and Erin, Travis?"

"Ninety minutes." He studied a spot on the far wall.

"Tell me about the baby." Her voice had softened.

He turned to meet her eyes and realized he didn't know if his director was a mother. Had she ever raised an infant? Watched it grow through the phases of childhood?

"He's a little on the thin side, curly blond hair, trusting eyes."

"Better. Will your report rule this a Baby Moses case?"

Travis didn't even blink. "The most unusual one I've ever seen, but yes. I believe it is."

"Good enough. What about Erin Jacobs? Give me your impression of her, and I don't want stats."

Travis needed to pace, but knew it would be impossible in his cubicle. Instead, he picked up the miniature basketball he kept near his computer and tossed it from one hand to the other.

"She operates an animal rescue facility, which I know nothing about. I suppose it's a real business, though it doesn't seem terribly lucrative."

"Being wealthy isn't a requirement for foster care parents."

"True." Travis couldn't hold back the anxiety in his voice as he pictured Erin. "She's young—unbelievably young. Twenty-two! What twenty-two year old wants an infant? She should be out doing whatever twenty year olds do, not taking on the responsibility of a child. She's not even married."

He squirmed under the weight of Moring's gaze, but he couldn't stop the rush of words now that they had begun.

"She has an obvious emotional bond to the child, which is totally understandable since she rescued him. I think it might be a mistake to encourage her attachment though. It will only hurt her more—hurt them both more—when we find a permanent placement."

Moring held up her hand like a traffic cop, stopping his flow of thoughts.

"Great. You've collected a lot of information. Let's take it one objection at a time. It seems to me her occupation might uniquely equip her for being a foster parent. You know as well as I do we are critically short of people willing to partner with us and help children."

Travis heard what she said, knew she was right, but didn't like accepting it. He remembered her description of the cabin, envisioned her going alone on the rescue. As always, his thinking froze.

"You plan on popping that basketball?"

He looked down at the object in his white-knuckled hands and forced himself to relax his grip.

"But she's awfully young for this level of responsibility."

"Point two. Her age. Twenty-two is young, but over half of our clients marry straight out of high school. Why does she seem particularly young to you? Is she immature?"

"No."

"Are you worried about her level of commitment as a foster care parent?"

"Not at all, but—"

"Then let's leave the age issue and move on to the fact that she is single."

Travis tried not to squirm in his chair, but found it difficult.

"We've dealt with single foster parents before. Do I need to name them for you?"

"Of course not."

"Why is Jacobs different?"

"Because she's single *and* young."

"Explain."

Travis began tossing the basketball back and forth again. "The single parents we have assigned foster children to have been older. They've had a long record of stability, and they've shown a history of wanting a family."

"Miss Jacobs doesn't want a child?"

"She wants *this* child, but she wasn't looking for one when she found Joshua on a porch."

Moring stood, walked to the door of his cube, then turned and looked at him. "You've been here eight years, Travis. You're one of the best social workers I have. Occasionally, an unusual case comes along. What is really bothering you about placing Baby Joshua temporarily with Erin Jacobs?"

"She doesn't want him temporarily!" The words exploded out of him as he shot out of his chair. "She wants him permanently."

"Which is not an atypical request. There's plenty of time for you to determine what is in the best interest of the baby. Don't get ahead of yourself on this one."

"But…"

"But what?"

"But if she does this, it cuts off so many paths for her. It limits so many options for the rest of her life."

Travis finally met his boss's gaze. He understood how his words sounded. Knew they flew in direct opposition to everything their pamphlets and television spots preached, but those weren't aimed at a twenty-two-year-old woman living across town on an ARK.

"We don't get to make those decisions for people." A smile split Moring's face, revealing teeth as white and perfect as the moon shining outside. "Erin will have the next three months to determine if this is what she wants, and you'll be there to guide her through the process."

As his boss walked away, Travis thought again of his boat waiting for him over at Sneaky Pete's Marina. He should have turned left. He would still have had to face the Jacobs case, but at least he could have done it from the bow of his boat. Some nights a little procrastination went a long ways.

———

Erin stood across the surgery table from Doc England. Both wore their lab coats, surgical scrubs, gloves, and masks. Doc was six inches taller and forty years older, but other than that they could have been twins—both entirely focused on the four-footed charge lying on the table.

She'd avoided asking the question as they prepped the four-year-old basset hound for surgery. She'd rescued him three hours earlier from behind a dumpster at the park, his back foot tied with a belt to an old tire. In trying to chew through the belt, he'd also gnawed his foot almost completely through to the bone.

"Do you think we can save him?" She pushed the emotion from her voice. Somehow she had to learn to take a more professional attitude toward this job or it would tear her up inside.

"I'd suggest euthanasia if I believed it to be in the animal's best interest. What did you name this one?"

"Boomer. As you heard, he has quite the voice." Erin positioned the light over the wounded leg. "His baying alerted the neighbors near the park. Though why they didn't call me two days ago, I have no idea."

"Folks don't usually call until they haven't slept a few nights. Boomer should be fine once we fix this leg. You sure you can assist with Joshua sleeping over there?"

Erin glanced over at the baby. He'd dropped off as soon as she'd fed him the bottle, so she'd set him in a basket usually reserved for her cat. She had, of course, lined it with fresh blankets.

"Yeah. He's out." She grinned at Doc. "He's been up since five. Helped me feed the animals. Could be why he's so tired."

"Sounds like you two are on the same schedule."

"I think so. Now if fancy-pants Williams will agree to let us be…"

As England began repairing the ligaments in Boomer's leg, neither of them spoke. When Erin had stitched the wound and wrapped the leg, Doc picked up the conversation right where they'd left off.

"Didn't care for the social worker, I take it?"

Erin stripped off her surgical mask and shrugged. "He's okay, I guess, if you don't mind pushy people who spend their days meddling in other people's business."

Doc's laughter filled the small surgery room, but neither Boomer nor Joshua seemed to notice. He sat on the stool and ran his thumb between his graying eyebrows. Erin resisted the urge to squirm as he studied her. Instead, she focused on tidying the already immaculate room.

She always suspected Doc could somehow see through the tight shell she kept around her life, perhaps because he had known her for so long. She still remembered the day she'd walked to his office with her older sister Dana and one half-starved kitten. He'd patiently told her what would need to be done to keep the animal alive.

"He second guessed everything I told him. Said I should have left Joshua there at the cabin and gone for help. What kind of idiot would have walked away from a baby?" She couldn't keep the contempt out of her voice as she swiped at the counter with antiseptic.

"Well now, we discussed this. It's their job to go over every single thing that has happened to the child, analyze it, and put a plus or minus in the column next to the person responsible. In their profession, it becomes something of a human equation."

"Hate math. Always have." Erin knew she sounded like a petulant child, but it did ease some of her anxiety. She glanced again at the large wall clock. "It's nearly ten. Why hasn't he called yet? What does it mean?"

"Lay it down, Erin." Doc's voice had grown soft like the blanket in Joshua's basket.

She didn't want to raise her eyes to his, but she couldn't resist. Blue, crinkly, and kind. Aged by sixty years. Patient and concerned. She had to fight the urge to run into his arms.

"You can't carry every burden, and you needn't worry about every outcome. Let the good Lord do that."

Erin nodded but didn't answer. She heard a rustling in the corner and turned to tend to Joshua. When the cell phone in her lab coat rang, she let out a squeak.

She checked the caller ID display and saw the number she'd programmed in the night before from Travis's business card. Child Welfare—Williams. Pressing one hand to the counter to still her shaking, she answered her smart phone and raised it to her ear.

Seven

Derrick glanced up to see Tara walking toward the yacht. His first instinct was to scream at her. How dare she show up here? This was his domain. He'd earned the boat—fair and square. Five years of marriage had tested his patience to the limit. Then she'd tried playing the baby card, as if that child could possibly be his.

He had to admit she knew how to dress though. In white pants, a navy top and that hat she looked as if she could have stepped off the cover of a boating magazine. The old codger on the boat next to his was certainly giving her a slow once-over.

"Derrick."

"Why are you here, Tara?"

"I wanted to talk to you… about the other night."

"There's nothing to talk about. I don't even remember the other night." He pulled down his ball cap against the noonday sun.

She stood next to the boat, as if she was uncertain whether she should board or not. "So you don't know what I've done."

"I don't care what you've done."

Usually Tara was the type to beg and plead. There was something different about her today though. Some of the girl he'd first been attracted to was back. He dropped the rag he'd been using to polish the boat.

"Why don't you come onboard? We'll take her out. It's been a while, huh?"

Tara glanced left and right, catching the eye of the old codger. Then she nodded once and stepped onto the boat.

Eight

E rin tried to match Doc's enthusiasm as she walked him
to his truck. Tried and failed. He was acting like a first
time grandfather, when she knew for a fact he had five lovely
granddaughters. Then it struck her. Did he think of Joshua as
his first grandson?

The idea left her frozen halfway between the porch and
his Ford F-150. Doc turned around and stared back at her
when he reached his truck.

"Something wrong?" He tipped his Stetson so he could
see her better against the glare of the midmorning sun.

"No. Not at all."

"Might as well fess up, girl." When he opened the door
of the brand new truck, the smell of leather wafted out and
spurred her feet forward.

"I can't believe Evelyn let you buy a new truck."

Doc's eyes twinkled nearly as brightly as the metallic
grey paint. "Now, Evelyn and I understand each other after
thirty-five years of marriage. I go along with those two-week

vacations she insists on booking every year, and she doesn't fuss when an old man wants a new toy."

Erin shook her head. She didn't need to admit the smell of leather made her dizzy and more than a little envious. A new car had been in her budget for three years down the road, but that had been before she'd rescued Joshua.

Joshua changed everything.

She glanced down at the baby in her arms as she stood near Doc's driver's side door.

"We'll help, you know." As usual, Doc seemed able to read her thoughts. "Evelyn called the church ladies this morning. They're talking about putting together a baby shower. She'll be in touch this afternoon."

Erin ran the fingers of one hand through her hair. She'd haphazardly pulled it away from her face with a headband, but already she could feel her curls escaping.

"I couldn't let them do that. Not after—"

She stepped back as Doc climbed into the truck, his laughter piercing the morning. "You ever try to stop Evelyn when she sets her mind?"

He started the truck, rolled down the power window, then closed the door. "Let folks help. It's what they want to do. There might be a lot of things you can do alone, but raising a child isn't one of them. At least it shouldn't be."

Erin stood back as he turned the big truck around, then made his way down her lane. He was right about her needing help. She knew that. Didn't make accepting it any easier.

She glanced at her watch as she trudged toward the barns. Two hours until she needed to be in Williams's office. He'd asked if she needed more time, but she'd been anxious to get this part over with. Once the papers were signed, once the foster portion was official, at least she'd have three months to prove her case.

Hurrying toward the pig pens, she groaned when she realized she couldn't wear the clothes she had on into the Child Welfare office.

Her anger rose as she replayed the conversation in her mind. Williams had been arrogant enough to ask if she had a safety seat for Joshua, even though she'd plainly told him last night that she did. As if she'd put the child in a car without a baby carrier.

It had been the first thing Doc had brought her.

Doc had been in her life as long as she could remember. What would she have done without her foster parents' oldest friend?

She'd certainly needed his help these last two days. No doubt she would in the future as well. She remembered Doc's warning about a baby shower and stuck her tongue out as she walked into the darkness of the barn. Depending on Doc and Evelyn was one thing, allowing the entire community to help her was different.

But how else would she be able to afford the stuff she needed to become an instant mother? She could tap her savings, but she'd sworn to only touch the small nest egg for an emergency. What if she spent it on clothes and furniture for Joshua and he became ill? What if she needed to retain legal counsel?

She set Joshua down in a cleaned-out trough lined with a baby pad and blankets—more emergency gifts from Evelyn. As the questions piled up in her mind, she stabbed the pitchfork into the pigs' soiled hay. Unfortunately, the hard work didn't bring her any solutions.

Normally, she would have called her sister, but Dana was on her honeymoon in the Caribbean. After all she'd been through, Erin didn't want to interrupt the rest her sister sorely needed. If she did call, Dana would cut the vacation short and fly back tonight. No, she'd e-mail instead. She would sound less emotional in an e-mail. And she'd call the minute they landed back in the US.

Joshua sucked on his fist as she cleaned out the dirty stall in the pig pen. He was a good baby. The important thing was she had been allowed to keep him for the next ninety days.

The other questions she'd have to put off until they needed answering. She'd focus first on making it to the Child Welfare office in time, signing the papers, receiving the court's approval, and hopefully nudging the lanky social worker out of her life.

In high school, she and Dana would have fallen into fits over him—plopped him right into the tall, blond, and handsome category. Erin was no longer that naïve, teenage girl though. She had repeatedly seen the havoc those sorts of men could wreak on households—pets, women, and children. She didn't consider herself a man hater, but she didn't need one around either. Seemed to her like the good ones, the ones like Doc, were rare.

Muck out the hay, change clothes, drive to the office. Good-bye tall, blond, and handsome. Then she could worry about how to gather up all the supplies an eight-week-old baby needed.

She cleaned and stored her tools, then picked up Joshua and walked out into the warm September sunshine.

One thing at a time, and the first thing definitely involved kicking off her boots caked in manure.

Though it might be fun to wear them into Travis Williams' fancy office—a nice little good-bye gesture.

———

In the end, she decided to wear a paisley skirt that reached well past her knees, a plain ivory cotton blouse worn on the outside, and a wide western belt she buckled over the entire outfit. Of course, she wore boots. She always wore boots. But she did trade her work boots for the clean ones at the back of her closet.

Basically, she threw on what she wore to every city council meeting she was forced to endure. Would it be that different to stand before a judge?

She had eyed the dress in the back of her closet, but only for a minute. With a fitted bodice, long sleeves that ended in lace cuffs, and a skirt that stopped above her knees and fit tighter than her leather work gloves, the emerald green number would have to wait. She was not aiming to impress Travis Williams. Well, she was, but a dress wouldn't accomplish what her mouth and temper had a good chance of destroying.

The drive into town was short and uneventful. As she unsnapped Joshua from his car seat, she thought back over the Internet research she had done. Babies were to sit in the back seat—it was a good thing she had an extended cab. The truck might be old, but it would do for their purposes. She licked her thumb and pushed down the blond lock of hair that insisted on poking straight up over his left eye.

"I suppose we impressed him enough, or we wouldn't be here, right Josh?"

The baby gurgled, then blew a bubble.

"Couldn't say it better, kid. Hopefully, our new caseworker will be a woman."

With Josh tucked in one arm and her purse strap slung over her shoulder, she paused in the sun long enough to steady her racing heart. She didn't pray exactly. She'd pretty much given up praying when Jules and Nina had died in the car wreck.

Her mind flashed back on the prayer uttered in desperation as she'd driven into the woods toward the cabin holding Joshua. Instead of analyzing why she'd fallen into a childhood habit then, she pushed the memory away and tried to gather all the positive energy she could. Not that she believed in positive energy either. Which might be the problem.

She didn't know what she believed in, though she recognized the fear coursing through her veins. Trying to draw peace from the warmth of the sun, she realized walking into the building in front of her scared her to death.

So she pulled in a deep breath, opened her eyes, and marched toward the front door.

As her luck would have it, Angela Drake sat at the receptionist desk, manning the phones. "Well, Erin Jacobs. You're the last person I expected to see walk into our office this afternoon."

Erin managed not to wince at the heavy perfume smell, drifting over the desk toward her.

"Hi Angela. I'm here to see Travis Williams."

Angela popped her gum, but she didn't reach for the phone on her desk. "Travis is our senior caseworker. He's single too. Yummy, isn't he?"

Angela leaned forward to share her gossip, though of course she didn't lower her voice. Erin could make out the tiny bit of red lipstick on her front left tooth, same as in high school. Some things never changed, including the anorexic body and the too bright dress.

"We used to have a pool going—how long it would be before someone caught him. Then the amount of money collected got so high I worried Keith might *borrow* it. You know Keith. He never could be trusted with money." Angela popped her gum again and ran her fingers through her perfectly straightened brown hair. "Remember when he ran off with our junior prom money? He claimed someone stole it out of his pocket while he made out with Belinda Swardowsky who never would have even talked to Keith let alone make out with him—"

"Angela, I—"

"So don't ask me why we trusted him, but we thought he'd matured." She pursed her lips and rolled her eyes in a coordinated effort. "Well, after two years Travis still wasn't married. The kitty had reached over a hundred bucks, and I knew it was my *duty* to tell them about the missing money from the junior fund. Travis rarely even dated by then, and all the fun was out of it, so we decided to get our money back and go spend it at happy hour. Come to think of it, I never see you at happy hour."

"Angela!" The girl's over-painted eyes widened at Erin's sharp tone. "I need to see Travis. Now. I have animals to feed before five, and this baby isn't going to wait very long for his nap."

Angela cocked her head at the baby in Erin's arm, as if seeing him for the first time. "Pretty baby, but you don't have to be snippy, Erin."

Picking up the phone, she rotated her office chair so she faced the wall and cupped her hand around her mouth and the receiver as if to keep Erin from hearing her private conversation. Hanging up the phone and turning back, she said primly, "Mr. Williams will be out in a minute."

Erin sighed and walked over to the waiting area. It was empty except for a woman with two children.

"Hello," Erin said.

The woman stared at her out of tired eyes, lanky black hair spilling out of a pony tail. She looked to be under twenty and in need of a good night's rest.

A toddler sat in her lap, knocking magazines to the floor, which she would reach over and pick up—only to have him repeat the process. The older boy sat at a table of Legos, quietly building a tall tower of blue blocks. He had to stand on tiptoe to add to it, but there was no energy to his play—no creativity in the design or choice of colors.

It all made Erin want to take Joshua and run back out into the sunshine.

Both children had runny noses and dirty clothing. Erin pulled Joshua closer to her breast, wondering if perhaps the children had a cold. Hadn't she read waiting rooms were the most likely places to catch a cold?

Her palms began to sweat as she looked down at the baby in her arms. She tucked the blanket more tightly around him to provide some measure of protection.

The possibility of rampant viruses galloping across the room scared her enough, but the haunted look in the woman's eyes was downright terrifying. What if her apathy was contagious?

The idea had barely formed in her mind when the door next to the reception area pushed open and Travis Williams walked through it. He was dressed in a light charcoal suit, starched white shirt, and Snoopy tie. All of which accentuated his healthy tan and sun-bleached hair. When his eyes met hers, Erin melted.

For a moment she forgot this man was her enemy.

In her need to flee the dreariness of the waiting room and the watching eyes of Angela, she jumped out of her chair.

Travis's eyebrows sprang up in surprise. His blue eyes twinkled as she practically ran across the room toward him. Erin briefly saw something there that reminded her of Doc— a kindness and affection.

"Erin. Joshua. Nice to see you two again."

His voice did funny things to her stomach. What was wrong with her? She pressed Joshua closer, trying to remember if she'd eaten. She couldn't think when Travis stood so close though. Every thought had flown right out of her head, leaving her dizzy with his scent—some combination of citrus aftershave, soap, and the outdoors.

Too late she realized he'd asked her something and was waiting for an answer. Glancing over at Angela, she wasn't surprised to see her old classmate had walked to the filing cabinet closest to them. No doubt so she could eavesdrop.

"I think I need to change Joshua," she murmured, hoping the excuse would cover her inattention.

"My office is through this door and upstairs, or we can take the elevator."

She followed him through the door without speaking and nodded toward the stairs.

"We have a large restroom with a changing station right around the corner." Touching her elbow, he guided her down the hall. His hand felt warm, even through her cotton blouse. Her pulse jumped, and she wondered if he could feel the thrumming of it through her veins.

She tried to focus on what he was saying. She heard the words Cowboys and Texans and somehow understood he was talking about football. He was trying to put her at ease. If she could make it to the bathroom, she could pull herself together.

"Here's the restroom, Erin. My office cubicle is to the right. Take as much time as you need." He again touched her arm, his blue eyes staring deep into hers, and then he turned and walked down the corridor.

She fled into the bathroom.

The changing table had high sides. She laid Joshua down, and with shaking hands, she popped a pacifier in his mouth, then moved to the rocker they had provided for nursing mothers.

Sitting down, she lowered her head between her knees.

She was having a panic attack.

Coming here, then seeing Angela, remembering high school, that poor tired woman with those two children. It had all been too much. It had pushed her right over like a tower of Legos. She—Erin Jacobs, who had single-handedly rescued alligators and put them back in the swamp—was having a panic attack over becoming a mother.

Then a big, strong, single male walks into the room, and she wants to run into his arms.

It would be hilarious if it wasn't so pathetic.

For the hundredth time in the last forty-eight hours, she wished she could call her sister Dana. Of all the weeks for her to decide to go on a honeymoon.

Nina always said God's timing was perfect.

What would she say about this?

Erin continued to suck in deep breaths of air as she stared at the blue-and-white tiled floor of the bathroom. She finally became conscious of Joshua's cooing.

Sitting upright, then standing, she stumbled over to stare down at him. There were many things she didn't understand, many more things she downright doubted. But one thing she remained convinced of—this baby belonged in her life.

She walked to the sink and turned on the cold water, ran it over her hands, and sprinkled some on the back of her neck. The coolness calmed her enough to lower her racing heartbeat.

By the time she reached Joshua's side, he'd spit out the pacifier and had plunged his fist into his mouth, looking quite pleased with himself.

"Yes, you're quite resourceful, little man."

Scooping him up, she hugged him to her and kissed the top of his head. Then she collected her wits, what she could find of them, and walked out of the bathroom.

Nine

Travis struggled with what to write in his notes as he waited for Erin to return from the ladies' room.

He'd been met in vastly different ways by clients over the years, but never quite like Erin had just greeted him. When he'd first appeared in the waiting area, she'd run toward him as if he held the sole life preserver as they were all drowning in the ocean.

Or had that been his imagination?

Hard to tell with the way his heart had jumped its regular rhythm. Erin Jacobs was one beautiful woman, which presented unique challenges of its own. Travis knew he could maintain a professional distance, but interpreting her moods in order to write his reports objectively might be difficult.

Once she'd reached his side, she suddenly looked lost as if maybe that wasn't where she'd wanted to be. Again, not the response Travis normally produced. He was used to clients being uncomfortable around him, but never terrified. The expression on Erin's face had pierced him through and through. How was he going to put her at ease when her moods shifted around like a puck on an ice rink?

So he'd talked football. Football! Like that made any sense.

During the last twelve minutes, and it had been exactly twelve because he'd been timing it, he'd only stared at his report pad, praying for wisdom.

He definitely needed it because Erin Jacobs and Baby Joshua were obviously not an ordinary case.

A light tapping startled him, jerking him back to the present.

Two heads—one auburn, one blond—peeked around the corner of his cubicle. "Are we in the right place?"

"Yes. Come on in." Travis motioned to the one empty chair he'd already cleared off. "Everything okay?"

"Absolutely." Erin smiled and looked directly into his eyes as if challenging him to declare her and Joshua anything but perfectly fine.

Travis nodded. "Great. As I explained on the phone, we need to sign a few papers, then run across the street to see the judge. After we receive her approval, I'll go over the process of the next ninety days."

He moved the desktop football goal so he could place the sheaf of papers in front of her. When she cast a sideways look at the game, he explained, "It puts some of my younger clients at ease. I have several—Nerf football, Nerf darts, maze bead games. I guess Joshua is a little too young."

She tilted her head and studied him, but didn't respond.

"What?"

"Nothing." She looked down at the papers, a smile playing on her lips.

"You don't believe the games are for kids."

Her smile grew, but still she didn't look up from the papers.

"Why don't you believe me, Erin?"

When she did look up, her brown eyes were laughing at him, and he didn't mind one bit. Though he knew the joke was on him, though he had no idea what the joke was, it was better than the confusion he'd seen written on her face fifteen minutes ago.

He leaned forward and lowered his voice. "So, I'm busted. What gave me away?"

His confession pulled out her laughter, evaporating any residual tension. "If the football goal was for your clients it would have been on the other side of your cubicle, where they could shoot from this seat. Since it's here, it must be for you to shoot… from your seat."

He sank back into his chair and studied her. "You're the first client to call me on that. Either you're the first to notice, or you're the first to realize I'm an overgrown kid."

Instead of answering, she fussed with Joshua. He noticed she handled the baby a bit more naturally than she had the day before, her hands moving over the infant lovingly and with the ease of a biological mother. He made a mental note to put a notation on his sheet about it.

"Moving helps me to think, puzzle things out. Working in this cube—some days I think I'm going to go completely nuts. The games help."

She met his gaze, nodded, and then returned her attention to the papers. "What does this clause mean?"

They spent the next twenty minutes going over the legal wording.

"Ready to go next door?"

Her eyes widened, and he noticed she clutched Joshua tightly, but her reply was firm. "Yes."

"Let's do this then."

Her death grip around Joshua relaxed the moment they stepped into the sunshine, but her face still looked drained of all color.

"I suppose it helps to have your office across the square from the courthouse."

"Doesn't hurt." He walked between her and the stopped traffic as they crossed at the light. Reaching to help her at the curb, he couldn't help but notice that her hand was ice cold.

She proceeded toward the steps of the Polk County Courthouse, the expression on her face looking like the caricature of a man headed for the gallows. It might have been comical if it hadn't tugged at his heart.

"Erin, wait a minute." He pulled her into the meager shade of a crepe myrtle tree. "This is a formality. There's nothing to worry about. Section 262 of the Family Code requires my office to request an initial hearing. The judge will appoint an attorney for Joshua—"

"How will I pay for—"

"Paid for by my office." He clutched her case folder with one hand and pushed his other into his pocket—anything to keep himself from reaching out and smoothing the worry off her face. "I explained this on the phone. We're seeking termination of the parent-child relationship, based on the fact that Joshua's mother voluntarily relinquished him under the Safe Haven law."

He watched her swallow, switch Joshua from one arm to the other, and knew she wanted to trust him.

"What if the judge says no? What if they take him away?"

"The police have searched and found no missing child report that matches Joshua. They'll continue to look, but at this point, there's nothing standing in the way of temporary placement."

She nodded, and a hint of color flowed back into her face.

"Are you ready?"

"Yeah."

"All right. Let's take Joshua to see the judge."

Walking into the courtroom, standing beside her as the bailiff read their names, Travis realized anew how intimidating the process could be. When Erin's moment before the bench came, she did herself proud.

Judge Boultinghouse was in her fifties, though only the spectacles she peered over hinted at her age. Thin hair fashionably dyed in a blend of light and dark browns reached to her shoulders. She wore the dignity of her robes well.

"I'd say Baby Joshua is lucky you found him, Miss Jacobs. We need more citizens willing to step forward and help raise our less fortunate children. Mr. Williams, I expect to see your full assessment within ninety days, including physicians and law enforcement reports."

"Of course, Your Honor."

When she stamped the papers, Erin jumped. Then the judge declared, "Next," and he thought for a split second Erin might throw her arms around his neck.

Her face lit up, the worry evaporated, and he was struck again with her fresh, absolute beauty.

"That's it?" She stood so close to him he caught the scent of the shampoo she used—something reminding him of honeysuckle in bloom.

"That's it. We can go."

She pulled in her bottom lip, trying to bite back the smile that wouldn't be tempered. Finally, she satisfied herself with burying her face in Joshua's curls.

"Let's go into the hall and sign the judge's papers."

They sat in the hard wooden chairs. She had signed everything, and he'd made her a copy on the clerk's machine and slipped it into an envelope.

They both stood and moved toward the doors. Then he upset her world one more time.

"Expect my first visit before Monday."

"Excuse me?" She'd been switching Joshua from one arm to the other, stuffing the envelope into her bag, and pulling the bag over her shoulder. At his words, her head jerked up and her auburn hair fell into her eyes.

Travis had the irrational urge to reach forward and tuck the curls out of her eyes so she could see better, so she could understand. Instead, he took a step back and spoke slowly, clearly. She'd processed a lot of information in one day. It was no wonder she was having trouble retaining it all.

"I'll make my first site visit before Monday. As we discussed, some of my calls will be scheduled, but some will be impromptu."

"I understand about the visits, but why will you be there?"

Over the course of the afternoon, the tension between them had eased until it was nearly gone. Now it had returned like a thick fog between them. Travis shook his head as if to clear his thoughts.

"Erin, I can't conduct the visits unless I'm present."

"But..." She looked around the hall, then juggled Joshua to her other arm. "Will you be there every time?"

Travis had viewed her college scores when he did a background check. He knew she wasn't dense. "How can I conduct a visit if I'm not there?"

"I thought the caseworker did the visits."

"Erin, I am your caseworker."

—

Erin stared at Travis Williams and tried to string words together to make a coherent sentence come out of her mouth. She tried once, twice, and then she gave up.

"Why don't you sit back down? I'll get you a glass of water."

She backed into the chair she'd just left and plopped into it. Better than falling onto the floor, which is what she would do if she trusted her legs another minute.

Travis Williams was her caseworker?

She could not have heard him right.

She'd made it through the last ninety minutes. She'd survived placing their lives in the hands of a judge, trusting their future to Travis's report. The knowledge that he would be out of her life, that she wouldn't have to look across the table at those blue eyes that seemed to want to probe deeper into hers than they had a right, well that knowledge had given her courage. She could endure anything for ninety minutes.

So she'd relaxed, even managed to be personable.

Because it had only been for ninety minutes!

She couldn't possibly tolerate the man for ninety days. Scheduling weekly visits? Showing up at her house unannounced? Visiting her during work hours?

Suddenly, all the things she'd agreed to on the pages she'd signed leapt out to her. While she'd been reading the papers she'd pictured a sweet, gray-haired lady coming by to check on her and Joshua. She had not pictured tall, blond, and handsome. She didn't need or want him in her life.

Travis appeared with a Styrofoam cup of water and pushed it into her hands. "Drink this. You lost all your color there for a minute."

She raised the cup to her lips and took a sip. Anything to put off speaking to him for another minute. How could she convince him she needed a different caseworker?

Then, as in so many other times in her life, she heard Jules's soft voice. "Never be afraid to ask for what you need, Erin. It can't hurt to ask."

Her foster father could not have envisioned the situation she was in now, but he'd been the wisest man she'd ever known, wiser even than Doc. She took another sip of water, aware of Travis's eyes on her, of Joshua's weight in her arms.

Drawing a deep breath, she set the cup down and pulled herself up to her straightest posture.

When she spoke, she looked Travis straight in the eyes so there would be no misunderstanding. "I don't mean to be rude or impertinent, Mr. Williams—"

"Travis." He smiled, clearly relieved she wasn't going to faint on him or go running off for another prolonged bathroom break.

"Travis. I didn't realize you would be my caseworker. That you would be the person doing the site visits. I thought you would hand my case over to another worker."

Understanding dawned on his face. Erin was tempted to look away as heat crept up her neck, burning her cheeks. It would be easier not to look into those blue eyes given what she was about to say, but this was too important. Ninety days! He had to know she was serious.

"You have been very kind to both Joshua and myself, but I personally would be more comfortable if I could have a woman caseworker. Perhaps someone older."

Travis started to interrupt her, but she put her hand up and stopped him. "It's nothing against you, and I realize this is an unusual request. It would be a great favor to me though if you could arrange it."

For the first time since she'd met him, the man was speechless. She took his silence as a better sign than a *no*.

Perhaps she should leave and allow him time to consider her request. Jumping out of the seat, she walked to the end of the hall. She had almost escaped when he spoke.

"I don't think I can do that, Erin. Once a caseworker is assigned, unless there is due cause, according to Section Eight of the Code, changing personnel is impossible."

She turned on him then, trying to think of what else she could say. What frustrated her was the knowledge that this man held all the cards, and he held her future.

So she said nothing. Instead she simply nodded, turned, and fled.

Ten

Erin pushed through the doors of the courthouse, back out into the waning afternoon sunshine, and walked straight into Chance Stubber of *The Livingston Daily*.

He raised his camera in front of his chubby, acne-pocked face and clicked twice.

"What are you doing, Chance?"

"Interviewing you and Baby Joshua. This is going to be bigger than any of your other stories, Miss Jacobs. This is front-page material."

Erin skirted around him at the same moment Travis walked out the door.

"What's going on?" he said.

"I'm reporting on the Baby Moses case." Chance turned toward Travis, snapping a picture of him, then holding out his recorder. "Do you have any comments as the caseworker, Mr. Williams?"

"I do not," Travis growled.

Erin had made it halfway down the steps. On hearing the tone of Travis's voice, she turned, curious as to what had riled him so. She was familiar with Livingston's small paper. Although Chance could be a nuisance at times, she also considered him harmless.

The young reporter took advantage of her pause and jogged to catch up, pushing his micro-recorder in her face.

"Is it true you found him on the porch of a hunter's cabin? Can you confirm you were actually on an animal rescue at the time?"

Erin had opened her mouth to respond when Travis swooped to her side, placing a steadying hand on her back, and towered over Chance.

"Miss Jacobs is leaving. This child's case is sealed by Judge Boultinghouse, and unless you want to walk inside and discuss it with the judge, I suggest you take your tape recorder and slither back to your van."

Erin forced herself to ignore the feel of his hand on her back and focused instead on the turf war between the two men. Travis scored points on physical intimidation. And though sweat had broken out on Chance's brow, the young man didn't back down.

"I wouldn't presume to break any of the Family Code Statutes, Mr. Williams. However, Miss Jacobs is free to share her story with the good folks of Livingston."

Erin thought she could hear Travis grind his molars together, though at least this time he wasn't pompous enough to answer for her.

Fortunately, Joshua did. He let out a cry, loud and lusty, which no doubt reached the inner chambers of the court, and he continued to wail.

"No, Chance." She glanced once at Travis, then over toward her truck. "I have no comment."

—

She was grateful neither man followed her to her truck. She settled Joshua in his seat, placated him with a pacifier, and drove out of the lot. She made it around the corner and three blocks down before her temper flared.

She checked for traffic, pulled carefully over into the fast-food parking area, partially lowered the windows, and slipped the transmission into park.

Checked the parking brake.

Checked Joshua, who was now sleeping sweetly.

She quietly stepped out of the truck, shut the door as gently as a whisper, then let loose like a tornado.

She ranted.

She raved.

She paced back and forth in the late afternoon sun, not caring if folks hustling in to get their burgers saw the crazy lady talking to herself. If she didn't let off some steam she'd go back and tell Travis Williams exactly what she thought, and what good would that do?

None.

Go by the book indeed. Ninety days of his visits, his snooping, his prying into her life. Twelve weeks! She'd have to put up with his smug face and GQ looks for twelve weeks.

She stopped her pacing and checked in the front window.

Joshua slept on, oblivious to her meltdown.

Which was how she wanted to raise him, completely oblivious to any hardship around him. The child had suffered enough.

She resumed her pacing and looked up to see a discount shopping center across the street. Travis would be checking to see if she'd set up a sleeping area for Joshua. She couldn't keep putting him in troughs and kitty baskets.

And he could stop by her place tomorrow!

She clamped her jaw together and walked around to the driver's door, wondering for the hundredth time if she should call Dana.

She wanted nothing more than her sister's arms around her. Her sister—who was now married. The thought of her new brother-in-law made her want to laugh and cry at the same time. She could finally stop worrying about Dana. Ben Marshall would see that nothing happened to her.

Which was a rather funny thought since her sister was the director of the Department of Homeland Security office in Taos, New Mexico. It was a small office, but it still had its share of danger, which was why Dana loved it. She'd fled Texas and all their family history and started over in New Mexico. Then Ben had come to work for her while she was chasing a lunatic. The timing had been perfect. Not only had he worked alongside Dana providing needed expertise, he'd fallen in love with her. He'd also been patient and waited until Dana realized she felt the same. Many late night phone calls had kept Erin apprised of the status of their relationship, and she hadn't been a bit surprised when they'd finally married. She'd been happy for them! Her sister deserved a normal life.

Erin started her truck and dried her tears. If Dana could go after the bad guys in northern New Mexico, she could take on one uppity caseworker who insisted on going *by the book.* The words caused her blood to boil again, but she refused to indulge in more crying. She needed to get home, finish her chores, and transfer funds to her checking account.

By the time she called Dana, she wanted to be able to say the nursery was all set up.

A sinking feeling churned in her stomach. How much money would it drain from her account to set up house for a baby? What if she had another emergency? Those were questions she couldn't afford to ask though.

She had committed to this path. The future would have to take care of itself.

—

Fifteen minutes later she pulled up to the ARK and wondered if she could wish herself invisible. Maybe she could hide inside the vehicle until the two ladies on her front porch left.

There wasn't even a miniscule chance of that happening. Evelyn had spotted her from the second gate and had stepped off the porch before Erin could put the truck into park. She might have been sixty, but the woman was slender and in great shape. A few inches taller than Erin, with straight, gray hair cut in a no-nonsense shag, she was every girl's wish for a grandmother.

No chance of sneaking away. Evelyn was already at the front bumper of the truck. Evelyn's sidekick for the afternoon, Shirley, was mere steps behind.

They both rounded Erin's bumper and peered in the passenger seat, opening the door as quickly as possible.

"Oh my goodness. Erin Jacobs. I can't believe you haven't brought this little man over to let me see him." Evelyn unbuckled Joshua faster than the barn cat ,Bitzy, could lap up a saucer of milk.

Erin slid out of the truck and walked over to them.

"How are you, Erin?" Shirley embraced her in a hug, pausing to look deep in her eyes and wait for an answer.

It had been four months since Erin had seen Shirley. The last time had been when her boxer had managed to wedge his head in between some boards underneath their porch. Embarrassment caused sweat to run in tiny rivulets down her back. She should have called Shirley to tell her about Dana's marriage.

There was a time when Shirley Smith had been a regular at their house. She'd been the closest thing Dana had to a best friend.

Now Erin looked into those familiar hazel eyes and felt something close to yearning. Shirley would be there for her if she'd just let herself open up, but opening up was hard. And dangerous. Safer to be alone. Safer to handle life without help than to have someone ripped from her world again.

A smile tugged at Shirley's lips. Her long red hair was pulled back in a ponytail, and her stomach protruded with the obvious signs of her third child.

Erin had wondered if she was pregnant when she'd rescued the boxer, but hadn't stayed around to ask. She remembered now that Shirley had made her promise to stop back by and had even left a few messages on her cell, but she'd never returned the calls.

"Are you okay?" Shirley asked again.

"I'm fine." Erin looked down at her boots and then glanced over at Evelyn before answering. "You look great. I didn't know you were expecting again. I should have called."

"You've been busy with the animals." Shirley's voice held no resentment, neither did she move away though Erin refused to meet her gaze. "Evelyn and Doc tell us about some of your rescues."

"Half of them wind up in the paper," Evelyn said, snorting.

"Not by my doing." Erin shook her head, thinking of Chance and their recent encounter. "I'd just as soon *The Livingston Daily* kept my name out of it."

"If those stories make people think twice about how they treat their animals, it's worth you suffering the spotlight, Erin." Evelyn had lectured her about this so many times, she didn't bother putting any scolding behind her words.

Shirley turned her attention to the baby.

"He's beautiful. Did you really find him on a porch?"

"She did, and thank the Lord she called Stanley, though I wish you had waited before going out there." Evelyn was the only one who called Doc by his given name.

Erin always had to remind herself who she was talking about, even after all these years. He'd never been Stanley to her but simply *Doc*. When she didn't answer, Evelyn managed to give her a disapproving look in the middle of cooing to Joshua.

Joshua stared up at all three women, blinking sleepily at the attention being showered on him. Small arms came up over his head in a stretch, then he plopped his right fist into his mouth and began to suck.

"He's a fist sucker," Evelyn observed in an approving tone. "That's good. Colton was a fist sucker, and I thought it was much more convenient than having to find a pacifier in the middle of the night."

She turned and carried Joshua back toward the porch, still fussing over the baby.

Following in Evelyn and Shirley's wake, Erin finally noticed the condition of her front porch. She sucked in a deep breath and stopped in the middle of the gravel path.

Eleven

"Better go back and get her," Evelyn said softly.

"Come on, Erin." Shirley placed one hand in the crook of her arm and tugged her toward the porch. "It's a few basic things. Folks wanted to help, and we knew you wouldn't abide a shower. So we brought it to you."

"A few things?" Erin's voice squeaked. She licked her lips and tried again. "You all must have bought out the entire department store."

Evelyn and Shirley's laughter filled the late afternoon. Their kindness, their very presence, should have drained some of the tension from Erin's shoulders. Instead, she felt her back stiffening and her shoulders bunching up. She didn't want this, didn't want to accept all the bags lined up across her front porch spilling over with the things Joshua needed.

The tears pushed at her eyes, but she fought them back. She didn't want to accept their generosity, although she knew she would.

She would for Joshua's sake.

"No, we didn't buy out the store," Shirley assured her. "First of all, *we* didn't do it all. Lots of people pitched in."

"Church folk and town folk." Evelyn had stopped on the porch steps. Her gentle voice carried out to them.

"Even old schoolmates," Shirley added.

When Erin turned on Shirley in surprise, she raised her hands up in defense. "They'd already heard about Joshua. He's the talk of Livingston."

"Secondly, it's not all new," Evelyn continued. "Like most babies, Mr. Joshua will have to make do with some gently used items."

"Used is fine." Erin continued to the steps and sat down on the bottom one. She once again felt the need to put her head between her knees. Motherhood apparently held more surprises than being an animal rescuer.

She realized that she needed to toughen up emotionally.

"Give me your keys," Evelyn said. "We'll take Joshua inside while you tend to the animals."

"Have you decided which room you want to make the nursery?" Shirley sat beside her on the step and wound her arm lightly through Erin's.

"The empty one," she mumbled. Fumbling in her purse, she handed the keys over to Evelyn.

It seemed to Erin that only yesterday she'd been walking down the road with Shirley and Dana. Wearing shorts and flip-flops, wandering to Doc's to watch him work with the animals. It was all she'd ever wanted to do. Dana had always teased her about it, but more afternoons than not they'd wind their way to his place, sit on the fence, and watch the horses.

It had made other things in her life simpler, cleaner somehow. The animals she could understand.

Her own feelings she didn't understand at all. Sitting on the step beside Shirley, she fought the urge to pull her arm away, jump off the step, and run to the barn.

She fought the urge to bury her head on her friend's shoulder.

Instead, she quietly confessed, "I didn't plan on being a mother."

"You don't have to be."

"Now that I've held him, fed him, looked into his blue eyes, it's as if I've promised him."

"Feeling like you owe someone isn't strong enough to last eighteen years, Erin. And motherhood doesn't stop when kids trot off to college." Shirley rubbed her belly with her other hand. "No one would blame you if you decided you weren't ready for this. Joshua is a wonderful baby. I'm sure a good family in Livingston would come forward."

A shiver ran down Erin's spine as the colors before her laced with Shirley's words. Though they were facing south, the setting sun splayed color across the entire southern sky, painting a dazzling display of reds, purples, even yellows, against the backdrop of wide open Texas blue.

She'd been that blue before Joshua.

She had thought her life was good, but it had been empty.

How could she explain that to Shirley, who she barely knew anymore?

"*I* want to be that good family. From the minute I picked him up from the washtub, I fell in love with the little guy."

"I can see why."

"What I'm afraid of though is that I'll let him down. It's one thing to take care of a bunch of animals. It's another to raise a child. I have no idea what I'm doing."

Shirley put her arm around Erin's shoulder, pulling her into a hug.

And though Erin couldn't allow herself to relax, a part of her reveled in the warmth of her friend's devotion.

"None of us have any idea what we're doing. Welcome to parenthood." Shirley rubbed her arm, then tousled her hair. "Joshua is lucky to have you because you care about him so much. The rest you'll learn."

Erin nodded, though she could feel the doubts surging, threatening to overpower her as they'd done in Travis's office.

"And you can call me," Shirley added.

"Keep your cell phone charged." Erin pulled in a deep breath. "I better see to my animals."

They both stood and walked up the steps.

Erin was still overwhelmed by the bounty of goods on her porch, but she'd deal with that after the chores. At least she knew she had two friends to help her—three if you counted Doc, which she did. The problem was she had forgotten how to be a friend. She didn't know any more about it than she did about being a mother.

It was a good thing Travis Williams wouldn't be probing into that part of her life.

Resolutely, she stiffened her shoulders and turned toward the barn. She needed to get to work, then she had a nursery to put together.

—

Erin was torn between lingering in the barn to avoid going back to the house, and going back to the house so Evelyn and Shirley would leave.

In the end, she did what she had to do. She cared for the two cows, four cats, three dogs, one goat, a llama, ducks, an iguana, several rabbits, and two horses that made up her ARK at the moment. Once done, she marched resolutely in the darkness back toward her house. Maybe she could thank them and they'd go.

Erin really did like Evelyn and Shirley, but somehow in the last year—in the year since Jules and Nina were killed—she'd grown used to being alone. Trudging up the steps of her porch, she removed her boots. On one level, she knew she'd need to change her degree of isolation now that she had Joshua. But it was something she'd have to think about later when he was older. Certainly not tonight.

Walking inside, the tantalizing smell of chicken nearly knocked her over, causing her stomach to growl. Evelyn stood at the stove, and Shirley emerged from what she'd come to think of as Joshua's room.

"I heated up a little of my chicken casserole for you." Evelyn turned to look her up and down. "I know you like it."

"Thank you. I'll have some later."

"All right. I need to get home and feed Stanley anyway. The man can perform surgery on any of a hundred different animals, but he can't heat a casserole." Evelyn shook her head but smiled as she said it.

"Erin, do you want to check Joshua's room? We only did the minimum." Shirley raked her fingers through her hair and retied it with her hair band as she spoke. "I figured some things you'd want to do yourself."

Erin peeked into the living room and realized all the bags had disappeared. She followed Shirley into the bedroom, reminding herself she needed to be gracious, she needed to accept help, she needed to keep her head about her.

Why was this so hard? For what seemed like the hundredth time since waking, tears stung her eyes.

Turning the corner into the room, her hand flew to her mouth, and she reached out to the doorframe for support.

"What you don't like, we could redo tomorrow." Shirley pushed stray red hair back behind her ear.

"I think Erin's overwhelmed." Evelyn's gentle voice behind her was like rain on the dry ground.

Erin closed her eyes and nodded, then forced herself to open them again and look around.

A crib stood in the middle of one wall, and Joshua was sound asleep in it. A mobile with horses hung over it. Next to the crib a changing table had been set up with a clean, white changing pad on it. A giraffe hung on a peg on the wall next to it. Partially unzipped, she could see it was filled with diapers. The shelf underneath was stocked with wipes and other things she couldn't even name.

An old dresser she had kept in the room had been topped with a puppy lamp and a blue lamp shade. Around the puppy's neck was a collar and a dog tag that read, "All God's Creatures."

"Jess came over and put up the crib while you were in the barns. He said you better stop by before this baby is born." Shirley beamed, her hand resting on her stomach for a moment, then moving to the dresser, indicating each drawer as she spoke. "I put the clothes in the drawers. Sizes he can wear now are in the top three drawers. Bigger sizes in the bottom two."

Erin pulled in a shaky breath, but didn't trust herself to speak.

"In the closet are a few more bags with things I thought you'd want to set out yourself. I also put the extra bags of diapers in there."

"Formula and bottles are in the cabinet to the left of the fridge." Evelyn walked over to check on Joshua. She reached down and adjusted the blanket covering him. "It's not like you were keeping a lot of food in this house, Erin Jacobs."

Shirley patted her on the arm as she walked out to the living room.

Erin thought Evelyn would follow, but instead she turned to her and handed her a book wrapped in brown paper and an envelope.

"The book is from me and Stanley. Read the inscription inside the cover when you have a quiet moment. The money in the envelope is what folks donated. Please don't ask me to return it. I wouldn't know who to give it back to."

Erin shook her head—left, right, left, right, left, right. She couldn't seem to stop. Her life had spun off on some cosmic orbit since she'd answered that 4:00 a.m. call. When would it resemble something she understood?

Evelyn's cool hands on her face quieted her thoughts. "Erin, look at me."

Erin swallowed and forced her eyes to meet the one woman she allowed to occasionally breech the walls she'd built around her life. "We're going to be here for you. Any time—doesn't matter when. You call."

Erin felt herself nod, even as she clutched the book and the envelope.

Behind her Joshua began to stir. She closed her eyes, grateful for the interruption.

"Take care of the baby. We'll let ourselves out."

Before Evelyn reached the hall, Erin managed a quiet, "Thank you."

She barely recognized the voice as her own.

Twelve

Travis pulled into the driveway of his parents' home—a typical 1950s brick that had been added on to several times—and wondered if he should have called and cancelled. He couldn't recall when the habit had started, but for several years now he'd stopped by on Wednesday evenings, always bringing dessert to compliment his mother's cooking.

Barbara Williams could cook as good a pie as any Travis could pick up in his wanderings, but she steadfastly refused to since George's diabetes diagnosis. Travis served as mediator by supplying his dad with sugar-free alternatives once a week.

"Dinner smells like my favorite—chicken."

His mom kissed his cheek, accepting the boxed pie. "I don't know why you spoil your father this way."

Travis shut the back door and set his keys on the counter.

"Because he appreciates his old man. That's why. One day I'll have a grandson who will in turn do the same for him." George Williams strode into the kitchen and held out his hand to his oldest son. After they'd shook, he pulled him into a bear hug. "Any chance you brought the real stuff this once?"

"Sorry, Pop. I'm with Mom on this one—sugar-free key lime."

"Can't blame a guy for trying. Still sounds wonderful."

"You're looking great. Lose more weight?"

His dad patted his waist line and grinned. "Joined the walking club at church. We go at it an hour every morning—sunshine or rain."

"Between walking and golfing, Dr. Lane says in six months there's a good chance he'll be off the insulin."

"Excellent." Travis pilfered a warm wheat roll from the stovetop and sat down at the table. The day's stress melted more quickly than the butter he spread on the top as he fell into the familiar routine of the home he'd grown up in. "What does he attribute the drastic change to?"

"Retirement. Seems I should have done it a long time ago." His dad grinned and headed toward the computer room. "Need to check on some day trades I made. Call me when dinner's ready."

His mom rolled her eyes and placed a glass of iced tea in front of Travis. "Phooey. He's been retired a year and had gained ten pounds. Truth is I was tired of him following me around all day like a puppy. I told him if he didn't get out of this house at least four hours a day, I was going back to work."

Travis eyed his mother over the top of his tea. Unsweetened but with a touch of lemon, it hit the spot. "Were you serious?"

"Absolutely. He was driving me crazy. I couldn't get anything done with him underfoot. When he caught me reading ads from the Livingston online paper, he dusted off his golf clubs. Then Fred convinced him to join the walking geezers."

"Geezers, huh?" Travis stood up and joined her at the sink. After washing his hands, he began cutting carrots and radishes for the salad as his mother took the chicken breasts out of the oven, sprinkled parmesan cheese lightly on the top, then popped them back in. "You two are amazing."

"Why do you say that, dear?"

"Most couples only bicker with each other. You two actually make healthy changes. It's good to see."

"Don't put us on any pedestal. We have our share of quarrels. Remember the time I locked him outside until he promised to paint the bathroom?"

Travis laughed as he picked up a cucumber. "I do. I was seventeen and came home to find Pop turning over every brick that lined the front garden, trying to remember which one he'd hidden a key under."

"I made sure I had both door keys."

"What I don't remember is why you didn't just paint it yourself? You've done plenty of projects around here."

"I tried, but the walls in that room are nine feet tall. Your father insisted I wait on him. I had bought a china-blue paint, brushes, everything, and after three months I'd had it. Finally, I pulled out the ladder and started myself, but he came home and caught me—carted all the stuff back out to the garage. I looked at half painted walls for six months."

"So you locked him out."

"Yes, I did. It made more sense than arguing."

Travis leaned over and kissed the top of his mom's head. "What's that for?"

"Because I think you're great. I see a lot of obstinate men and women. Most of them aren't as creative with their stubbornness."

"God did give me a sense of humor with my bull streak."

The dinner was exactly what Travis needed. Only a few times did his mind return to Erin Jacobs and Baby Joshua. If his parents noticed he occasionally lost the thread of the conversation, they didn't say anything.

After his dad left for choir practice, he helped his mom with the dishes. It was when he'd dried the last dish and was hanging up the towel that she brought up his inattention.

"I should have known I couldn't slip anything past you."

He pulled her into a hug, the top of her head not quite reaching his chin.

"Parents are paid to notice these things, son. I'm assuming it's your job, unless you've taken the time for a personal life and haven't told me."

Travis laughed as he retrieved his keys. "My personal life—the boat and the guys—are fine."

"Can you talk about it?"

His mom followed him out into the night. It was all so comforting that Travis wanted to stay. The sound of crickets filled the evening air. A basketball bouncing next door brought back the familiar urge to lose himself for an hour in the sport, in any sport.

Unfortunately, he still wouldn't have any answers for Erin after that hour. He sighed and ran his hand through his hair.

"Must be a bad one."

"First time I've had a client ask for a different caseworker." Travis leaned against his Chevy Blazer, stared at his mom, and tried to shrug it off.

She put both her hands on her hips, which had rounded a bit since she turned sixty, and demanded, "Are they crazy? You're the best caseworker in Polk County."

"I'm glad you're not prejudiced."

"They don't have to believe me. Have them ask your boss—the tall woman."

"Director Moring." Travis had to smile at the look of outrage on his mother's face. He should have known she would go to bat for him.

"Exactly. She'll tell them you're the best."

"Actually she assigned me to the case."

"Well, there you have it. What kind of fool—"

"Actually I think I've somehow stepped off on the wrong foot with this new mom…" Travis's words trailed off as he watched his mom's head jerk up.

She stepped closer, put her hand on his arm, and peered up at him in the darkness.

"I don't suppose you'd be talking about the younger Jacobs girl?"

Travis felt his jaw tighten so that an ache started up his molars. "Mom, you know I can't talk about my clients. It's a violation of HIPPA laws—"

"Stop. You don't have to tell me anything. Besides, I've already heard most of the details through the church's prayer chain. Those girls have had a hard life."

"There are two?"

His mom mirrored his position, leaning against her red Ford Fusion and crossing her arms. "Dana's the oldest. Erin's the youngest. Didn't you go to school with one of them?"

Travis frowned and ran his thumb over his bottom lip. "I knew her name sounded familiar, but Erin is very young—twenty-two."

"You probably knew Dana."

Travis shook his head. "We had a small class, four hundred kids. I don't remember her."

"Well she wasn't an athlete, and you were all about sports in those days."

"If she's as beautiful as her sister, I think I would remember her." The moment the words escaped his mouth, Travis felt the heat crawl up his neck.

His mother's gentle laughter spilled out into the night, mingling with the neighbor's children and the slight breeze in the trees. The tension in Travis's shoulders began to ease, though he still had no idea what he would do about Erin's request.

"They were pretty girls in a simple kind of way. And their foster parents were good people. Jules and Nina Brown went to our church."

It was Travis's turn to be surprised. "I remember Mr. Brown. He taught my Sunday school class a few times."

"I expect he did."

Travis stared into the night, trying to put the pieces together. "Didn't they—"

"Yeah. They were killed in a car accident about a year ago. You were down in Florida visiting your brother at the time."

"Wow. And they were the girls' foster parents?"

"Had been since they were very young."

Travis waited for his mom to continue, but she didn't. It wasn't like her to hold back. He knew there was a reason for her reticence, but he couldn't resist asking.

"Why were the girls in the foster care system?"

His mother sighed, but the night had grown too dark for him to read her expression. "I don't know if it's my place to share that family's pain. It happened such a long time ago."

"Mom, this client of mine has petitioned to adopt an infant she found."

She repositioned herself against the car. "Someone called today from the church—said there had been a baby found. Your father took the message. I sent a donation over, but I didn't realize immediately it was Erin who found the child. Then the phone started ringing off the hook. You know how a small town is. People are worried about her."

"It's my job to determine if she can provide a stable and healthy environment. For the next ninety days, I'm going to have to visit her at home and work."

"The ARK," his mom said softly.

"Today she asked me to assign her a new caseworker, preferably a female. I believe there's absolutely no grounds for her request. Director Moring agrees and wants me to remain on the case."

Travis stared out at the streetlights that punctuated the darkness before continuing his thought.

"I'm wondering if this particular case—this woman— might have a problem with men and male relationships. If she does, then I'm not sure I can approve placement of an infant boy permanently in her home. Obviously, I need to dig further into her history based on what you've said."

Travis paced up and down between the two cars, his concerns over the case taking more legitimate form as he verbalized his thoughts. He stopped and turned back toward his mom. "If there's anything you can tell me, anything that will help me make a good decision for Baby Joshua, then I would appreciate it."

His mom was silent for so long, Travis almost gave up hope. When she finally did speak, he could tell she had slipped back in time.

"You would have been eleven when it happened. I didn't know Mrs. Jacobs—the girls' mother—very well. Of course, Livingston was smaller then, and they lived on the edge of town. She came into church a few times. Always sat at the back. I remember her bringing the older girl—Dana. I also recall the first time I noticed she was pregnant with Erin."

She pulled in a deep breath, and Travis felt a shiver go down his spine as she pushed on, unearthing Dana and Erin's story.

"Part of the reason it's so hard to tell is because we all blamed ourselves afterwards. Asked what we could have done to stop it. As a community you want to think you would notice. As a church, we're commanded to be a family. We should have intervened, but we didn't. We were all busy with our own lives."

"What happened to Erin's family, Mom?"

"After Erin was born, Mrs. Jacobs stopped coming to church at all. One of those things where people slip away and you don't really notice—in the front door of the church, out the back. It's one of our biggest sins."

He moved beside her, stood shoulder to shoulder with her, and waited.

"When it happened, Erin was two or three, so Dana must have been closer to ten. You can check the papers for the exact dates. The father was a heavy drinker. Everyone knew it. He'd been seen in town overdoing it, even picked up a couple of times and made to sleep it off in the city jail. Overall he wasn't a mean drunk though. At least that's what we told ourselves. Then…"

She fiddled with the glasses hanging from a chain around her neck, and Travis felt the hairs along his arms stand on end. He pictured Erin's brown eyes staring into his, the way she had run across the waiting room to him. He tried to envision her as a three-year-old child, and the image cut him like a chisel piercing his lung.

"Then what?" Travis had heard of and even witnessed many instances of abuse. He steeled himself against one more.

"Then one night he killed her, killed the girls' mother. Somehow Dana was able to get Erin out of the house and run with her into the woods. Mr. Jacobs followed them there, but he passed out before he could hurt them. I believe it was a miracle. He would have killed them too."

Travis realized he was clenching his car keys when the metal pierced his skin. He forced his hand to relax, took a steadying breath, and let the information sink in. Tried to reconcile what he'd heard from his mother with the young woman who had stood beside him in court a few hours earlier.

"Dana managed to dash back to the house and call the police. They found the girls there with the mother's body."

"And the father?" Travis heard the hard edge behind his words. It was the voice he used when he had to testify in the courtroom, when he had to keep his anger in check.

"He's been in the state pen in Huntsville ever since. Convicted of manslaughter."

"I had no idea." He looked again at the basketball goal, longed for something, anything to throw—or punch. "None of this showed up on Erin's preliminary report. It wouldn't though since it happened while she was a minor."

"A dozen families from our church would have stepped up and taken those girls. Jules and Nina wanted them most though. They'd never had children of their own."

"Did they love them?"

"Oh my, yes. As if they were God's prize for forty-five years of work on this earth."

Travis again ran his hands through his hair. "How could I not remember any of this?"

"You never paid much attention to the news unless it had to do with sports." His mom squeezed his hand as he opened the door to his Blazer and rolled down the window.

"So she has a sister here in town?" Travis asked.

"No. Dana left as soon as she turned eighteen. First for college, then for a government job in the west. Erin stayed with Jules and Nina."

"Then they were killed."

"Yeah."

A mourning dove called out as the hard facts of Erin's life settled around them.

"I don't remember seeing her at church," Travis said.

"No. I don't suppose Erin ever took to church much. She'd come dutifully at Easter and Christmas with Jules and Nina."

"Until they died."

"I haven't seen her since."

Travis nodded and started his Blazer. "Tell Pops to take it easy. Thanks, Mom."

"Sure, honey."

Travis drove home more slowly than usual, trying to piece it all together. His life had been relatively calm with few upsets along the way, unless you figured in the occasional dislocated shoulder or sprained ankle.

Why was it some people, like Erin, suffered not one but two such tragedies in their lifetime?

And how was he, Travis Williams, supposed to decide if she now possessed what it would take to be a fit mother?

Thirteen

Derrick was glad he had switched to Scotch and water hours before. Beautiful day on the gulf, there was no reason not to. Tara had begged him to take her back to shore, but he wasn't cutting his trip short for her.

Now she sat across from him, arms crossed and a familiar stubborn look on her face. She'd never change, and he'd been a fool to think it was possible. Then she started in again about the kid, and something inside of him snapped.

He lunged for her, but she jumped away at the last second.

"I told you to shut up about that."

"Why? So you can ignore your responsibilities? It's not too late. I can get him back. I can tell the police it was all a mistake and that—"

He caught her before she could finish the sentence, and then she was clawing at his hands, trying to remove them from her throat. He squeezed tighter. At least she wasn't nagging him anymore. Maybe she'd pass out and he could have some peace.

With the last of her strength, Tara raised a knee and rammed it into him.

Derrick staggered backward, anger turning his vision red.

Then the game was on, like so many times before. If he wasn't so angry, he might actually enjoy it. On their second lap around the boat, she slipped, grabbed at the rigging and missed. There was a splash, and then he was staring down into the water. The inkiness of the waves merged with the blackness of the night.

"Tara?"

He collapsed onto the bench, reaching for his drink. Had she even been here? Had he imagined the entire thing? Then he looked at the seat opposite him and saw her hat.

Fourteen

On Friday morning, Erin looked up from cleaning out the llama's stable area and bit down hard on her lip.

She'd been going over Dana's e-mails in her mind. Dana had always had a knack for looking at things logically. After her initial shock at becoming an aunt, she'd followed with a short but effective list of things Erin could do to insure cooperation from a government agency.

Leave it to Dana to think within the lines.

She'd also offered to come home early—to which Erin had immediately replied *no.*

Then she'd insisted both she and Ben would both be there for the formal hearing, to which Erin had gleefully replied *yes.*

Things were looking up... until Erin actually did look up and had to bite down on her lip.

It was the one way she knew how to keep from saying words she should not say in front of Joshua. Even at two months—and two months seemed correct based on the baby book she'd poured over—children absorbed the meaning behind your words.

According to the book, children were like sponges.

They took in everything. Absolutely everything.

Frightening.

When she was eleven she'd brought home a baby duck. She'd gone off to school the next day and returned to find the duckling sitting at her foster-mother's feet, watching her wash dishes. After that the duck had followed Nina around like a shadow.

Doc had explained to her the concept of imprinting all those years ago, and Erin found herself thinking about it again—thinking about the duckling and Nina, Doc, and Joshua.

From the way Joshua watched her expression now, she suspected the baby book was spot-on. That book had given her nightmares.

Who had donated it to her?

Not her most immediate problem.

No, her current trouble was walking toward her barn in khaki trousers, white dress shirt, and another too loud tie. She leaned against her pitchfork. How many men dressed like that?

"I've been in the animal business too long," she muttered to Joshua. "Or not long enough. Depends on how you look at it."

Joshua kicked his feet, which were covered with frog shoes. He blew a bubble when the frogs rattled, which they did each time he banged them against the car seat. Great invention—toys disguised as shoes. The monkey hat perched atop his head temporarily erased the frown from Erin's face.

"He must have found a sale on khaki pants. Why can't he wear blue jeans like a normal person?" Erin thought of hollering out so Williams would know what stall she was in, then decided he'd find her eventually. Why rush it?

By the time he did, she'd worked up quite a sweat punching the fork into the hay, picturing the leather seats of his Blazer. She knew it was childish and unfounded, but it did wonders to ease her stress. Best of all she didn't have even a hint of an anxiety attack like she'd had in his office.

"Good morning, Erin, Joshua."

Her heart rate had kicked up a notch as he walked into the barn, but no doubt it was from the exertion of cleaning out the stall. "Good morning, Travis."

She liked the way he always spoke to Joshua, but she was not going to focus on his good attributes. She was planning to answer his questions, speed through his checklist, and be done with him.

"Obviously, this is an unscheduled visit." Travis smiled and held up his clipboard and pen. "I'm here to take a few notes, ask a few questions, and watch you interact with Joshua. Then I'll be out of your hair."

Erin leaned on her pitchfork and studied him. Perhaps it was the fact she was in her element standing in the fresh hay. Could have been she felt a tad safer knowing she'd bought herself ninety days. Whatever the reason, she felt slightly less intimidated by him, which left plenty of room for her irritation to rise.

"So you're saying I don't have to change clothes for this visit?" She didn't bother pointing down to her muck-covered, knee-length boots.

She knew his eyes would follow, and they did.

From there, Travis worked his way up her patched overalls to her Houston Astros baseball shirt and corresponding hat. Her work gloves were only six months old but felt as familiar as a kid's favorite baseball mitt.

His eyes met hers, and color crept into her cheeks— probably from the heat in the barn though it was a cool seventy-five.

"Nope. No need to change clothes. This is your job, so you just go on doing it. I'll say hello to Joshua and watch."

She had hoped he'd be embarrassed by the difference in their clothing style, but there was no chance of that.

He walked over to where she'd fashioned a baby table on top of the old work bench and buckled Joshua's car seat to the top of it.

Erin continued working, but they were in a corner area of the barn. She couldn't help noticing the way he first talked with Josh, then checked the type of rigging she'd used on the baby seat—no doubt wondering if there was any way Joshua could work his way out of the contraption.

She ground her teeth together, reminding herself of Doc's words. It was his job to check on Joshua's safety.

Why did he irritate her so much?

Why couldn't he stay away?

She supplied Cocoa, her llama, with fresh food and water and moved back over to the table.

"Where to now?" Travis asked, standing close enough she could smell how clean he was, not to mention how masculine. She took two steps away.

"Pig pen." She said it with a gleam in her eye. Truthfully, the pen was fairly clean already, but she was hoping he'd change his mind and leave.

Instead he placed a hand to his stomach. "Great. I've always had an affinity for bacon."

She somehow resisted rolling her eyes and had just begun to unbuckle Joshua's seat when her cell rang.

"The ARK," she fairly barked.

As soon as the hysterical woman started talking, she had pulled out the notepad and pen she kept in her back pocket at all times.

"Calm down, ma'am. Tell me again where you're located." She copied the address and calculated how long it would take to transfer Joshua and his things to the truck, then drive to the southeast side of town. "I can be there in thirty minutes. Don't allow anyone near the animal. Keep your dogs in the house or they might attack."

She listened for another minute, at one point holding the phone away from her ear and grimacing. She allowed the woman to continue for as long as it took her to store the supplies she'd been using in that area of the barn.

"Ma'am, I'm hanging up now. Keep everyone away from the area."

Shutting the phone, she turned to Williams, trying to repress the grin on her face. "I guess we'll have to reschedule another time."

"Why would we need to do that, Erin?"

"I just received an emergency rescue call. I need to go to a site in southeast Livingston, and I have no idea how long it will take."

"Great. I'll ride with you."

"Ride with me?" Her voice had risen an octave, and she sounded ridiculously like Minnie Mouse. She cleared her throat and tried again. "What do you mean ride with me?"

"I mean I'll go with you on the rescue. Part of my job is to observe you in your place of employment—that would include the ARK. It would also include going out on calls with you."

Erin was grateful she'd put up the pitchfork, or she might have felt tempted to poke him with it. "So you're going to tag along?"

He actually grinned at her. "Sure."

She unbuckled Joshua's entire seat and stomped from the barn. The man was impossible. She refused to look at him as she made her way across to the porch and sat down.

Pulling off her boots and socks, she sat the dirty boots under the outside faucet and ran water over them. Scrubbing them with the brush she left hanging there for just that purpose used up some of her frustration. Then she looked at Joshua, and he blew one of his bubbles—the biggest one yet.

The laughter which escaped from her filled the morning, wiping away her angst like a needed rain clears the air. She picked the baby up and hugged him, then turned and saw Travis studying them.

"You don't even know what we're rescuing," she said, shaking her head as she stood there in dripping feet.

"Does it matter?"

She closed her eyes for a minute. The morning sun slanted through the trees, warming her back. Joshua snuggled against her chest, melting her heart.

"No. I suppose it doesn't. It'll take me ten minutes to get ready."

"May I look at Joshua's room while I wait?"

Since it would do her no good to say no, she nodded and escaped into her home.

—

Travis held the front door open as Erin picked up Joshua and her backpack, along with the baby bag. He didn't offer to help, which was difficult for him.

In his personal life, he'd always offer to carry a bag for a woman. There was certainly something about Erin Jacobs that made him want to open doors, carry bags, even offer to muck out llama stalls. Fortunately, he'd been able to squelch that urge.

The manual plainly stated he was there to observe. It wasn't a question of having good manners. His job was to monitor how well she managed on her own with Joshua. He couldn't objectively assess her situation if he helped her with everything.

So, instead, he watched her struggle with the backpack, diaper bag, and baby.

He noted with a check of his pencil that it wasn't much of a struggle. Whether it was because she was already used to juggling a myriad of items with her ARK full of animals, or because motherhood came naturally to her, she was adjusting to the demands well.

When they reached the Chevy truck, she snapped the baby carrier into the car seat. Turning around faster than he expected, she almost ran into him.

"I assume you'll be taking your Blazer?"

"I'd rather ride along with you if that's okay."

She placed both hands on her hips and glared up at him. "What if I said no? What if I said you bothered me and asked you to go away?"

Travis looked down into Erin's face and had the most frightening moment of his eight-year career with Child Welfare.

Erin's defiant look would have convinced the casual observer. In fact, a more intelligent man might have taken a step back. Why then did he have an overpowering urge to step toward this woman? He wanted desperately to push the auburn curls out of her eyes, gently wipe the worry from her face, and suggest she relax.

He wanted to cradle her in his arms.

All because his mother had told him Erin Jacobs' past. He understood the anger directed toward him for what it was—a shield against any man who might hurt her.

"I'm not the enemy, Erin. Our procedures state I'm to stay with you for a minimum of two hours when I make site visits."

Hands still on her hips, she stomped her small foot. It took all the restraint Travis possessed not to smile at the gesture.

"Why? Why do you have to stay two hours? I have a job to do and a baby to raise."

"And I need to see you're capable of doing both before I can recommend Joshua be placed in your permanent care."

His final words stopped her cold. She brought up her chin and glared at him in the mid-morning light.

"Fine. But I'm not used to having people tag along while I work. Don't blame me if you get hurt or, or…" She tripped over the words, then gestured at his clothes as if they personally offended her. "Or dirty."

Still glaring at him, she made her way around to the driver's side of the truck and pulled herself up into the seat using the grasp bar. She did not bother to see if he was inside, but she did buckle before she put the vehicle in reverse.

Travis wasn't a bit surprised when she cranked up the radio and the cab of the truck was filled with the smooth voice of George Strait singing about Mexico. Erin Jacobs would not be comfortable with silence, not as long as he was around.

And casual conversation at this point would not be an option.

—

They stopped outside a ranch-style house in a subdivision with half-acre lots. Erin consulted her notes only once, confirming the house number. She checked on Joshua no less than six times. The baby slept through the entire ride.

Finding the house was no problem.

A mother and three children, all preschoolers, met them at the end of the gravel drive. The woman looked to be about Erin's age, and Travis wondered how she could possibly have had three children so quickly. It wasn't the first time he'd wondered that, and he was sure it wouldn't be the last. Then again, living in this subdivision, she and her husband must be doing well financially.

Erin rolled down her window.

"I saw her through the trees not five minutes ago." The woman shifted one child from her right hip to her left as she spoke. "She was on the back part of the lot."

"Take your children and move inside."

"I don't know how it happened. I was putting out wash on the line, and I turned around and saw her. We've noticed her hanging around the lot before, limping. This time she had the thing around her head and was going crazy. I think she was bleeding."

"I need you to go inside with the children, ma'am."

"Will she be okay?"

"That's what I'm here to see. Move inside until I signal you it's okay to come out."

"She banged her head—ouchie hard." The oldest preschooler rubbed the top of his head, demonstrating the spot.

"Will you put a bandage on it?" The middle girl had to pull her thumb out of her mouth to ask the question.

"I might," Erin admitted.

"Will it have a Snoopy like mine?" She held out her arm to reveal a tiny Snoopy Band-Aid over an invisible hurt.

"Or a Garfield like his tie?" The oldest pointed to Travis.

"Probably no Snoopy or Garfield. Maybe you two could draw a cartoon picture while we wait."

The thumb popped back in and the tot looked up at her mother with widened eyes.

"Sure. You both can color while Miss Jacobs works."

Some unspoken communication passed between the two women. Travis had seen that before as well.

Of course, he'd experienced the same thing with guys on a basketball court, but it was different with women. With them it was more like the passing of a dinner dish. It was less hurdled communication than it was something trusted.

The woman hurried off with her children into the house, and Erin parked the truck in the circular drive.

She was all concentration now, and he nearly forgot his notebook. It was a pleasure to watch her work.

Reaching into the back of the truck, she pulled out a full-sized hiking backpack he hadn't noticed before. It was crammed full, and he wondered how she'd even be able to lift it, but she swung it on with no problem, then clipped the hip belt and breast strap.

"How much does that weigh, Erin?"

"Forty-five pounds," she said with the widest grin he'd seen from her yet. "I know what you're thinking, and it was too heavy for me at first."

She removed the carrier portion of the car seat—Joshua still intact—and began walking around to the back of the house. Travis actually had to trot to keep up with her.

"At first?"

"Right. I tried all different ways of carrying what I needed on rescues. Some workers carry Go Bags, but I depend on my hands and found a bag slowed me down too much. Plus my upper body strength isn't very good to be honest." She met his gaze, her smile holding, as they walked across the wooden deck and started through the back woods.

Her smile seeped into him and threatened to penetrate his professional demeanor. He had to glance away and remind himself to be objective.

"Once I learned to distribute the weight properly in an overnight pack, it was simply a matter of increasing the weight slowly."

He was about to ask her what all was in the pack when she held up her hand to stop him. They had reached the edge of a stand of pine trees, and he immediately saw what had caught her attention as well as what had brought them there.

A yearling deer stood in the clearing approximately twenty yards from them. She limped slowly between two trees, shaking her head back and forth, trying in vain to dislodge the plastic lid caught around her head. Streaks of blood ran from a tear on her left ear, and her eyes had a crazed look Travis had seen once before in a deer.

As a teenager he'd shot a young buck, but it hadn't killed the deer. His grandfather had shown him how to track it. By the time they'd found the buck, it was nearly crazy from the injury. Travis had taken the mercy shot, but the look in the deer's eyes had haunted him for a long time afterwards.

Caught up in the memory, he didn't immediately notice Erin had placed Joshua's carrier on the ground, unzipped her pack, and pulled out a disassembled rifle.

Fifteen

Travis put his hand on her arm to stop her, but Erin shook him off.

"Erin—"

"Shush."

Still monitoring the yearling, she assembled the rifle and inserted a tranquilizer dart.

"Erin, don't."

Fitting the rifle to her shoulder, she looked through the scope, pulled in a steadying breath, and took the shot.

The deer dropped instantly.

"Stay with Joshua."

"But—"

She left him talking to himself. If he was going to insist on tagging along, the least he could do was watch Joshua for five minutes. She placed the rifle carefully on the ground, picked up the pack, and left without a look backward.

Erin was pleased with the shot as well as the yearling's reaction to the dosage. She checked the deer's respiration,

gently pulled the plastic lid off her head, and put a field splint
on her leg.

Then she jogged back to where Travis and Joshua
waited.

"I'm going to bring the truck around."

"Erin—"

"Three more minutes. Tops."

Fortunately, there was a clear path to drive in, though
she had to jump the curb to get into the clearing. Once there,
she picked up the yearling. She estimated the deer's weight at
less than thirty-five pounds, which wasn't a surprise given
she'd injured her leg some time ago.

Gently, she placed the young doe into the crate she kept
in the truck's bed for just such emergencies. The poor thing
still hadn't awakened. Chances were she would before they
made it back to the ARK, so Erin administered an additional
sedative.

She was about to drive the truck over to where she'd left
Joshua and Travis when she looked up and saw him walking
toward her, carrying both the baby and her rifle.

Adrenaline still rushed through her veins from the
rescue. It had gone more smoothly than she'd expected.
Often she had to wait in the field for hours before even
spotting the animal she was there to save.

Now she was looking forward to the rewarding part,
caring for the animal. This is what she had trained for. Her
mind was there, thirty minutes down the road, back at the
ARK.

So it was a complete surprise when she realized the look
on Travis's face didn't match her own. She hadn't expected
him to understand or even really appreciate what she did, but

that had been a nice shot. Why the look of fury as he walked toward her?

Her own mood plummeted as she realized a confrontation was looming.

The infuriating part was she had no idea what she'd done.

Then she heard Joshua's cry.

Jumping out of the truck, she hurried toward him.

—

Instead of taking the carrier from Travis, Erin unbuckled Joshua and pulled him from it, and cradled him in her arms. "What's wrong with him?"

"How am I supposed to know?"

She didn't bother to look up and check his expression. There would be time to puzzle out his mood later. Turning her back on him, she walked back toward the truck, laid Joshua across the front passenger seat, and began to undress him.

His earlier crying turned into outright screams. Their pediatrician's appointment wasn't until tomorrow, but she could already tell this boy had healthy lungs.

"We need to talk, Erin."

She barely understood his words uttered through clenched teeth.

Travis had been leaning in to try and speak to her over Joshua's wails. When she fully opened the soiled diaper and its odor filled the cab of the truck, he gasped and took a step back.

Erin smiled down at the baby. It was pretty nasty stuff.

"You're all right, little man. Hang on. I've got you covered."

Joshua's bottom lip trembled, and an occasional whimper continued to escape, but the full blown bellows seemed past. She taped up the dirty diaper, dropped it into a plastic grocery sack, and double tied the top, then set the whole mess in the backseat floorboard. If Williams wanted to ride with them, he could enjoy the ambience.

"Erin, I need to talk to you."

"Did you get snake bit back there?" She picked up Joshua, snugged him to her shoulder, and turned to face Travis. "What is wrong with you?"

Travis had stored her pack behind the driver's seat and was crossing back around to the passenger side. They met in the middle.

Erin traditionally avoided confrontation. She was an intelligent woman, and the right side of her brain screamed at her to back down from a fight with her caseworker. But her defenses were up. For some reason, when it came to Travis Williams, backing down never seemed a viable choice.

"What's wrong with me is I'm upset to see you put a child in danger."

Blood rushed into Erin's ears. She actually shook her head as if she could dislodge the sound of the wind. "What?"

"You heard me."

"You think I put Joshua in danger?"

"Think it? I saw it, remember?"

"Of course I didn't."

"You left me to watch him while you ran off like some Crocodile Jane on the hunt." He was no longer the calm and composed cover guy.

Erin would have laughed if she didn't recognize the risk here—risk of losing the most important thing in the world to her. The child fighting against sleep as he burrowed into her shoulder. She stared in horror at her caseworker.

In his frustration, Travis had put both hands in his sun-bleached hair, and it now sprang out in different directions like some punk rocker. With each word, he leaned closer to her, then backed away as if she might be contagious. The entire display was comical.

What he was suggesting was not.

She turned, walked back to the truck, and snapped Joshua's carrier into the baby seat, then placed him carefully in it. When she thought she'd calmed down enough to face Travis, she walked back to where he stood.

"I did not put Joshua at risk. I was doing my job, and at no time was that baby ever in danger of being hurt."

"How about when you were packing a rifle while you carried him?"

It was a good thing the rifle he referred to was safely repacked or she'd hit him with the broad end of it right now. "The rifle was disassembled, Travis. If you've grown up in Polk County, you've been around rifles long enough to know they cannot hurt anyone disassembled. On top of that, it's a tranquilizer rifle."

He stopped at the far end of his pacing and stormed back toward her. "You shot a hurt deer, Erin, with an infant less than three feet from you. He could have charged. Deer go crazy when they're hurt. I've seen it myself."

"I use a combination of Telazol and Xylazine. There's enough immobilizing drug in the dart to bring down any deer for twenty minutes. The worst possible scenario was a miss, in which case she would have sprinted the other way."

Erin looked into the truck at Joshua, now sucking on his pacifier and fighting sleep, her heart tapping a triple rhythm. If she had put him in danger, she wanted to know it. But she hadn't. Had she?

"I'm proud of what I did here this morning. There was an injured deer, I located it and made a perfect shot. The deer is loaded, her leg splinted, and we're on our way to the ARK. You've seen what I do. Isn't that why you came along?"

"Erin, according to the manual, I am supposed to observe you. Only observe you." Travis sighed, apparently gaining some control over his anger. "Maybe I was wrong about what I said earlier about the rifle. But the fact remains you left Joshua with me to run off and get the truck and load the deer. You left him with me for ten minutes."

"You're angry because I asked you to watch Joshua?" Erin's voice rose an octave. She fought to bring it down. "Please tell me you are kidding."

"I'm not supposed to be his babysitter." The words were soft but no less harsh because of it. "What would you have done today if I hadn't been here? How would you have handled the situation? That's what you need to ask yourself. Would Joshua have been safe then?"

Travis continued to the truck's passenger side, leaving Erin standing there in the light of a once perfect morning.

———

Travis didn't speak as Erin pulled the truck around, honked the horn, and waited for the woman to come back out of the house. He did note she didn't leave the truck to go in and talk to her.

How had he managed to lose his composure so badly back there?

He simply could not remain detached around this woman. He'd told Moring he wasn't the person for this case, but she'd insisted. He was surrounded by stubborn, unreasonable women. Which was why he should be on his boat, the one place a man is safe.

Erin pulled out onto the blacktop and still he didn't break the silence. One part of him wanted to make notes from all he'd seen in the last hour. Another part knew he wasn't likely to forget any of it.

She'd made the perfect shot. His grandfather would have been proud. The yearling had gone down easily.

The look on her face when she'd made the shot, well that was where his trouble had begun.

He glanced at her now. All the delight was gone, but it had been there. He'd seen that look of joy on plenty of faces before—mostly kids when he told them they were placed with families. Seeing it on Erin's face, watching her at work, it had reminded him of how he used to feel about his job, scratching the surface of some guilt he did not need to face today.

As if her complete absorption in her job wasn't bad enough, she'd jogged away, leaving him with Joshua. Dedication to a job was commendable, but attention to a child always came first. That was when his temper had begun to get the best of him.

"I'm sorry I left Joshua with you." The windows were rolled down a quarter inch, allowing the breeze to tease the auburn curls of her hair.

She turned and looked at him, the anger still simmering and warring with something else—her pride? Yet Erin Jacobs did not strike him as a prideful person. Stubborn, hard-headed, determined to go it alone, possibly even impetuous, but not prideful. She glanced in the back seat, swallowed, and gripped the wheel.

"If you hadn't been there today, I obviously would not have left Joshua alone in the woods. I don't know what I would have done. You were there, so I left him with you—without thinking." She had been steadfastly refusing to meet his gaze. Finally, she turned to look at him as she turned into the lane on her property. "I don't know the rules yet, Travis. But I want Joshua, and I'm willing to learn your way of doing things if that's the only way I can keep him."

He tried to glance away from her deep brown eyes, searched to remember what he'd been so angry about. Since he couldn't, he merely nodded.

She drew in a deep breath. "Not exactly a stellar first visit." She pulled up to the cattle gate and tugged her baseball cap down as she set the truck in park and jumped out to open it.

By the time she had maneuvered through the second gate and closed it again, he'd collected his thoughts and his objectivity. "You're right about this being a learning process. I shouldn't have lost my temper back there. But according to the manual, I am here in an observation capacity—"

Erin pulled the truck next to his Blazer and jammed the transmission into park so hard he feared it might break off the lever. "If we're going to go by that manual so closely, you might want to get me a copy of it."

She was out of her side of the truck before he could respond, which was probably a good thing. He moved to his vehicle and took a few minutes to write some notes about the morning.

By the time he was finished, she'd disappeared with Joshua and offloaded the deer.

And she hadn't asked for his help.

He found Joshua sound asleep in his crib, sides safely up, baby monitor on. How she'd managed to set up the baby room so quickly he had no idea. He made a note on his pad to ask her.

His mother had told him about the church bringing a few items, but this looked as if she'd been eagerly awaiting a baby for months.

On his way out of the room he stopped and stared at the antique dresser next to the door. Two items sat on the top—a child's lamp in the shape of a puppy topped with a pale blue shade and a Bible.

Was Erin Jacobs a believer? If so, it would go a long way toward easing some of his reservations about this situation. Suddenly, he realized another piece of the anxiety puzzle that had been keeping him awake nights.

Erin was probably quite capable of giving Joshua everything he needed and learning all the skills to be a good parent. What she lacked was a safety net. Every parent needed a family, friends, or community of believers to back them up should they become sick, lose a job, or just need emotional support.

Erin struck him as a little tugboat out on the ocean, determined to do everything on her own.

He knew she had no immediate family in the area.

So far there had been no evidence of close friends clamoring to her aid.

But if she were a believer, if she had a church family to help her during those times every person struggles...

He reached for the Bible and opened it.

On the first page the inscription read—

Erin, God has a plan for both you and Baby Joshua. He promised as much in Jeremiah 29:11. And he doesn't expect you to fulfill that plan alone. We love you and are here for you and Josh.

Evelyn and Stanley England.

Travis closed the Bible, looked back at the sleeping baby, and went in search of Erin.

Sixteen

Erin didn't glance up from the yearling when she heard Travis approach. The more she thought about the morning, the more her temper threatened to explode.

Best to avoid eye contact.

"How's the doe?" He stayed on the far side of the stall, but she could feel his eyes on her. No doubt mentally he was checking off some item on a list she couldn't see.

"She'll recover." Erin tapped the baby monitor at her belt so he could see. "I haven't abandoned Joshua in case you were wondering. In fact I heard you walking around his room earlier."

Travis sighed and moved across the barn stall, stopping when she looked up and pierced him with her stare. At least she hoped he felt pierced. She was struggling to convey with her eyes what she was holding back with her tongue.

Raising both hands, palms out, he backed up two steps. "I'm not the enemy. Let's speak openly here."

"Oh, you want to speak openly? All right. If we're speaking openly, you *act* a lot like the enemy—most of the time in fact. So how would I know you're not? I haven't seen any evidence you're trying to help me, though you're awfully good at pointing out things I do wrong." She tried to stop the words flying from her mouth, even as she worked to keep her hands at her side instead of gesturing in front of her like the conductor of some grand orchestra.

"You know I've heard and read about the child welfare Gestapo." When he flinched she pushed on, satisfied her words were finding their mark. "I never thought I'd be subjected to your tactics. That's one of the reasons I went into animal science. I knew I didn't have the personality to be so mean to people. At least with animals I know the client wants my help. I know who's on my team, who's pulling for my side."

Travis had crossed the area between them and was in her face in a split second. "You're on the animal's side, right? Are you telling me you haven't seen what people can do to their pets? You haven't witnessed firsthand the way they can neglect and abuse them? Think about the worst thing you have encountered, then multiply it times a hundred. Imagine it done to a child like the one sleeping in your home this minute."

Erin needed to pull her eyes away from his, wanted to step back from the raw emotion she saw there, but she couldn't. She could only shake her head softly back and forth, denying the truth in his words.

"What, Erin? Say it."

"This is different."

"How is it different?"

126

"Because I'm not like them."

Even as the words burst out she knew how feeble they sounded. She knew what he would say next.

"And how am I to know that?"

He raised his hand, and she thought for a moment he meant to brush away the tears tracking down her cheeks. Instead, he ran his hands through his hair in frustration, then reached into his pants pocket, pulled out a travel pack of Kleenex, and pushed them into her hands.

She turned away from him, feeling foolish and spent. When she'd wiped her face and pulled in several cleansing breaths, she squared her shoulders. What was it about Travis Williams that attracted and repelled her so? Why couldn't he go away and let her be? But she knew the answer to the question pounding through her head. She'd seen it in his eyes not two minutes ago.

He was Joshua's protector, for better or worse.

He wouldn't go until he was sure about her.

She loved Joshua, wanted to provide a home for him, but she'd never envisioned the process being this hard.

Turning back to Travis, she walked over and sat beside him on a wooden bench that ran against the back wall.

"I feel as if I've birthed a child," she confessed. "I had no idea my emotions would be all over the place like this. I'm afraid of all sorts of things that never concerned me before—like burglars and car accidents and apathy."

Travis's eyebrows arched at her last concern. "Apathy?"

"Never mind. I've heard about post-partum, but I thought that was a hormonal reaction to giving birth. I haven't physically birthed a baby."

"Erin, your body doesn't know that. It's playing catch up. You're going through the same physiological changes as a woman who has gone through nine months of pregnancy and labor."

She considered his words, then hiccupped as another sob lodged in her throat. "I've always been so in control and decisive."

When he didn't break the silence, she felt the need to justify her emotional display.

"From the time I was young, really ever since..." Backtracking she folded the Kleenex she'd nearly shredded. "Since I can remember almost, I was the one who took care of everyone and everything else."

"Do you feel it's your duty to raise Joshua?"

Although the question was gentle, Erin's head snapped up. She fought to push away the defensiveness threatening to coil up her back. Something told her they were reaching the heart of the matter here, and she didn't want to blow it with her temper.

"No. It's not my duty. It's not that at all. I love what I do. Saving things and making them well is as natural to me as..." She looked at Travis for an example, but there was nothing she knew about this man, so she glanced around the stall instead. The yearling lay curled and dozing in the hay. "As natural as it is for that doe to lie curled when it sleeps. No one had to teach her that. It's instinctual."

"And caring for Joshua is instinctual to you?"

"I don't guess you can tell it from the way I've been acting, but yes—it is. When I hold him in my arms, it's as if two pieces of a puzzle have snapped together. I knew it the minute I picked him up. Somehow he is meant to be in my life."

She met his eyes as she uttered those last few words. She had known Joshua belonged with her from the very first night when she walked across the porch of the hunter's cabin and looked into the washtub. Perhaps that was some of what frightened her. To look into your destiny, to be caught up in it when you were simply doing your job.

Well, it was terrifying.

She drew up a little straighter. "I suppose I'm a little confused about how I can be so sure he belongs with me, and yet so inept at following or meeting your standards."

"While at the same time you're dealing with all the feelings of being a first-time mom."

Erin felt her head nod and wondered if she sounded crazy. What would he write in his report now?

"I admire your certainty that Joshua belongs with you. Most foster parents have some doubts." Travis stood and paced the length of the stall. When he turned and walked back toward her, she could tell by the frown line between his blue eyes that she wasn't going to like what he was about to say.

"I'll be honest with you. The biggest obstacle I see to placing Joshua in your home is you *are* so independent. You've created a very efficient, independent little world here. An ark."

She clutched the bench she sat on, felt the splinters from the wooden seat scratch her palm, but she let him finish.

"Babies need more than one person though. I'm not saying a single mom can't raise a baby and raise it well. What I'm saying is every person needs a safety net of friends and family. You're bound to eventually get sick or be called out on an emergency rescue where it wouldn't be prudent to take Joshua."

"I won't get sick, and I'll find someone to watch Joshua for those rescues."

"Everyone gets ill some time." When she didn't respond, his frown line deepened. It highlighted how tan he was, and that irritated her.

Why was she aware her caseworker had a good tan? He had a social life. So what? She needed to focus on the demands he was laying out for her life.

"I'm glad you're willing to find some sort of sitter for Joshua during your most challenging calls. I don't think you quite understand what I'm saying though."

She launched off the bench like a rocket.

"You're saying I need a man. Why don't you spit the words out? It's the same with everyone—you, Evelyn, Doc. Well I don't, all right? Why can't this world accept that a woman can survive on her own? I've been making it on my own for years, and I can and will raise this child by myself."

She hadn't realized she was in his space until she needed to tilt her head back to throw her final words at him. He was shaking his head, which meant he was not listening, only waiting to respond. She wanted to force him to hear her—had a sudden irrational urge to grab him by the shoulders and shake him.

"Child welfare does not suggest single moms get married in order to be approved for placement."

"That's what you just said." Her voice rose over his.

She took a step forward.

He took a step back.

"It is not what I said. I'm suggesting you rejoin the community around you. You might not have family in the area, but surely you could find a church or community group. People who would provide a backup and help you with raising a child."

"Who do you think provided everything in the nursery?"

Travis stopped short, a look of confusion momentarily wiping out the expression of certainty he usually wore.

Erin would have laughed if she wasn't so furious at him. How dare he judge her life?

"I meant to ask you about that. I wondered how you managed to put his room together so quickly."

"Not alone. I do have friends. Put that in your book. Write it down. Erin Jacobs has friends." The tears were close again so she crossed her arms and bit her bottom lip. She felt childish but better.

"Tell me their names, Erin."

"What?" Surely she had heard him wrong.

"The names of the folks who helped you. The people who brought the things for Joshua. What are their names?"

She stared at him for ten seconds, then twenty. When she was sure he wouldn't rescue her by changing the question, she turned and walked out of the barn.

Seventeen

The body search had continued for three days.

By the time the police left, Derrick had set a record for sober days. A record he intended to end as soon as Detective Carmichael got off his back.

The man was intent on pinning Tara's death on him, but Derrick hadn't forced her on to the boat—the old guy in the berth next to his had been happy enough to testify to that. He also hadn't pushed her off, at least not that he could remember. And why would he?

He did care about his ex-wife. He loved her in his own way. She was simply too difficult to live with.

"We are going to rule the death an accident, Mr. Pitcher."

"Well, it was an accident."

"But we retain the ability to re-open the investigation." The man stepped closer, and fear tripped down Derrick's spine. This fool had the ability to send him away, a place that Derrick had heard enough about. He had no intention of going to prison. He planned to spend the rest of his days out on the open water.

"Should any additional information come to light, I'll be back."

Derrick forced a smile. "I hope so. Losing Tara, well, it's a terrible thing. If you find that it wasn't an accident, then I'd like to see the person responsible—"

"Save it, Pitcher." Carmichael's voice was soft but solid as an iron rail. "Save it for someone who believes you're innocent."

Then he turned and walked away.

Eighteen

Travis and James took the stairs two at a time, waving at Angela but not stopping to chat.

"The woman looks at you like she could eat you up with a spoon," James ribbed him.

"Don't start with me."

"Kicking my butt around a racquetball court for an hour did not improve your attitude, bro. Maybe you should have eaten lunch instead of an energy bar."

Rather than answer, Travis slapped him on the back and continued around to his cubicle, then dropped his keys next to his shoulder bag.

He spied what had been left face open across his keyboard. The growl he emitted caused James to pop his head up over the top of the partition.

"Problem?"

"Have you seen this?" Travis shook the paper clutched in his hand, feeling blood rush to his face and thrum in the veins at his temple.

"Can't say I have. Mostly carries local school news, obits, general small town stuff."

"He's done it now—little acne-pocked shrimp of a boy." Travis opened the paper and slapped it down on top of a stack of folders.

"I warned Mr. Chance Stubber." He spat the name as he snatched up his keys. "I told him this case was sealed, but no, he had to splash Erin's picture across the front of his paper anyway. Because she's a beautiful woman, because she'll sell papers, he thinks he has a right. We'll see who has rights."

He had pushed open the door to the stairwell when he heard Moring. "Williams, my office. Now."

The look on Director Moring's face said her lunch wasn't settling any better than Travis's. Of course, she'd probably *had* lunch. She at least appeared calmer than Travis felt, meaning she didn't resemble a wild bear.

"He took the photo as we walked out of the initial hearing. I told him the case was closed and Miss Jacobs had no comment."

Moring's right eyebrow shot up. "Was Miss Jacobs incapable of speaking for herself at the time?"

Travis reached for his tie, adjusted the knot, and rephrased his explanation. "No, of course not. I merely suggested she might not want to speak with the papers since the judge had sealed the case. Erin agreed."

Moring studied the photo for a moment, then sat back in her chair and peered at him over her steepled fingers.

"The photo, even the story, is not our problem."

"But their privacy is at stake, and Joshua's anonymity—"

She cut him off with a wave of her hand. "Everyone already knows. I heard about it twice, and it hasn't even been a week—once while I waited for my car to be serviced and once in the grocery checkout line. Word travels quickly. *The Livingston Daily* was merely reporting what everyone discussed over their back fence yesterday."

Travis glared at his boss, but held back any retort. He was starting to realize his initial course of action would feel great but solve nothing. Pummeling the adolescent reporter would only earn him a formal reprimand.

"No, I didn't call you in here to discuss the front page story. I was contacted this morning by the Methodist DeBakey Heart and Vascular Center." She paused, stood, and walked around her desk. When she took the seat next to him, Travis had the irrational urge to check his cell phone, see if he'd somehow missed a call from his parents. Why was she speaking to him about the most reputable heart hospital in Austin?

Sweat broke out on his brow.

"They have an elderly patient there—a Mrs. Dorothy DeLoach."

"The name is familiar." To Travis his voice sounded as if it were coming from the far end of a tunnel.

"Mrs. DeLoach is from Huntsville, though she's been in an assisted living facility in Austin for the last several years. She does, however, still follow the local news." Moring reached out and tapped the newspaper on her desk. "When she saw this, she insisted the hospital staff contact us."

"Why? What... I don't understand." Travis stood, unable to contain his agitation.

"Mrs. DeLoach believes Joshua is her great-grandson."

"How—"

"Travis, sit down."

He walked back across the room and willed the thoughts stampeding through his brain to slow.

"Until this morning, Mrs. DeLoach thought she had no living relatives. She's eighty-six, by the way."

Travis told himself he had to remain objective, forced his heart to remember that Joshua belonged in the best possible environment—and that might be with his biological family.

"Two days ago, her granddaughter, Tara DeLoach, was declared dead."

"Dead?"

"Lost at sea and presumed dead. It's the reason Mrs. DeLoach is back in the hospital. She sounds like a tough woman, but understandably the shock took its toll. I spoke with her briefly, as well as the attending physician and the detective assigned to the case."

"How did the granddaughter die?"

"Apparently a boating accident."

Travis stared at the carpet and tried to assimilate all the information Moring was throwing at him.

"And no one has been looking for this baby?"

"According to Detective Carmichael, there are some domestic issues, but they're ruling Tara's death an accident. I want you to take Joshua—and if possible Miss Jacobs—"

"Jacobs?"

Moring held up a hand, unaccustomed to being interrupted.

"It's a request, not an order. DeLoach is not petitioning for custody of Joshua, but she would like to meet Jacobs—"

"That flies in the opposite direction of standard protocol!" Jumping up, he stuffed his hands in his pockets.

"Would you please *stop* interrupting me? This is a unique situation. I realize customarily there is no contact between birth parents and foster parents; however, as I was saying, Mrs. DeLoach is not petitioning for custody. She wants to meet Miss Jacobs, and after speaking with her physician, I don't believe she has long to live."

Moring stood and moved back behind her desk. "Should she decide to fight this, and she certainly has the financial means to do so, she could tie it up in court for many years. Take the baby to see her. Use your charm, if you have any, to persuade Jacobs to go with you. Go tonight if you can, but no later than tomorrow."

Travis tried to think of what to ask next, but came up blank. His world was rocked, and he could imagine what effect this news would have on Erin and Joshua. He had turned to go, when Moring called him back.

"You've always been a good dresser, Travis. I assume you wear those ridiculous ties to put children at ease. DeLoach is old money, very traditional. See if you can borrow something a bit more... normal."

—

Erin clutched Joshua as thunder rattled the windows and lightning split the night sky outside the hospital. Walking down the softly lit corridor, glancing at the framed oil paintings artfully placed along the walls, she had the tipsy feeling of walking through a dream. The Methodist hospital was certainly unlike any other facility she'd ever visited.

Travis's hand at her back kept her steady. Tonight he wore his court suit, but this time with a demure, midnight-blue tie. She glanced down at her burgundy blouse and calf length, denim skirt.

"You look fine." His eyes met hers as they stopped outside room 321. "Ready?"

She nodded, and he knocked on the door.

A surprisingly strong voice commanded them to enter.

Erin doubted the story no matter how many times she replayed it in her head, but she couldn't deny the way Mrs. DeLoach's eyes shone with love when they landed on Joshua.

Her skin faded to nearly the whiteness of the sheets. Dorothy DeLoach wore a rose- colored nightgown. Eyes sharp and bright blue—the exact color of the babe Erin held in her arms—peered out of a face wizened by a life's worth of age lines. And though her hair was thin and wispy, it had been carefully combed.

"Joshua DeLoach," she proclaimed. "It is good to see you before I leave this life behind."

Her words held no bitterness. As she spoke, she patted the linen coverlet. "Bring him to me, please."

"Mrs. DeLoach. This is Erin Jacobs, and I'm Travis Williams."

"Yes, of course. The young caseworker Director Moring told me about. She didn't mention you were so tall."

Erin moved closer to the bed, her heart tripping with the rhythm of the rain against the window. This woman had the ability to rip her world apart.

"Stop trembling, child. I read about you in that paper. You've rescued alligators, haven't you?"

"Yes, ma'am."

"If you're brave enough to handle a beast with teeth powerful enough to rip your arm off, you can approach one very old lady." She reached out, and Erin placed her sleeping baby into her arms.

"He's grown so since I saw him last." Tears pooled in her eyes, but didn't spill. "Joshua—you were named after your grandfather. Never forget that, dear one. I did not know what happened to you, but I believed God would watch over your soul and he has. He has little Joshua."

Erin sank into the chair beside the bed, no longer trusting her legs to hold her. Only Travis's hand on her shoulder kept her from flying apart.

When thunder again rattled the windows, Joshua squirmed, opened his eyes, and peered at his great-grandmother.

"I will see Tara soon, and I will give her your love." Now the tears did fall, trailing down her weathered cheeks. She made no move to brush them away, neither did she apologize for them. Instead she sat there, quietly weeping, as Joshua reached up and touched her with his tiny fingers.

Travis retrieved the box of Kleenex from her bed stand, and Erin pulled a bottle from the diaper bag at the same moment Joshua's first cry joined the music of the storm outside.

"Would you like to feed him?"

"You take him, dear. It's been over thirty years since these hands have fed a baby. Tara was the last in fact."

"Can you tell us about Tara, Mrs. DeLoach?" Travis perched on the chair on the opposite side of the bed. "If you feel well enough to talk about this."

"At my age, it's important to talk about things while you still can." The old woman peered out the hospital window, out at the lights of the Capitol dome. "Tara was, is, my granddaughter. I say *is* because even though she no longer exists in this life, she continues in the next."

"What happened?" Travis leaned forward as Erin settled Joshua into her arms and resisted the urge to clap her hands over her ears.

"Tara grew up with her parents in Livingston."

"Did she go to school there?" Erin asked. "I feel like I should know her, but the name... it's not ringing a bell."

"Probably because at school she went by her first name—Abigail."

"Your granddaughter is Abigail DeLoach?"

"Yes."

"I think my sister knew her. They didn't really run in the same circles, but I'm pretty sure they shared a few classes. Once... one time she came over to our house. We'd rescued an owl, and she wanted to see it. That's why... why her voice was familiar."

"And also explains why she contacted you. Tara never would have left her child with someone she didn't trust." Mrs. DeLoach plucked at the cover. "My granddaughter married badly. She was convinced life had passed her by. Her parents had died, and she thought she was alone—but she wasn't." She slapped the coverlet for emphasis. "When a nice looking man came along, gave her attention, she fell for him. Without learning anything of his past."

Joshua cooed as he sucked greedily on the bottle.

"But I checked Derrick Pitcher out, and I didn't like what I found—a few petty charges dropped, bad associates, blank spots in his history. More than that, he was a little too interested in my fortune. Money had never been an issue between us before..."

Erin met Travis's gaze and waited for Mrs. DeLoach to continue, caught in the web of her story.

"Your money became an issue?" Travis asked gently.

"After she married Pitcher? Oh, yes. The first year he blew through Tara's annual allowance in two months. She made excuses. The second year I issued an ultimatum, but she chose her foolish dreams over family—family! I always knew she'd come back." Her lips began to quiver. She raised her head higher, and Erin had a glimpse of the proud woman she once was. "And she did—three times."

"With Joshua?" Erin asked.

"Not the first time a little over a year ago. She'd been married to Pitcher for nearly five years. With no children to inherit her fortune, and no yearly allowance, the man had begun to show his true colors."

"Infidelity?" Travis's voice took on its edge. Both women glanced at him.

Mrs. DeLoach only scoffed. "Yes, and worse. Oh, Tara never told on him. Heaven knows why she'd still protect the man. The second visit was four months ago. She was quite pregnant by then, with dark circles under her eyes. That's when I started working on little things for the baby—like the blanket with his name."

Erin flinched at the mention of the blanket, another puzzle piece slipping into place.

"So Pitcher is Joshua's father?"

"Not according to him. In fact, he divorced her when he found out she was pregnant. Claimed it wasn't his child, and

I talked her out of paternity testing. The fewer ties between my grandchild and that man the better. It was the one time she listened to me. Their divorce was final before Joshua was born. Seems he didn't want to be inconvenienced by a child. Tara wore hope like a cloak she'd bought at Macy's though. She thought when he *saw* the baby he'd change his mind."

"He didn't."

"Oh, no. Wouldn't even look at him when she took Joshua over there. So she moved back to Austin and found an apartment close to downtown."

"You said she visited you three times."

"The last time was two weeks ago." Suddenly, she looked her full eighty-six years—tired and more than a little sad. "There was something wrong, something worse than usual. She wouldn't tell me what, except to say Pitcher had contacted her. He needed money, which was normal. She was nervous, very protective of the baby."

Mrs. DeLoach raised her eyes to Travis's, then sought out Erin's and reached out a trembling hand to her. "I sensed a desperation in her. I told her we could handle Pitcher. I reminded Tara she could always depend on her family and her roots."

Her voice grew feeble as her strength wilted. She seemed to fade into her pillow though she never took her eyes off Joshua. "Those are the two things you can trust— your kin and the place you come from. She told me she loved me, but I knew that. Never doubted it. Families love each other, take care of each other, no matter what."

"You didn't see her again?" Travis asked.

"I didn't, but I will. One glorious day I will."

Nineteen

Travis visited the ARK again six days later. He found Evelyn England caring for Joshua while Erin was at the Huntsville State Park.

"Alligator made its way on to the interstate where a car spotted it. She went to retrieve the poor thing and put it back in the lake."

Travis felt all his blood drain to his toes.

Evelyn shook her head and actually wagged a finger at him. "You knew she rescued more than cats and dogs."

"I read the article in the paper, but I thought the alligator part was journalistic exaggeration. Is that safe?"

"Wouldn't be for you or me."

Evelyn sat in the porch swing, rocking the baby. She hardly looked the grandmotherly type, since she could probably pace him in a marathon, but silver peppered her hair and lines created a mosaic around her eyes and mouth each time she smiled down at Joshua.

"How long have you known Erin?"

"Since she was a child."

Though her answers were short, her tone was friendly. Travis took that as a good sign and sat down on the top step of the porch.

"Mind if I ask you a few questions?"

Evelyn raised Joshua to her shoulder. "Sounds to me like you already asked two. Might as well get them all out of your system."

"Will she be a good mother for Joshua?"

"Yes."

Travis ducked his head. "Care to add anything to your response?"

"No need. I answered your question."

He liked this woman. In fact, she looked familiar now that he'd studied her a bit. "Do I know you, Mrs. England?"

"You should. I've watched you grow up at church."

Travis punched the air with a fist. "Sunday school. Second grade."

"You were a rowdy one back then. Not nearly as tall, of course."

"Growth spurt hit in junior high."

Evelyn rubbed Joshua's back and let the memories settle around them. Their church was growing larger every year. In addition, Travis usually attended the early service. He bet Evelyn attended the more traditional eleven o'clock one.

When he finally spoke, it was as much to himself and the birds flitting in the crepe myrtle tree as it was to Evelyn. "Moring told me early on that Doc England was sponsoring Erin, and repeatedly Erin has mentioned Doc—somehow I didn't put two and two together. Didn't connect her Doc with the man who patched together Gus when he caught his leg in that hunter's trap."

"I guess it's been a lot of years since you've visited his office."

He glanced up at the woman sheepishly. "Don't think I've crossed to the dark side and started using one of those new vets in town. I don't even own a pet. Haven't since I moved out of my parents' house."

"I imagine you're busy enough with the children you oversee, and Doc is actually starting to shuffle patients off to those new vets. He can't take care of every animal in Livingston, Texas. It's one of the reasons he was happy to see Erin open the ARK."

"He helped her?"

Evelyn shifted in the porch swing and lay Joshua on her legs. "Erin doesn't accept help unless she's in a corner. In case you haven't noticed—and I'm betting you have—she's a might independent. But those two have been close since…"

Her voice trailed off and the expression on her face grew distant.

"Since Erin's foster parents died?"

"Hard times. Erin pulled back from everyone after Jules and Nina passed. She even stopped talking to Doc, but she held herself together for the ARK. Her passion for saving hurt animals goes beyond what most of us put into our job. I would think it's something you could understand."

Travis leaned back against the porch pillar. He would have never believed he had so much in common with Erin Jacobs, but it seemed their personalities matched on more than one level. Not that he considered himself an ideal candidate for a parent. He put so much into his job, there wasn't much left for a family.

"Given she does have a job requiring more than the average nine to five, do you think now is the right time for Erin to be a mom?" He leaned forward as Evelyn looked down at Joshua and traced his face with her finger.

Instead of answering him, she walked into the house. He could hear her in the nursery, speaking softly to the baby.

When she walked back out, she held two glasses of iced tea. She sat beside him on the step and picked up the conversation as if ten minutes hadn't passed.

"Right now, Erin has more on her plate than she can say grace over. But God has a reason for what he brings into our lives and His timing is perfect. It's not an accident the mother of Joshua called Erin, or that Erin has such a love in her heart for this baby."

Travis started to protest, but Evelyn stopped him with a touch of her hand on his arm.

"Drink your tea, son. I know it's your *job* to examine this from every angle. God has also placed you at a crossroads though, and that's your *mission*—to help Erin through this time. I'm sure you'll find a way to do both."

It was a good thing Evelyn had brought the tea, because suddenly, Travis found his throat painfully dry. She'd just managed to put all the uneasiness, all the anxiety he'd struggled against for the last nine days, into a one-minute declaration. Then she made the solution sound as simple as the flight of the sparrows in front of him.

That, he heard a voice in his heart whisper, was the essence of faith.

—

Erin returned home feeling satisfied with her work. The gator was unharmed and safely back in his habitat, and she was exhausted.

Once at the house, she wanted nothing more than to sit on the floor and play with Joshua. First though, she had chores.

Thankfully, Evelyn insisted on staying while she tended to the animals. She'd walked back into the house and practically fainted at the smell of homemade chicken and dumplings.

"Eat. Joshua couldn't wait for you, and I'm meeting Stanley at the Burger Shack later. It's his favorite Friday night junk food." Evelyn sat across from her, holding Joshua and feeding him his bottle.

"Little man looks sleepy."

"He took a very small nap earlier."

Evelyn continued to feed Josh as Erin ladled herself a bowlful of dumplings and collapsed at the table.

"You look exhausted, sweetie."

"Gators can do that to you."

"Sure it's just the gators?"

Erin shrugged and concentrated on blowing on the spoonful of dumplings.

"Young ones can be exhausting—"

"Especially when you're alone?" Erin's tone was sharper than she'd intended, but if Evelyn noticed she ignored it.

"I felt pretty alone when mine were young. Stanley had signed on with Dr. Dunn, and he was at the clinic twelve to fourteen hours a day. Most nights, too, come to think of it.

Livingston was more rural then..." Evelyn shook her head, lost in the memory.

"Those were precious times, but I wouldn't want to go back. Unless you've been there, you don't know the loneliness of rocking a crying baby when you're so tired you can't hold your own head up."

Erin smiled and ate the bite of chicken and broth. On her tongue it turned into something beyond food—rich and creamy, exactly what she needed. If heaven were a soup it would be chicken and dumplings. The thought surprised, then amused her.

"You can laugh about it now. I guess Joshua's been sleeping well the last week."

Erin didn't bother to correct her. No use trying to explain her daydreams over a bowl of soup. "He has been sleeping well."

"Might end when he starts teething. At least it did with my children."

"I read that in the baby book." Erin reached for the cornbread. All of a sudden she was famished. Had she eaten lunch? She knew she'd had breakfast, because she'd eaten cereal while feeding Josh his bottle.

"Baby books are one thing. Life is another." Evelyn retrieved a washcloth from the drawer near the sink, warmed it under the faucet, and proceeded to clean Joshua's hands. He endured it until she went for his face.

His cries were loud and piercing as he squirmed this way and that to avoid the cloth.

"I need to bathe him tonight, Evelyn. I don't know why he hates to get his face wet. I have to give him a pacifier to distract him, and still, if I'm not fast, I get those screams."

"Might consider earplugs during bath time."

"For Josh?"

"For you."

Evelyn handed Erin the baby and planted a big kiss on his tear-stained cheek. In response, Josh snuggled into the space between Erin's shoulder and neck.

"He's a charmer, all right." Evelyn walked over to a side table and picked up a business card. "Speaking of charmers, your caseworker stopped by this afternoon."

Erin rolled her eyes, but she took the card.

"He wants to see you and Joshua in his office Monday at ten in the morning. If that time won't work, he said to call and reschedule."

Erin ignored the headache forming at the base of her neck and focused instead on the feel of Joshua in her arms. His snuggly warmth and fresh smell, everything about him was right. And it almost made up for having to see Travis Williams on Monday. On second thought, it did *not* make up for that.

Evelyn was already collecting her things in the living room.

"Thank you, Evelyn. I don't know what I'd do if I couldn't call you at the last minute for the big cases."

"Don't be silly."

"I'm being serious. Travis told me he wouldn't approve Joshua's placement unless I made different arrangements."

Erin led the way out onto the darkened porch, more so that she wouldn't have to look into the older woman's eyes than for any wish to hurry her off.

"What else did he say?" Evelyn's voice was stiff, defensive.

It made Erin want to reach out and hug her, but she didn't.

"That was about it." She didn't want to go into the entire *needing a social safety net conversation.* She still had no clue what to do about that. She wasn't ready to put an ad in the Livingston paper asking for friends.

"Any other word from Mrs. DeLoach?"

"DNA testing will be back next week, but I was convinced. She's Joshua's great-grandmother." Erin tucked her hair behind her ear. "We went to see her again yesterday. She and Joshua have the exact same color of eyes."

Evelyn turned abruptly and peered at her in the porch's dim lighting.

"You don't have to do that, Erin. No one expects you to cart this baby back and forth to Austin."

"If you could have met her…" Erin gazed out past the stand of live oak trees. "She's a very sweet old woman, and she lights up so when she sees him. I needed to pick up some supplies anyway."

"Supplies UPS could have delivered."

Erin didn't bother arguing with her.

"Remember we're out of town until Wednesday, going to see the grandbabies in Dallas." Evelyn's voice took on the no-nonsense tone. "Are you sure you'll be all right here? There's a storm due in this weekend."

"I have extra feed stocked for the animals *and* the humans. We'll be fine."

"You call the church if you need anything."

Erin nodded, but they both knew she wouldn't. She hadn't been back at the church since Nina and Jules's funeral.

It wasn't like the good folks of the congregation had been beating a path to her door, and she couldn't blame them. Truth was they didn't have much to offer each other. No, going back through the church's doors didn't appeal to her.

So how would she establish a social safety net?

Shirley would allow her to renew their friendship, had encouraged her even, but the woman's hands were full with her own family and the menagerie of pets and cattle they had. Add in the charity work she did, and Erin didn't believe she needed another project.

Evelyn and Doc were all she had right now. They'd have to be enough.

After watching Evelyn drive away, she placed Travis's card on her desk. Monday morning. She frowned. At least she had something to look forward to after the long weekend—another chance for Angela to gossip about her, perhaps another depressing family to watch in the waiting room, maybe even experience another panic attack.

She was grateful it was three days away.

Who knew what could happen in that amount of time.

Twenty

Erin's coughing started in the wee hours of Saturday morning, same as the rains.

She fed herself canned chicken soup, wrapped up when she went to the barn, and tried not to cast a worried eye to the darkening storm clouds.

The forecast called for possible flooding.

She'd lived in Livingston all of her life and dealt with all types of weather. After taking care of her animals, she was determined to enjoy her day off from rescue calls. She was looking forward to spending quality time with Joshua. She closed the window blinds, turned on all her lamps, and shut the storm outside—for a time.

Saturday night she pulled on her rain boots and stepped into water up to her calves.

Checking the baby monitor in her pocket one more time, she trudged toward the barn. Once before she'd had to move the animals to higher ground, but never at night, and she hadn't been sick then.

She clenched her teeth together against the chills racking her body and hurried toward the dogs.

How had the water risen so quickly?

She shouldn't have napped with Josh. The idea of resting her pounding head had been too tempting, and now her animals might pay the price.

—

Travis backed his boat into the slot beside his parents' driveway. They'd built an extended covered area—ostensibly for an outside patio spot, but the dimensions perfectly fit Travis's boat. Unhooking the Skeeter, he watched the water flowing down the street.

He preferred keeping the boat at the lake, but the way this fierce storm had blown in, he felt better with it on high ground. He'd allowed himself few luxuries in life. The Skeeter was one of them.

In the driving rain, he ran the few feet to the back door, and still he was soaked when he stepped into the kitchen.

"Going to be a record-setter." His father nodded toward the small television on the kitchen counter. The sound was muted, but the weatherman's charts needed no explanation—rain, rain, and more rain.

"Thanks." Travis accepted the mug of steaming coffee and sat down at the table. "Ever seen a storm like this one?"

"When you were a kid."

"We had moved your bedroom to the back patio because your little sister was due in November." His mom pulled a large pan of fresh cookies from the oven. Their sweet scent filled the kitchen.

"I remember. One day I had a bedroom, the next I

didn't." Travis crossed his ankles and settled in for the story.

"You loved the patio." His dad laughed. "By late October when we closed it in and made it a real room, all you did was complain."

"As long as it was a patio, I felt like I was camping." Travis fell back into the memory—a time when he had no obligations, no children depending on him and his judgments.

"The rain that year came up over the back steps." His dad reached for the cookies, but his mother passed the plate to Travis.

"These cookies are for church. You can eat the bowl of fruit that I cut up for you."

"It flooded my room," Travis said, attempting to get his father's attention off the sweets.

"You ran into the house like the hounds of hell had lit out after you."

"I thought they had. I'd turned six that summer. Dreamed I'd fallen into a lake and couldn't swim, then woke up to a lapping sound." Travis stared out the window at the sheets of falling rain. "Strange how I can remember the fear of that nightmare after all these years."

"Some dreams grip you that way." His mom sat down at the table and studied the television as if she could change what she was seeing there. "This will be a strain on folks. Anyone you need to check on?"

"No." Travis patted his shirt pocket. "All my cases have my cell phone number."

"I didn't ask about your cases." His mom's voice was soft, but the reprimand was there nonetheless. "I asked about the *people* you're looking after."

Travis met his dad's eyes. Neither dared smile for fear

of a slap on the back of the head, but an understanding passed between them. "I hear you, Mom. I'm not their pastor though. I'm their caseworker."

He pushed his chair back and kissed her cheek. "You two sure you'll be all right here?"

"Snug as two owls in a tree," his dad declared. Walking him to the back door, he placed a hand on his back. "Which one you worried about?"

Travis froze, one arm in his jacket. "Why?"

"You didn't touch the cookies—a sure sign you're worried. Don't have to talk about it if you don't want to."

Sighing, he finished slipping his jacket on and picked up his keys from the countertop. "Erin Jacobs. She lives out of town, alone. All those animals to tend to, and now she has an infant."

His dad nodded and stood beside him, studying the rain. "Should you go and check on her?"

"She'll call if she needs me."

Travis hugged his father and stepped out into the rising waters.

—

Sunday morning dawned dark. The rain continued to fall in sheets, and Erin had trouble remembering why she needed to push her way out from the shelter of her covers.

Then Joshua's cries broke through the last of her dream fog. As awareness splashed over her, she struggled to fight her way free of the mass of quilts. They felt like hundred pound weights. Before she managed to sit completely up, a hacking cough seized her and threatened to throw her back into bed.

Joshua's cries escalated from the "I'm-hungry-alarm" she'd become accustomed to into sobs. Erin stared at the baby monitor as if it could offer answers before stumbling toward the hall.

The room seemed to tilt, rocked back and forth like the deck of a ship, then finally righted itself.

Holding tight to her doorframe, she wiped the sweat from her forehead, grabbed her robe from the chair, and hurried toward the nursery.

He quieted the minute she peeped over his crib. Tears still gleamed on his cheeks, but he popped a toe into his mouth and smiled.

"Hey, baby boy. You okay?"

For his answer, he giggled, exchanged one foot for the other, then reached for her nose.

"I suppose if I'm contagious you've already been exposed. But I hope you don't catch this, Josh. I would be a bad, bad mommy to give you this virus, darling." It was the first time she'd used the word *mommy*, but it felt sweet on her tongue. Somehow it eased the aches tormenting her body.

She changed his diaper, reached into the crib to pick him up, and marveled at the coolness of his hand against her cheek. Instead of heading for the kitchen, she gave in to the weariness threatening to overwhelm her and sank into the rocker.

Gazing out the window, she wondered how she'd ever manage to tend to the animals today in this storm. How much had the waters risen? Where would she find the energy? She could barely walk across the room. How would she make it to the barns?

If she were a praying person, she'd pray.

Hadn't helped much a year ago, and she wouldn't resort to it now. No use being a foxhole believer.

She had prayed the night she'd found Joshua. The thought hovered like a whisper, but she pushed it away.

Joshua began fussing in her arms. Erin glanced at the clock on his dresser. Somehow she'd managed to sit there for half an hour.

"Bet you're starving. Am I right?"

It took the strength of a power lifter to carry him to the kitchen and place him in the reclining highchair. Feeding him the bottle sapped the rest of her energy. She wouldn't make it to the barns this morning.

Returning the formula he hadn't quite finished to the refrigerator, she closed the door and leaned her head against it, reveling in its coolness.

Her teeth began to chatter, and she clamped her jaws tight. In the background she could hear Joshua gurgling. Soon she'd need to clean him up, move him back to his crib. The tears rolled down her cheeks.

She hated her weakness.

Why did she have to get sick now? During a flood? When Joshua and her animals needed her?

Nina's voice, soft and gentle in her ear, whispered, "God's timing is perfect, Erin."

Rubbing her palms across her cheeks, she pushed away from the refrigerator. She might be stubborn, but she wasn't a fool.

Doc and Evelyn were out of town. Shirley was too pregnant and had a family of her own to worry about. Not to mention her husband would have his hands full with their pets and cattle.

That left one person she could call.

She picked up the business card and ran her thumb over the name—Travis Williams, Child Welfare. Beneath his business address was listed his work phone and cell. Doubting he'd be at work on a Sunday, she grimaced at the cell number.

It galled her to call him.

She could think of a dozen reasons *not* to ask for his help.

Her gaze tracked around the kitchen. In slow motion, like a film advancing frame by frame, the room once again began to tilt then spin. Darkness claimed the morning as what little light had pierced the darkness fled and thunder rattled the windows.

Rain beat a rhythm against the roof.

Even as she reached for the counter to steady herself—willed her heartbeat to slow in its headlong rush toward panic—Joshua lay in his reclined highchair, batting playfully at the toys on the tray. He remained blissfully unaware of the danger increasing around them.

Joshua was the one reason she would put aside her pride.

Downing two more Tylenol, she pulled her cell phone off the charger. If ever a situation qualified as an emergency, this one did. She pressed the *on* button and stared at the display in disbelief.

NO SERVICE AVAILABLE.

Pushing away from the counter, she walked to the wall phone. Sweat broke across her forehead as an ominous silence filled her ear.

The line was dead.

"Don't panic. We'll drive out. Go for help."

She dug deep and found enough strength to lift Joshua from his chair. Within ten minutes she had them both bundled up and in the truck. Though the house was on the highest part of her property, the water was up to the running board.

She didn't allow her mind to think about driving through the cattle guards. Instead, she cranked the truck, pulled it around, and started down her lane.

Though the clock on the truck's dash flashed nine in the morning, she had to turn on her headlights to make out the lane. Thunder rumbled and lightning split the sky.

She refused to think about the animals on the ARK. She'd drive Joshua to safety and take herself to the doctor. The animals would be frightened but okay for at least twenty-four hours. The water wouldn't reach them in the ARK, where the barns were set on even higher ground than the house. She'd set out additional food last night. They would be fine. The milk cows would be suffering, but there was nothing she could do about that.

Erin was so busy considering the needs of her animals, she didn't at first recognize the lake blocking her path.

Fever, exhaustion, doubt, and confusion took what she saw, tried to process it, and failed.

She shook her head, thinking maybe she'd lost the lane.

Then she saw the fence posts and stared in horror at the top two inches. The rest were submerged in the rising waters that blocked her only way out.

Twenty-One

Travis tapped his pen against his keyboard and checked the time on his computer monitor once more—fifteen minutes after ten. Unable to resist, he picked up his phone.

"Any sign of Miss Jacobs, Angela?"

"Again, no. I would have called you if she'd arrived."

"Try to get her on the line for me."

Travis hung up before their receptionist had a chance to editorialize any further.

He'd spent the day before caged up in his apartment, and now he was paying for it. He felt itchy. Why hadn't he gone to the gym instead of spending the day on the couch watching sports, hoping Erin Jacobs would call?

How had the woman managed to care for her menagerie of animals in this flood?

Any other new mom, any other single mom, would have called him scared to death when the skies dropped twenty-six inches of water in less than three days.

Not Erin Jacobs.

His only calls had been from his mother, two clients who wanted him to deliver meals (he'd referred those to Meals-on-Wheels), and James inviting him over to watch a game (he'd passed).

No calls from Erin, and now she was fifteen minutes late.

When his phone rang, he pounced.

"Williams."

"I tried Erin's number, Travis. Lines aren't working out her way. Phone company reports they've been down since yesterday morning."

"What about her cell?" Travis began combing through his file for her number.

"Tried it already. Nothing."

"What do you mean nothing?" Travis's voice boomed, temporarily muting the steady drone of rain against the windows. He launched out of his chair, looming a good head taller than the sides of his cubicle.

Seeing everyone within shouting distance turn to stare at him, he muttered into the handset, "I'll be right there."

One minute later he was standing in front of a wide-eyed Angela.

"I tried. Both numbers aren't working."

"You mean you didn't get an answer."

"No. I mean they weren't working."

"How is that possible? Our phones are working. Erin Jacobs lives in the same town we live in, correct?"

"Calm down, Travis." Angela slid a bright red fingernail down the front page of the newspaper and stopped below a sidebar. "It says here some landlines and cellular companies are experiencing temporary outages."

"Unacceptable." Determined to keep his cool, he gritted his teeth together.

"Gosh. I'm sorry, but there's a flood going on if you haven't noticed." Angela leaned back, cocked her head, and looked at him inquisitively. "It's only an appointment. Maybe she forgot. I'm sure Erin will reschedule. What's got your spine up?"

Travis tamped down his temper, drew a deep breath, and stepped back from Angela's counter. He paced away from her, stared out the window, and uttered a prayer, but the itchiness didn't lessen. It intensified.

Running a hand through his hair, he turned back to his receptionist. "I'm worried about Erin," he confessed. "She was *early* for her last appointment. I think she'd at least call—"

"If she could," Angela pointed out.

"Exactly." Travis nodded, relieved they were finally working together.

"Do you want me to call emergency dispatch? Have them take a run by her place—"

Travis stopped her hand as it reached for the push buttons of the phone.

"Emergency personnel have enough to do in this kind of flooding. You could be right—maybe with all she had to do at the ARK, she forgot. My next appointment is after lunch. I'll run out and check on her."

Travis jogged back through the door toward his office, grabbed his keys, jacket, and cell phone—at least his worked. As he rushed past Angela's desk, she waved him over and shoved her keys across the counter toward him.

"Jimmy insisted I bring his truck today."

"Jimmy?"

"My brother."

"Oh, yeah." Travis tried to think of something to say and couldn't. Jimmy was about as redneck as they came—from his work boots to his John Deere hat and pinch of chewing tobacco. In his mid-twenties, the boy had already experienced several brushes with the law.

"If I remember right, to get to Erin's you have to go through some pretty low spots. Your Chevy Blazer is high, but not as high as Jimmy's truck."

"You mean the—" A grin spread across Travis's face for the first time since realizing Erin wasn't going to show for her appointment.

"Yeah, it's that old Dodge Power Wagon he enters in the four-wheeler competitions—408 engine, larger pistons, heavier axels, even waterproofed. Why do you think he still lives with my parents? He spends all his paycheck on his *hobby*. Says he's even made it up a seventy-degree slope. Any more than that, and you'll flip over."

Travis gripped the keys in his hands. "Thanks, Angie. I owe you."

Then he was gone, flying down the road like a superhero in a transformer machine. He had no problem ignoring the strange looks thrown his way. First of all they were rare, since most sane people had stayed off the roads. Secondly, he was high enough that he could look down on the roof tops of the cars he passed. He felt them though—people wondering about the nut in the off-road vehicle.

He waited until he'd left the central part of town to see what the truck was able to do. Though the water had started to recede, it still remained two to three feet deep in some places. At first he would slow down as he went through it, but the truck's wheels never lost traction. It was like driving a subterranean vehicle. He would almost enjoy it if his heart rate would slow down.

The closer he got to Erin's place, the deeper the water became on the flooded roads and in the pastures.

Then he turned on her lane, stopped the truck, and stared—mouth wide open. The truck idled, growled practically, as if its engines were eager to take on the lake in front of him.

But there was a cattle guard in the middle of that lake. No way he could push that guard open given the amount of water it was standing in—unless he wanted to crash through it, and he'd never achieve the speed needed to manage that.

He tried his cell.

NO SERVICE AVAILABLE.

The rain had lightened somewhat, and he thought he saw a light on in the house at the top of the hill.

There was another way to Erin's house. There just wasn't another *road* to Erin's house. If you had an all-terrain vehicle though, you could get there via the back way—up the hill.

Jamming the gears into reverse, he spun the truck around and circled the farm road to the back side of the ARK.

Like one magnet drawn to another, he felt a pull now that he was powerless to resist. He'd reach Erin's house to check on her and Joshua if he had to swim. First though, he'd try driving off-road.

Looking at a ten percent grade and a river of mud, chances were he'd slide right back down. So he muttered a prayer, pushed the gear shift into first, and punched the accelerator.

When he gained the hilltop, he crashed through an old fence behind the barn. A dilapidated three-foot wooden fence couldn't stop him. Adrenaline pumped through his veins as mud sloshed beneath the truck's oversized tires. He was so elated to have made it to the top of the hill and onto Erin's property that it took a minute for what he was seeing—or not seeing—to register.

There were no animals in the pens.

No dogs in the dog run.

The horses didn't poke their heads out from the barn. In fact, the barn was closed up tight.

He cracked his window and rain slapped him in the face, but he didn't hear a single moo.

The ARK was silent.

Where were the horses? Ducks, rabbits, and cats might be quietly curled in a corner. But horses and a llama should be making a ruckus.

Spinning the truck around in the lane, he downshifted once more. Erin's house loomed in front of him in the noonday darkness. The one light he'd seen from the cattle guard—from the *lake* in front of her house—still shone through the porch window.

Why hadn't she noticed him? Even through the rain, she should hear the diesel engine of Jimmy's truck. She should be looking to see who the idiot was trespassing on her property.

He tried to swallow the panic rising in his throat. Wiping his sweaty palms against his pants leg, he studied her house and considered his next move.

Surely there was a logical explanation.

Maybe she'd left when she saw the water rising.

Erin would never leave her animals—they were here somewhere. She was here.

With the conviction that something was wrong, and thanking God he'd found a way to make it this far, he drove the truck steadily through the remaining three hundred yards of water and mud to her porch. When he finally cut the engine, the soft patter of rain against the metal roof of the truck almost unnerved him.

Still no sign of life.

He sloshed his way through the mud and up her porch steps.

No one answered his knock, and the door was locked when he tried the knob.

He peered through the slim window that ran the length of the door and saw another light on in the back room.

He pounded on the door. "Erin? Erin, it's Travis Williams. Are you in there?"

He rattled the door and tapped on the glass. Still no one answered.

Looking around the front porch, he spied a plastic frog sitting next to the swing, lifted it up, and removed the key.

Unlocking the door, he stepped inside.

Silence blanketed the home.

"Erin?"

His boots echoed on the wooden floor as he crossed the room. He had an overwhelming urge to stop them, knew he was tracking mud across her pine floors.

But the silence and an urgency spurred him forward.

Through the living room, down the hall, to the darkened nursery.

Joshua's crib stood empty. The blanket with tiny horses had been tossed in the corner.

The monitor light blinked on, and through it he could hear tiny, whimpering sounds—not cries really, not something he could hear from the other room. He leaned closer to convince himself it wasn't his imagination. The whimpers stopped, then started again.

He no longer called out.

His pulse thundered in his ears as he strode down the hall, his legs growing heavier with each step.

Her door was cracked slightly.

He reached out his hand, again petitioned God for mercy, realized he'd been praying since he'd crashed through the fence, and pushed open the door.

Twenty-Two

Erin woke to Travis kneeling beside her bed, his hand on her face, deliciously cool fingers running across her brow. He whispered something she couldn't make out, but it didn't matter. All that mattered was the comfort of his skin against hers.

She curled toward his hand and let her eyes drift shut.

Then Joshua's howls pierced through her fever. She struggled against the weight holding her eyes shut. Pushed at the mounds of covers pinning her down.

Why couldn't she sit up? Joshua needed her.

"It's all right, Erin. I have Joshua. Lie back and rest." Travis framed her face with his hands.

She was powerless to resist the delicious chill his hands brought to her face. Closing her eyes, she replayed the dream again—she'd been lost in a desert and alone.

But now he was here and with him relief.

She sank back into her pillows.

"Joshua—" Her voice sounded like someone else's. Pine needles scratched at the inside of her throat.

"He's in my arms. See? Josh is right here. You're burning up. I need to bring your fever down."

"Josh first." She croaked. "I've been feeding him."

She pointed to the cooler and bottle warmer by the bed. It was all she'd been able to think of the night before when the worst of the chills had hit. Realizing they were stranded on the ARK until the waters receded, she'd premade bottles, brought in ice and a cooler, and stored them beside her bed. The bottle warmer had been in the bag in Josh's closet.

Then she'd set in a supply of diapers.

They'd spent the last twenty-four hours huddled there.

She finally met Travis's gaze and hoped he understood that she'd done her best.

"He's fine—only wet. I'll change him."

She heard the heavenly sound of a diaper being pulled off and nearly cried because she didn't have to lift her arms to do it. Falling back into the abyss, her last thought was something else needed to be done. Something urgent.

When she woke again, Travis was pushing the hair back from her face. He worked a wet cloth around her forehead, cheeks, mouth—she had the bizarre urge to bite it. Anything to feel liquid in her throat.

"Drink," she murmured.

He nearly jumped off the bed when she spoke.

"I have water right here."

Helping her sit up, he held the cup to her lips. The water was delicious, cold, better than a thousand ice cream shakes. She tried to take the glass from his hands and gulp it down.

"Easy. Try a little at first."

She nodded, rested back against the pillows, and studied his face.

"Josh?"

"He's fine. You fell asleep again, so I washed him up and fed him another bottle. He's asleep in his crib now."

She nodded, satisfied. "Thanks."

"You're welcome."

She tried to understand why he was there, how he'd come to help them, but it took too much effort. Instead she said, "You look worried."

"You're burning up, Erin. Can you take these Tylenol?"

She nodded and took the caplets from his hand. When she reached for the water though, she shook too badly to hold it. He again brought it to her lips and held it for her while she quenched her thirst.

"I need to take you to town, but the flood…"

Then it all came back to her. She remembered trying to leave with Joshua, and the lake at the bottom of the hill.

"Phones?"

"Still out. I guess they have been for some time."

"Since yesterday. How did you reach us?"

"Angela's brother has a monster mud truck." The familiar grin returned to Travis's face, and somehow it brought her more comfort than anything so far. She knew if he could smile in the midst of this, they'd be fine.

"Mud truck, huh?" Her voice cracked again, and she began to cough, deep and painful, sounding as if she were coughing up her lungs.

Travis jumped up and stuffed his hands in his pockets. He tried to hand her the glass of water, but she shook her head no.

"You need to be in a hospital. Your fever, I don't know how high it is, but it must be over one hundred. And you look terrible."

"Thanks."

"You know what I mean." He sat back down as her coughing subsided. "I was scared senseless when I walked in here and saw you lying there curled around Joshua."

She saw him look down at the floor and clench the fist that lay on her quilt, but he held the words he wanted to say.

"I know," she whispered.

His head snapped up, and his eyes searched hers.

"I know you were right. When you said we need…" Her hand fluttered out of the cover, gesturing toward the empty room around her. "Other people. When you said we can't do this alone."

The dam inside her burst open, tracking hot tears down her cheeks.

She glanced away because looking in his eyes hurt too much, and she wouldn't be able to say what she'd rehearsed all night. Instead, she studied the scene out her window where the rain continued to fall. She could admit she'd been wrong, had finally found the right words she owed him—in the moments she'd been lucid. But she couldn't look in his eyes while she did it.

She needed a moment to compose herself and stop the tears that insisted on falling like the rain.

—

Travis realized he shouldn't allow himself to get any closer to Erin.

Their relationship had already become too intimate. He understood the rules governing relationships between caseworkers and clients and knew their purpose.

But the last fifteen minutes had been packed with too much emotion for even the notoriously distant Travis Williams to stuff inside. Seeing Erin in that bed, her body curved protectively around Joshua, with the infant supplies stacked neatly near her on the floor—he had felt like a fist was squeezing his heart and feared it wouldn't stop until it burst.

Then Joshua had moved his tiny hands and reached up for him.

Is that what Erin had seen the night she'd found him on the porch?

When Erin had turned her face toward his, he'd felt the double blow. Somehow they had both worked their way past his defenses. He understood now how much she loved this child. He didn't fully know how such a thing could happen so quickly, but it had. Seeing her physically suffer, and not be able to do anything about it, tore at him. On top of that she was hurting emotionally. How could he not reach out and comfort her, just this once?

Even if it was against the rules.

Tenderly, he ran a thumb along her jaw and felt her shiver. She turned her face into his hand as she had before.

He longed to pull her to him and cradle her in his arms.

Instead he said, "Look at me, Erin. Tell me what's wrong."

"Joshua and I shouldn't have been here alone. I shouldn't try to do this by myself. What if I had di... di...

died? What would have happened to him? I need a ne... ne... net."

When she finally turned her eyes to his, he meant to pull his hand away. Instead, he found himself pushing her hair back from her face, trying to soothe the agony he saw written there, and finally doing what he swore he wouldn't, pulling her to his chest.

As he rocked her back and forth, her sobs doing more to drench his shirt than the rain had, Travis realized he was losing his heart with each beat of hers. Some part of his mind knew that even as he whispered nonsense words and clumsily patted her back.

Finally, her well of grief seemed to run dry, and he was left holding what seemed to be her shadow. The heat from her fever radiated through her clothing, penetrating the blankets between them. When she began shivering, he pulled the comforter around her.

He used his thumbs to dry the tears on her cheeks. She glanced at him for a moment, then buried her face against his chest. She started shaking against him again, and he worried her fever was spiking, knew he needed to move her soon.

"Listen to me. You wouldn't have died, okay? And someone would have come. Doc would have checked on you."

"They're out of town." Her voice was a wail, tearing from her throat, and he realized how all alone she must have felt, how terrified she'd been since the rains had begun. "And the phones didn't work. I moved all the animals to high ground—locked them all in the barn, set out extra feed, even managed to milk Kizmit and Bells. I tried to leave, tried to drive out, but the road was blocked. I came back, and Joshua was so heavy. Then the next time I tried to get to the animals, I couldn't. The water was too high."

Her sobs once again interrupted her story. He thought she'd been cried out, but like the clouds outside the window she had more to give. He waited another minute, two, until her breathing returned to normal.

Then he scooched back and held her face in both his hands.

"You did great, honey. You were very smart to bring Joshua in here with you. And the phones would have come back on eventually."

Now she did raise her eyes to his, and he saw the smallest glimmer of hope there. He had the overwhelming urge to gently kiss her lips, to bring even the tiniest of smiles to her, but he didn't.

He'd crossed enough lines today.

"Yes, you need a network. I'm glad you understand the importance of having others to call, but you did the right thing with what you had. Now tell me what I need to do with the animals, and then we'll get you and Joshua to town."

Twenty-Three

Erin looked at the doctor and stubbornly shook her head. The IV had helped tremendously. Whatever meds they had mixed with the saline solution had improved her condition dramatically after only a few hours—enough for some of her willful streak to return.

"I can't stay tonight," she insisted. "Now please sign my release papers, or give me that form saying I understand I'm leaving against your advice."

"But Miss Jacobs, perhaps you don't understand how severely dehydrated you were. We've seen this happen before in flu cases. You're feeling better now because of the fluids and the medicine we've pumped into your system. Tonight the fever will rise again. The next twenty-four to forty-eight hours will be rough."

Erin didn't blink. Instead, she pushed the button to call her nurse and scooted to the side of the bed. "I have a baby, doctor. And there's no one else to take care of him. Plus an ARK full of animals. I can't stay."

Doctor Bandal's eyes widened at the word ARK. He was a young, middle-eastern man, with a gentle demeanor. Sighing, he picked up her chart and began writing a notation.

The door opened with a swoosh and her nurse Jamie entered, followed by Travis who was holding Joshua. Her heart kicked up at the sight of the two of them. She was grateful the doctor didn't have her on a heart monitor. He'd never let her go. She took a deep breath and smiled at them though Travis remained standing across the room.

"Good news?" he asked.

"What can I do for you, sweetie?" The nurse was a no-nonsense, grandmotherly type.

"I need this IV taken out," Erin said, attempting to maneuver out of the bed while still holding the back of her gown together.

"Is Miss Jacobs going home, Doctor?"

"Apparently." He scribbled three prescriptions and set them on the tray beside her bed. "Do not try to tend to your animals in this weather. You will have a relapse, and you'll be back here before the sun is down tomorrow. Am I clear?"

Travis juggled Joshua to his other arm. "Why are you leaving? Are you that much better?"

The doctor crossed his arms, but didn't speak.

The nurse actually tsked. Erin hadn't heard anyone tsk since, well, since Nina had passed away. The sound shot through her heart like an arrow from a bow.

"What am I missing here?" Travis asked as he once again switched Joshua to his other arm. The baby had begun to fuss and squirm as soon as he'd spied Erin.

"I'm not at liberty to say, Mr.—"

"Williams. Travis Williams."

"So you're not Mrs. Jacobs' spouse."

"No!" They both shouted the word simultaneously, causing the doctor and nurse to exchange a quick glance.

"Then, of course, I cannot share Miss Jacobs' medical information with you." The doctor shook Travis's hand, even as he managed to send a disapproving look toward Erin. "It's nice to meet you though. I am Dr. Bandal. Perhaps you could talk to my patient and remind her how ill she was when she entered this facility."

"Erin—"

"There's no use ganging up on me. I'm going home." Erin heard the petulant tone in her voice, but held her ground.

"Doctor, you might not be at liberty to say, but I suppose I'm free to hazard a guess. Is our patient going AWOL?"

Again the tsk as Jamie removed the IV and applied a Band-Aid.

"It's the baby," Erin explained to her. "I'm a single mom, and there's no one else to care for him."

"No one else looks like a tall drink of water to me, hon." The observation was offered in a girl-to-girl whisper, but in the sudden quietness her words carried—probably out to the hall and down to the nurses' station.

Travis had been attempting to settle Josh. At Jamie's comment, his gaze found Erin's. She was powerless not to look at him—look and remember how his arms had felt around her. For a moment, she had actually stopped being afraid.

That moment was over though, and it was time to stand on her own two feet.

Again grasping the hospital gown from the back, she put her toes on the cold linoleum floor, grimaced, and stood.

"Erin, where—"

She made it three steps before the room began to tilt.

———

Travis almost resented the doctor for reaching Erin's side before he did. Of course, he had to dash around the bedside tray while holding on to Joshua.

Plus he had been standing across the room. He'd hoped it would help him maintain his professional distance—something he hadn't done a very good job of all day. Looking out at the inkiness of the night sky, it occurred to him he would do better to start afresh tomorrow.

By the time he reached Erin, Dr. Bandal and the nurse had lowered her back to the bed.

"I'm fine. I was only dizzy for a minute."

"This is what I'm speaking of when I say you are not ready to be dismissed from my care. What if you were at home and had such a spell? What if you were carrying your son?"

Travis knew the doctor had hit his mark when Erin pulled in her bottom lip to stop the tears.

She hadn't cried again after he'd held her in his arms, but he'd seen her almost break down twice. Once as they passed the barns on the way back down the hill. He'd spent two hours tending to her animals, and he assured her they were fine. He'd even managed to milk the cows, which he considered a real achievement. Passing the barn, she'd bit down hard on her bottom lip, gazed at him as if he'd paved a path to the moon, and reached out to touch his arm.

When the tears had pooled in her eyes, she'd pulled her hand back and tucked it under the blanket he'd wrapped around her.

The second time she'd almost burst into tears was during her admittance downstairs when they'd asked her to list her next of kin.

Watching her now, Travis realized Erin's pride had taken quite a few blows these last few hours, and the dark circles under her eyes were evidence of her exhaustion.

"Could I have a few minutes alone with Erin? Perhaps we could reach a compromise."

The doctor nodded as he jotted a final notation in her chart. "I need to speak with two more of my patients. Have the nurse page me if you have any questions."

Nurse Jamie leaned in and whispered something to Erin he couldn't make out. Erin sniffled, but continued to stare at the wall.

As she walked past Travis, she stopped and took Joshua's hand. "You are one beautiful little man. Yes, you are. And you have your mother's curls—don't you?"

She patted Travis's arm as she continued out of the room, her soft-soled shoes nearly soundless on the floor.

Travis waited for Erin to raise her eyes to his before he approached her bed. Then instead of perching next to her on the mattress, he pulled over a chair.

Seeing the longing in her eyes as she gazed at Joshua, he again marveled at their bond. How could he have ever doubted these two belonged together?

"Let me hold him."

"I don't think that's a good idea."

"If he were going to catch this, he already would have."

Arguing with her was an exercise in futility. Raising the bedrail, he gently laid Josh next to her. Automatically, her arms formed a protective circle around the baby and the clouds of worry in her eyes lifted, as if holding Josh righted the world.

Sitting in the chair, arms propped on his knees, he peered through the bars of the railing. "Erin, I think you know you shouldn't go back to your home right now—at least not alone."

She didn't answer or take her eyes from Josh, but she did nod slightly.

"Is there anywhere else you can go? Any friends who would let you stay with them for a couple of days?"

The tears started from the corners of her eyes and tore at his heart. She wiped at them with the heels of her hands.

"When will Doc and Evelyn be back?"

"Wednesday." Her words whispered defeat.

They both knew in two days she'd either be ready to go home alone or she'd be in the hospital's intensive care unit.

Travis did not have all the answers to his clients' problems, never claimed to be able to solve all their issues. He did like to appear confident in front of his cases though. Somewhere in the last eight hours, Erin Jacobs had ceased being merely a case. Maybe she never had been.

So he leaned forward, placed his head in his hands, and he did something he usually only did when he was alone—he silently prayed for guidance.

Lord, I can take Joshua from Erin now for a few days. Put him in an emergency home, but I don't believe that's what you'd have me do. I can see her love for this child. Thank you for urging me to her house, for sending me there in time. Thank you for taking care of these two through the night. I know you have a place and a person to care for them until Erin is well, Lord. Help me to guide them to that person.

When he lifted his head, Erin was studying him.

"I'm going to step into the hall for a minute. Will you be okay?"

"Yeah. Do you have a pacifier for Josh?"

He smiled and unzipped the quilted baby bag he'd been carrying around for hours. "Happen to have one right here."

Her fingers brushed his as he passed it over the rail. Electricity jumped up his arm, sending warmth through his body.

He needed to focus, needed to make the call.

"I'll be right back."

Twenty-Four

Travis gazed with longing at the basketball standard as he unloaded the last of the groceries.

"Pick up that ball, and I'll hit you with these bananas," his mom threatened. "I need the rest of this food in the kitchen. Then I want you to find the playpen in the garage and wipe it down nice and clean for Joshua."

Travis longed to drop the bags and rub at the tension headache that had begun an hour ago. Instead, he picked up a third bag and trudged toward the back door of his parents' house. His mother had done too much for him in the past three hours to argue.

As he walked into the garage, a hand reached out and clapped him on the shoulder.

"I'm actually enjoying having a baby in the house again." His father smelled of machine oil and leather. He'd been tinkering on their 1953 Ford truck again. Just thinking of the classic eased some of the tension in Travis's shoulders.

"Of course it's only been a few hours and the little guy has slept the entire time. I might feel differently tomorrow."

Travis looked around at the stockpile of junk. "I'm supposed to find a playpen? Before Joshua reaches puberty?"

"Check the back corner if you can get there. Let me carve you a path."

"Stay where you are, Dad. One of us needs to be close enough to the door to call for help when the whole pile comes crashing down."

"Every spring I say I'll clean this out, then the fish start biting and I can't make myself do it."

"Don't blame you there. Who wouldn't rather sit by the lake than clean up this mess? Personally, I'd rather be shooting some hoops." Travis pushed aside a bicycle with a flat tire, a broken dining room chair, and a wheelbarrow full of old pottery.

"Saw you eying the stand. First time the rain's stopped in three days. We could turn on the outside lights, run a few layups. Does wonders to ease a man's tension."

"You're not helping. Mom wants the playpen now. Volleyball sets and lawn darts—we could start an outdoor camp with all this stuff."

His dad laughed, cleared off the top of a short filing cabinet, and sat on top of it. "When your sister's kids come in the summer, they like to dig around in here. It's like a treasure hunt for them."

Travis made a secret vow to enlist his nephews in organizing the clutter come June. Twenty bucks a piece and he would never have to face this catastrophe again. Spying what looked like a playpen leg, he pulled, only to be bonked on the head when a slippery slide and three inner tubes cascaded down.

"Careful. We don't want to end up back at the hospital after you finally busted out... what was her name?"

"Erin," Travis growled. Why did Joshua need a playpen anyway? With a mighty yank, he pulled the thing free, sending a shower of dirt into his face.

"Yes, Erin. Seems like a lovely girl. Shame that she's all alone."

Travis stopped, his anger suddenly cooled by his father's words.

"You're right, Dad. It is a shame she's all alone. I appreciate you and mom taking her in until she's well."

His father waved his hand as he moved forward to help Travis through the path they'd made. "Your mother loves to help, and you know we couldn't turn away anyone who really needs us."

Travis stepped out of the garage, breathed deeply of the clean night air, and looked again at the basketball goal. He still would enjoy a game, but his need to pound the court had passed.

"Have I told you and mom how much I love you lately?"

"Not that I can remember." His dad grinned at him, a twinkle sparkling in his eyes. He picked up the water hose and began squirting off the playpen. "Your mother's right inside though. I'm sure she'd be happy to hear it."

Travis looked at the lighted window over the kitchen sink, but he didn't move toward it. Instead, he backed up to his dad's new Ford truck, leaned against it, and crossed his arms. Then decided to stick his hands in his pockets. Nothing felt right though. He pulled his hands back out. It was as if he'd outgrown his own skin. He watched his father turn off the water and rewind the hose.

"Best just to say what's on your mind."

"You ever cross the line in your job?" The words shot out of his mouth before he'd formed them in his mind.

"Well, now. Let me think." His dad joined him next to the truck. Together they studied the house, and something about his closeness eased the ache in Travis's soul.

"There were times I did what I thought was right, then later I wasn't so sure."

Travis felt his head bobbing in the darkness, reminding himself of one of those crazy bobble-head dolls in a car window. "Exactly. What else can a man do? It's not like they give you a manual. I mean they do, but it doesn't cover everything." He crossed his arms the opposite way, then finally let them hang at his side.

His dad reached out and cupped the back of his neck, though he had to reach up to do so. "Manuals are written by men, son. Seems like God is always throwing new situations at us. Or maybe we manage to find new messes to tangle up in."

Travis let his head fall forward and allowed his father to massage the knots in his neck. He felt like a boy again, running home and expecting his parents to make things right. His father telling him everything would be okay. The comfort was easier to accept in the darkness.

"Is caring about Erin that big of a problem?"

Every muscle in Travis's body went taut. He stepped away from the truck and stared at his father.

"I care about all of my clients."

"First one you ever brought home." The words were a kindness, not an accusation.

"She didn't have any other options. I explained—"

His dad raised his hands, palms forward, in that age-old sign of surrender. "Tell yourself what you want. You can stuff it down until you have a crick in your neck and everyone but your old man believes you. I've never seen you look at a woman the way you look at Erin. I expect that scares you."

"Yeah, it scares me," Travis said, forgetting to deny his feelings. "I'm her caseworker, Dad. I can't afford the luxury of caring for her or Joshua personally. I need to be objective and approve or disapprove her case before a judge. Then I'll probably never see her again. How can I afford to care for her?"

The last words threatened to strangle him.

His dad stepped forward and clapped him on the back. "God has a purpose and a plan. Never doubt that."

Travis could only stuff his hands into his pockets and stare out into the night.

—

Erin woke to bright sunshine, streaming through yellow curtains, and the sound of Joshua cooing as someone talked baby nonsense to him.

That would be Barbara Williams, Travis's mother.

Running her fingers over the seam of the handmade quilt, tracing the pattern of the purple and rose tulips, Erin allowed herself to luxuriate in the fact she did not have to immediately jump out of bed. Maybe she should, but she didn't have to, so she wouldn't.

She had the uncanny sense of lying inside a pat of butter. The walls were painted a warm yellow and trimmed in white molding. A well-framed print adorned each wall, except for the one directly across from her bed. It contained a ten-by-ten square with a three-dimensional mosaic of sorts—a collection of found items it seemed.

Erin pushed back the quilted cover and padded across the carpeted floor to stand in front of the mosaic. It wasn't large, but its simplicity and placement on the wall drew her attention. That and, of course, the objects it contained.

A button in the shape of a heart. An old cross. A flower. She reached out a finger to touch the star-shaped emblem and trace the letters placed carefully atop the stone, h-o-p-e. Positioned beneath this word was one final item—a carving of Christ.

With the sun warm on her face and her hand on the mosaic, she noticed what she could not have seen from across the room—a word etched repeatedly into the background of the ten-by-ten square. *Grace*. Only the one word written in an old script. *Grace*.

The morning's rays had warmed the stone. Standing there, her fingers tracing the letters, the warmth traveled up her arm. Inexplicably, the ice around her heart began to melt, and she was powerless to resist it.

She no longer wanted to resist it.

Joshua's murmurs from the other room blended with the aching in her heart. The tender words of Nina and Jules always seemed to run through her mind, even when she tried to push them away—even when their bittersweet memory pierced her like a scalpel meeting bone.

In the last week she'd learned that memories were sometimes painful, but loneliness hurt much worse.

She needed all her memories of Jules and Nina—could no longer afford to push them away. The child in the next room was a gift, and grace? Her fingers retraced the word. She needed grace as surely as she needed to rise from the bed today.

She bowed her head, drew in a deep breath, one that went past the aches of her losses, and prayed the only prayer she could remember. The simple one she had learned kneeling between Nina and Jules during Communion.

The words poured from her like a cleansing rain, lifting her heart in that shaft of light so she didn't stop with "for thine be the kingdom and the power and the glory forever," but instead, she sank to her knees in the soft carpet and thanked God for sending Travis to rescue her and Joshua.

For sending her to find Joshua.

For prompting Joshua's mother to call her in the first place.

Once she began thanking God, it was difficult to stop. She might have stayed there until her knees cramped had it not been for the tap on the door and Barbara's head popping in, followed by Joshua's smile.

When Erin didn't rise from the floor, Barbara walked over and sat on the chair.

"I stood to look at the mosaic," Erin tried to explain, wiping at the tears on her cheeks as she smiled for Joshua. "Next thing I knew I was on my knees."

Barbara nodded in understanding. "The mosaic has had that effect on me more than once. I found it at a market in

Newport. George wanted to put it in the living room, but I thought it needed the light."

She reached out and touched Erin's forehead. "How do you feel?"

"Better." Erin sniffled, laughed, then kissed Joshua's hand. "Better than I've felt in a long time."

"That's good to hear, honey." Barbara waited a beat, then handed Joshua over, folded her hands on her lap, and beamed at her—the woman's smile fitting into the room as naturally as the tulips sewn into the quilt. "Mr. Joshua has had his breakfast already. I had the idea he wanted to see you, but if you'd like I could take him into the living room to play while you shower."

Erin buried her face in Joshua's curls, inhaled deeply of his smell. For once the joy she felt at having him wasn't tainted by the burden of worry over how she'd care for him. Somehow she knew their situation would work out.

"Thank you."

"He's no problem at all. We like to read books. Don't we, Joshua?"

"I meant thank you for everything."

"I knew what you meant, and it's still no problem."

As Erin shuffled down the hall to the shower, she realized how sick she'd been. Pausing halfway to catch her breath, she studied a row of pictures lining the wall—family pictures. It was difficult to tell who the babies were, but once she'd pegged Travis, she backtracked.

It looked as if he was probably the second child, because in the very first picture Barbara was holding an infant in her lap and a toddler stood by her side. These were followed by Travis in kindergarten, Travis in Little League with his bat proudly held over his shoulder. Sometime after Little League a baby sister appeared. Then Travis in high school—playing basketball and baseball, smiling for an academic awards ceremony.

In each photo either his father or mother stood behind him, proudly resting a hand upon his shoulder for the picture. Until the last one. She stepped closer and felt sorrow splinter in her chest as she recognized the college she had attended for one year. Travis was graduating—cum laude from the looks of it.

In this photo he'd become the man she knew. He had outgrown his parents, and so he stood a little behind them and rested his hands lightly across the backs of their shoulders. Otherwise, the smiles were identical to the ones in Little League.

Erin closed her eyes and tried to slow the hammering of her heart. She had never experienced the domestic scene displayed on this wall. Her life had been filled with a toddler's horror, yearly visits to a judge, and her sister's valiant attempts to make whole what her father had torn apart.

Jules and Nina had done their best though.

She would do the same for Joshua.

With God's help she would.

Twenty-Five

Erin walked into the kitchen, feeling more like her old self than she had since the fever began four days before.

"Tea or coffee?" Barbara asked.

"A cup of hot tea would be wonderful. Thank you." She bent and planted a kiss on Joshua, who was propped in an old-fashioned high chair. Excited to see her, he kicked his legs.

"The shower helped," Barbara noted.

"It did. I feel almost like an animal rescuer again."

"How did you choose such an interesting career?"

Erin laughed as she accepted the hot tea and slice of warm cinnamon bread, suddenly realizing she was famished. "Thank you. I suppose my career choice was Doc England's doing."

"I guessed as much. He speaks very highly of you."

"Doc and Jules were very close." Erin sipped the chamomile tea. She braced herself against the tightening in her chest that always accompanied memories of Jules and

Nina, but it didn't come. Studying Barbara's kitchen, she thought she knew why. Who could be sad sitting in the midst of a bird's nest? Feeders hung outside every window. As she watched, a goldfinch hopped to the tube nearest her and pecked at its breakfast.

The nature theme echoed throughout the kitchen, with placemats touting different types of woodland birds, window valances displaying nests photographed in the wild, even the salt and pepper shakers imitating male and female woodpeckers.

"Like birds?" Erin asked.

Barbara smiled and sat down on the other side of Joshua. "I do, as a matter of fact. When the boys were small, I used to worry about every little thing. My grandmother was eighty-seven at the time. She would remind me that God even looks after the sparrow."

"Sparrows?" Erin pressed her tea cup to her lips, staring over the rim at Barbara.

"Are not five sparrows sold for two pennies? Yet not one of them is forgotten by God. Indeed, the very hairs of your head are all numbered. Don't be afraid; you are worth more than many sparrows." Barbara laughed, reached out, and retrieved Joshua's pacifier from the tray where it had tumbled beyond his reach.

Erin could tell the words had transported her to another time, another place. "Sounds like something from the Bible, but I've never heard it before."

"Luke, chapter twelve. The disciples are in a tight spot, and Jesus is trying to comfort them, encourage them. He's also telling them not to fear death."

"Doesn't sound like much of a pep talk." Erin ran her finger along the top of her cup, but didn't dare look up into Barbara's eyes.

"There are worse things than death. Jesus knew that, and the disciples were about to learn—as was I." Barbara hesitated while two more finches settled at the feeder. When she continued, her voice brimmed with precious memories. "Granny Ruth would visit me, always quoting Luke before she left. I'd nod and pat her hand because I loved her more than I loved chocolate mint ice cream, but I thought her a little senile at the time."

She stood and refilled their cups with fresh tea from a small white pot that was covered with a quilted tea cozy. "Then Travis's brother, Tommy, died of a ruptured appendix. I believed my world had ended. Wanted to curl up in bed and never rise. Granny Ruth showed up in my room one day, reminded me God hadn't forgotten Tommy, but only needed him home sooner than the rest of us. God never forgets his children, she said. I don't know if I understood what she was saying, but I did crawl out of bed and wash my face—that day and every day after."

They both sipped their tea and watched the goldfinch that had been joined by three others with less color.

"Granny brought me my first feeder that day. She set it up outside this window."

"That feeder?" Erin asked.

"Oh my, no. This was over twenty-five years ago. Feeders don't last more than five or ten years, what with all the storms they withstand. God's love does last though. I learned that eventually, but it took many hours of sitting here, watching God's miracles. Travis's sister was born four years later."

"So God took one child away and replaced him with another?"

Barbara's eyes crinkled into a smile as she folded and unfolded the paper napkin. "I don't believe so. Tommy was never mine to begin with, Erin. We're given children to love forever. We're entrusted with their care. One child, one person, can never be replaced by another."

When she raised her eyes, Erin was surprised to see no tears there. Would she ever learn to lean on God that way? She'd only this morning learned to stop blocking him out.

"So tell me about your ARK."

The smile again spread across Erin's face of its own accord. She accepted the change of subject as a gift.

"When I think about it, my love for animals began with Jules. He'd take me with him into the barn, mostly to get me out of Nina's hair. When I'd find some little bird or rabbit, he'd help me to sneak it back into my room."

"Jules and Nina were lovely people," Barbara said as she retrieved more bread. "I can't tell you how sorry I am about what happened. When they passed, we were all shocked. I remember coming by to see you. I don't suppose you even recall that. You looked as if you'd been carried away in the same ambulance."

Erin looked up in surprise, studied Barbara, then shook her head. "You're right. I don't remember anything from those weeks. I'd barely started the ARK, and I was so glad to be back in Livingston. School wasn't... it wasn't a good fit for me. Being home and with the animals was what I was supposed to do. I thought we had years left to spend together."

Barbara nodded. "And Jules and Nina were so healthy."

"Yes." Erin bit her lip, more to stop the words than for fear she might cry.

"When you try to bottle up what's circling round in your mind, it pecks away at your insides."

Erin's head jerked up. Again the smile spread across her face. It felt tight and unnatural like new skin over a fresh wound.

"I've been angry at God for so long," Erin admitted. "Angry about Nina and Jules. Angry about… things that happened even before their accident. Then this morning, something happened. It all seemed to drain out of me onto your guest room floor. I realize that sounds crazy."

She glanced up at Barbara nervously, suddenly remembering this woman was her caseworker's mother.

"It doesn't sound crazy at all. God works in mysterious ways. Sometimes he takes our anger and robs us of it when we least expect it. I remember feeling like I was trying to walk one legged without my crutch after Granny shamed me out of bed."

Erin felt her head nodding. "Without the anger, I don't understand how I feel. It's as if this thing has lived curled inside of me for so long, and now it's suddenly missing."

Erin stopped, sipped her tea, and tried to put thoughts into some coherent order.

"Everything that's happened since Nina and Jules died—Joshua coming into my life, getting sick, and…" her hand fluttered out taking in herself, the baby, their jackets hanging near the back door.

She wanted to add how she felt about Travis, but this was his mother she was talking to. The woman was so perceptive she probably suspected anyway.

"I'm not sure I understand," Erin mumbled. "It's like seeing a lot of puzzle pieces from the back. I'm a bit overwhelmed."

Barbara reached across the table and covered Erin's hand with her own.

Erin looked down, and the image of their hands moved something in her chest.

Something that had been hard and achy for nearly two years.

Something Joshua had melted the ice around, and Travis had come dangerously close to touching.

"The important thing, I think, is you're willing to study those pieces. God will help you figure out how to put them together."

Twenty-Six

The sun had reasserted its place in the sky by the time Travis and James reached Erin's place.

Before Travis could jam the Blazer in park, James jumped out of the truck, sloshing through water and mud to open the cattle gate.

"I'm surprised we can pass through this way." James climbed back in the truck, but leaned forward, pointing to the debris on the fence indicating the high water mark. "How high was it yesterday when you came out to check on Jacobs and the baby?"

"Over the road. I would have never made it across in this Chevy."

James sank back against the leather seat and studied him as they climbed the road to the house. "I would have filled your boat with gas for a month to see you driving Jimmy's mud truck."

Travis tried to stop the grin spreading across his face and failed. "Wouldn't want to own one of those monsters.

Probably gets five miles a gallon, but that baby took the back hill with no problem."

James laughed and banged the dashboard with his hand. "Travis Williams, the next Polk County, Mud-Wheeling Champion. The office would love it."

They crested the hilltop, passed the house, and continued toward the barns.

"Nice of you to do this for Jacobs. Never known you to get involved to this degree." When they stopped and got out, James pulled on his old work gloves and began unloading bags of feed.

Travis ignored the remark, since he hadn't worked up a good explanation in his own mind. If he couldn't justify his behavior to himself, how could he rationalize it to his best friend?

He didn't get involved in clients' lives. He called the appropriate authorities. Somehow, this time that seemed like an intrusion into Erin's privacy. He'd picked up the office phone twice, and both times he'd set it back down in the cradle.

Travis stared at James a moment longer; he'd followed his directions well enough. Old jeans with a tear in the knees, a stained Houston Astros tee, and over that a long-sleeved orange flannel shirt that had seen much better days. A Houston Texans ball cap covered his usual crew cut. The boy was dressed to work. Good thing, as they had plenty to do.

He jammed his own baseball cap on his head and nodded toward the pig pens. "You're going to be glad you wore those old work boots." Travis grabbed two forty-pound bags of oats and headed toward the barn.

James didn't need a lot of direction since he'd grown up helping around the place where Travis's uncle lived near Dodge. As teenagers, they'd had great fun saying they were "Going to Dodge" or "Getting the heck out of Dodge." James had spent many a Saturday on that farm, which was probably why they worked so well together now.

They were able to knock out Erin's chores in just over an hour. Each time Travis lifted a sack of feed though, he tried to envision her slender arms doing the same and failed.

The work was grueling.

He'd never considered himself sexist, but he didn't understand how someone so small and fragile could do such physically demanding labor day after day.

Then he reached Kizmit, who he had fought with the day before, and the pressures of the last forty-eight hours caught up with him.

The milking cow gave him a crossways look and started bawling. She stamped her foot and stepped sideways, knocking over the stool he'd placed beside her.

Travis started laughing, giant guffawing sounds that had him holding his sides and bending at the waist. He couldn't have stopped if someone had threatened him with a shovel. Meanwhile Kizmit was getting more worked up by the spectacle in front of her.

James appeared, his boots covered with horse manure, a pitchfork in his right hand. "What's so funny in here? You're disturbing my stride."

"Kizmit," was all Travis could mutter as he leaned against the barn wall laughing and tried to catch his breath, feeling like a runner who'd just completed a marathon.

"What did you do to that cow, Williams? Looks like she's seen a slaughterhouse." James dropped his pitchfork, walked to the Holstein, and ran his hands down her back, then along her side, murmuring in her ear as he did so. "I thought you said you milked her last night. Her udders are near to bursting."

He righted the stool, grabbed the pail, and began easing the cow's misery.

"I tried," Travis gasped, collapsing against the far wall. "Kizmit and I have a history."

Three cats suddenly appeared beneath James's feet, rubbing against his boots, meowing pitifully. Their cries nearly drowned out Travis's groans.

"Get a grip, man. Find me some saucers for these cats."

"I'm on it."

Travis retrieved the saucers and placed them within range of James's milking, which he was accomplishing with irritating ease.

"I'm going to need an extra bucket." James threw him a reproachful look.

"Don't blame me." Travis's hands came up in a surrender gesture. "I did try. That cow hates me."

He rummaged around in the tool room and came up with an extra bucket.

"Scald it in the sink. Use hot water first, then disinfectant, and rinse with more hot water." James had filled the first bucket by the time he returned. "I thought Jacobs ran an animal rescue operation. Who ever heard of rescuing a dairy cow?"

"Kizmit came with the place." Travis moved to the next stall, tossed fresh hay to Bells, and began mucking out her bay.

"If I'm going to be this sore tomorrow—and I am going to be too sore to properly use a mouse in the morning—you owe me. Come clean about Jacobs. There's something you're not telling."

When Travis still didn't answer, James persisted. "The least you can do is explain why I'm abusing my office-weakened physique."

Travis plunged the pitchfork more deeply into the stack. The muscles in his forearms strained against the weight of the hay, but it helped to balance the heaviness in his heart.

James was right about one thing. He did owe him, and he needed to talk to someone.

"You know this involves Baby Joshua."

"Right. Jacobs found him on a porch. Old lady in Austin claims she's his great-grandmother. No parents have appeared. You've been on it what—a week?"

"A little more." Travis plunged the pitchfork deeper. Sweat ran down his back. He wondered if there was enough labor in this barn to ease the restlessness in his heart.

"Man, if you clean any more hay out of this stall, there won't be anything left for that cow."

Travis looked up and saw James standing in the opening, the day's last light falling on his back and casting him in shadow. He didn't have to see his friend's expression to know it was filled with concern.

"Yeah, I guess you're right."

James milked the second cow as quickly as he had the first.

When James was finished, the two men walked outside and sat on a bench overlooking the house, the front meadow, and the newly expanded pond thanks to the flood. The sun setting over the scene cast it in a more gentle light. From their perch, it was hard to tell the difference between a road that had been washed out and a creek. There was a difference though—one was the result of destruction.

"I never found my footing on this case. From the first night I came out here, I was floundering. Erin's young and vulnerable. How does she do this work on her own? It took you and me nearly ninety minutes, and she doesn't weigh a buck fifteen. How can Erin do all this and provide for a child?"

"So you're not going to recommend placement?"

Travis reached down and pulled a weed from the ground, popped it in his mouth, and chewed. The bittersweet taste reminded him of when they were kids and the biggest decision they had to make was which pond they'd fish in on Saturday.

"She loves Joshua and would do anything for him. They have a connection I've only seen between birth mothers and their children. Her commitment to him is unlimited."

"So you're recommending placement." James pulled out his pocket knife and began cleaning the muck from his boots.

"I honestly don't know at this point. It's a toss-up."

"Tough case. Most are clear cut, but occasionally we get one that's difficult. Ask Moring to step in and evaluate."

"It's not that simple."

"Meaning?"

Travis hunched forward, palms flat against the wooden bench. When he raised his eyes to the horizon, he saw clear skies and a Texas sunset stretching for miles. Inside though, he felt muddled, as if the storm were only beginning to brew.

"I can't believe this." James snapped the pocket knife closed and stood, then walked a few steps away. When he turned, the familiar grin Travis had come to expect played across his face. "The famous Travis Williams has fallen, and on top of that you're tongue-tied about it."

"This isn't a high school crush," Travis growled.

"Obviously. I remember your high school crushes, and you were fairly loud-mouthed about all three of them. Since then there's only been Melissa. After she moved away all you've done is work. I'm happy for you." He trudged back to the bench, propped a foot on it, and slapped his friend on the back. "Cheer up, man. It's not as if you've been sentenced to the gallows. There are worse things than falling for a woman."

"I'm her caseworker, James. I've already broken at least three different regulations by helping her directly this way. We're supposed to stay objective. Not to mention it's totally inappropriate for me to feel the way I do about Erin."

"I noticed it's *Erin*, not Miss Jacobs." James looked as if he'd found a bar of gold under the pigs' feeding trough.

Travis glowered but refused to rise to the bait. What was the use?

"Okay. I can see you're taking this very seriously. There's no chance you could have her case transferred to someone else?"

"I tried the afternoon Moring first gave it to me. She's pretty dug in that I handle it."

"So handle it, get to know her, and once the temporary placement is over then you can date her."

"Erin doesn't want temporary placement of Joshua. She wants permanent placement."

When Travis's words settled in, James let out a long whistle, then dropped into a slouch beside him on the bench. "Which means you'd continue making site visits for a minimum of one year."

"Exactly."

"I'm beginning to appreciate the desperate look in your eyes." Then James voiced the two questions that had been running through Travis's mind for days. "Have you told Moring how you feel about Erin?"

"No."

"Have you told Erin?"

"I've known her less than two weeks. It seems ridiculous…"

"Right."

The evening sounds settled around them as the animals bedded down for the night.

"I want you to meet her, James. She's the smallest thing, but strong. You know? Her hair is this shade of reddish brown with all these natural curls that make you want to sink your hands into it." When James didn't interrupt, Travis couldn't stop the words from tumbling out—words that had dammed up inside him over the last ten days. "It's her eyes that suck me in though—eyes the color of my morning coffee. You can tell she's carrying the world's weight, but she'd never say so. She looks at me like she's handled it forever and she'll keep handling it for as long as necessary."

He slumped back against the barn's wall, the last of the day's warmth draining from it as the final bits of his resistance fell away. "When I walked into the house yesterday, I found her lying in bed, curled around Joshua. I thought maybe I was too late." Tears pricked at his eyes and he blinked them away. "That's when I knew she'd already managed to get under my skin—way under. I was so terrified, I couldn't cross the room, couldn't even breathe. Kept staring at the covers waiting to see them move."

He tried to think of how to describe the way Erin felt in his arms, how she completed him. But there were no words. Instead, he stood, stuffed his hands in his pockets, and stared out into the darkness.

"I don't know what to do about this. I'm her caseworker, and I swore to do a job and take care of children, to always put them first—including Joshua. So what am I supposed to do about Erin?"

He thought his friend wasn't going to answer him, began to wonder if he should have admitted all his feelings. Then Travis stood, grabbed the back of his neck, and squeezed hard.

"I don't know, man," James said. "I'm fresh out of advice, and anything I could tell you would be worthless anyway because I've never been in this situation. But I will pray with you. I have a feeling God has a plan, even when we have no idea what it is."

"What if it's a plan I don't like?" Travis asked.

"One more thing we'll have to pray about."

Twenty-Seven

Erin sat on the couch that had seen better days. A sunflower slipcover brightened the furniture and blended perfectly with the accumulation of knick-knacks on the enclosed back porch. She had been sitting there for the better part of an hour, since she put a sleeping Joshua into his playpen, with a novel lying face down on her lap. The porch was softly lit with lamps.

"I thought you might want a lap blanket." Barbara handed her an ivory-and-blue afghan.

"Did you knit this? It's beautiful."

"Guilty. George says I've knitted enough scarves and blankets to warm the free world, but I find it a relaxing thing to do before bed. Settles my worries."

Erin smiled and let her hand follow the pattern. Since their talk at breakfast, an easiness existed between them that Erin had only shared with her foster parents and Evelyn and Doc. She was beginning to realize perhaps that was her fault. Perhaps she had chosen to isolate herself, and people were genuinely kind if she gave them a chance.

"If my fever doesn't return tonight, and I feel sure it won't, I plan to go back to the ARK tomorrow."

Barbara turned from where she stood, gazing out over the backyard. As usual her eyes twinkled, and Erin found herself wondering if she'd ever find the woman's depth of peace. "I figured you'd be thinking along those tracks. Knowing your stubbornness, I've already started putting together a few meals so you won't have to cook, and there's no use arguing with me, Erin Jacobs."

Barbara walked across the room and embraced her in a hug. "It's been nice having you here. I don't see my own children and grandchildren enough since they live over in San Antonio. Promise me you won't be a stranger."

Unable to speak around the lump in her throat, Erin nodded and pretended to be cold so she could fuss with the blanket.

"I best go check on George. He wants to watch one of those shows he taped on that new-fangled DVR we ordered, but he hasn't quite figured out which remote to use to replay it. I have plenty of job security in this house." Chuckling, she walked back inside, the door banging lightly behind her.

Relieved to be alone, Erin wiped at the tears clouding her eyes. How long had it been since she'd felt someone's embrace?

There'd been Travis's the day before, but she'd basically thrown herself at him when he'd arrived at her house.

Her cheeks burned in embarrassment, and her tears felt like water on a fire as they tracked down her face. She pressed the palms of her hands against her eyes, pushed at her grief, and reminded herself she had plenty to be thankful for—things she could pray about right now.

Pulling in a deep, shuddering breath, she tried to remember how to pray. It had helped so much this morning while standing before the mosaic and again at lunch. She needed that peace now more than ever. How had she begun?

She was focusing on what words she should use, wiping again at the tears that seemed to fall from an unlimited source, when she heard someone shift.

At the same moment she smelled the light combination of woodsy aftershave and soap.

Her heartbeat took off like a rocket, and she searched her memory for how long he'd been standing back there. Since Barbara had left? Had he seen her crying?

Pulling the blanket closer around her, she drew her shoulders back.

"You might as well sit down if you're going to stay."

"I'll go if you'd rather be alone." His voice was soft, too gentle, and she knew he knew.

She was instantly submerged in the memory of his arms around her, felt her cheeks flame, and wished the porch were darker. "No. We need to talk."

"If you're sure you feel up to it." Travis walked around and sank into the old oak rocker. It held his weight easily as he folded himself into the chair.

Her mind flashed back to the first night she'd met him— the wicker furniture, him fidgeting and knocking things over when he moved. Looking around she understood Barbara had created a haven where her family would feel comfortable.

"What are you thinking about?" Travis brushed at the dirt on his jeans, but his eyes were locked on her face.

Laughing and crying at the same time, Erin wiped

futilely at the tears that refused to be stemmed. "Remembering you sitting in that ridiculous wicker furniture on my porch."

"Thought I'd break it. Didn't you?"

"Yeah." The tears became a flood. She folded her arms across her middle, grasped her elbows to still the shivers coursing through her body. Any moment now she would literally fly apart in front of him, and she had no idea why.

"Hey. Don't do that. Erin, it's okay." He moved beside her on the couch. "Sweetheart. What's wrong?"

He clumsily patted her back with one hand, while searching in his pocket for a handkerchief with the other.

"Never mind. I'm fine. It's like I'm this faucet with no off valve. You're going to think I'm too emo… emo… emotional to be a mother." She brought the afghan up to her eyes and rubbed, which only succeeded in making them itch and burn.

"Hang on. Just—" Travis jumped up from the couch, grabbed a box of tissues from the table near the rocker, and shoved it onto her lap. Instead of returning to the rocker, he sat back down again beside her on the couch. "Mom said you had a pretty good day."

"I did," Erin admitted, pulling out several tissues and blowing her nose.

"So why the tears?"

"Honestly, I don't know." She paused, wondering if she should tell him about the mosaic, about her prayers, but when she searched her mind for words to express what had occurred earlier she came up blank.

"Are the lights bothering you? You keep squinting, and your eyes are really puffy. Would it help if I turned one or two off?"

She nodded, knowing that was only half the truth. She had trouble talking to Travis when every time she looked into his china-blue eyes her heart tripped a double beat. She needed to settle her emotions, wanted to clarify things, and it was hard to do when she had to meet his gaze.

The truth was she was a coward.

Travis walked around the porch, turning off lamps until just the one behind them remained lit. The softer light soothed her. She could look out over the backyard and make out the pine trees, even see an occasional bird swoop down in the near darkness. She took a deep, trembling breath and started over as Travis settled again beside her.

"I had a wonderful day. Your parents have been more than kind to me. Your mother helped me to work through some... important things today."

"If my mom made you cry, I'm going to have to go in and talk with her."

She reached out and slapped at him. "No, silly."

Travis captured her hand in his and rubbed the back of it with his thumb. "Good. I know you've been through a lot in the last forty-eight hours. I wanted this to be a time for you to recharge."

Erin tried to swallow, failed, and tried again. She felt as if a tennis ball were lodged in her throat. She had the wild urge to snatch her hand away, and at the same time she hoped he would keep holding on to it forever.

"Your mother came out and handed me this afghan—a blanket she had knitted with her own hands." She looked him fully in the face then, hoping he would read there the words that were too painful for her to voice.

"Sometimes it's the little kindness that works its way through our defenses."

Erin nodded and stared down at his hand covering hers. Did he have any idea what effect his touch had on her?

"I feel raw inside and out." She swallowed around the tennis ball, forcing the words out while she had the courage. "Two weeks ago my life made sense. I can see now that was because I kept it very simple, completely closed. I put myself on an ARK—literally."

———

Erin paused, pulled her bottom lip in and worried it. Travis knew they were at a breakthrough moment. He certainly didn't want to push, but he had prayed so hard she would accept God's help in her life.

Seeing her struggle like this, it reminded him of the time he'd kept a baby bird in his room under a heat lamp. He'd watched it fight its way through the tiny shell. Only nine years old, he'd run to the kitchen for a spoon to crack the shell and help the fella, but his father had stopped him and told him he'd be weakening the bird.

So he waited and watched Erin struggle.

It nearly broke his heart.

"Then I received the call from Joshua's mother. I didn't realize God was telling me it was time to join the world again." She looked at him and smiled. Tears still shone in her eyes, but they didn't spill. Glancing back out into the night, she continued, her voice filled with wonder. "I was so afraid driving through the forest to find him. I didn't tell you that before. It was as if I had this premonition something big was about to happen, and maybe it was my last chance to turn around."

She turned her full attention to him and clasped her other hand on top of his so he had trouble concentrating on her words. "What if I had turned around? What would have happened to Joshua?"

"I don't know, Erin." He reached out, touched her face though he knew he shouldn't. "God has plans we can't know. He was watching over Josh."

She nodded and another tear slipped down her face. He wiped it away with his thumb, but she didn't seem to notice. She was still on the back porch of the hunter's cabin. Still considering what might have been.

"Once I saw him, held him, I knew my life would never be the same, and I was terrified. I wasn't ready, and part of me wanted to hide. Do you know what I mean?" She turned her pleading gaze on him, and Travis had to focus to breathe.

He nodded and ran his thumb over the back of her hand.

He knew all about hiding from God.

It hadn't worked for him either.

"When you came along—"

"Was that a bad thing?" He wanted to snatch the question back as soon as he asked it.

"I don't know." Her hand—the one he hadn't claimed— went to her lips, her throat, then finally settled on her lap. "If you hadn't come to the house and found me after the flood—"

"I would have found you." The image of her still form curled around Joshua in the bed continued to rob him of sleep.

The silence stretched between them until he didn't trust himself any longer. The need to pull her into his arms again nearly overpowered his common sense.

He stood and walked to the windows.

"I know you've been right about so many things you said to me. Spending the day here with your mom, talking with her about Nina and Jules, it's helped me to see they wouldn't want me living such a solitary life. I'm going to try and do things differently—because I need to in order for you to approve Joshua's placement, but also because I think it's what God wants me to do."

He turned and stared at her. The single remaining light haloed her hair, which was tousled from running her hands through it as she'd told her story. She'd pulled the afghan around her to ward off the night's chill, and it gave her the appearance of a child huddled there on his mother's couch. But he knew Erin Jacobs was no child. The circles under her eyes and the steadiness in her gaze combined to assure him how seriously she'd considered every word she had just said.

"You've had some major changes."

"Yes. I have."

The need to be near her overwhelmed him. He stuffed his hands in his pockets, took a step back, and bumped into the window frames.

"There's one more thing though." She continued to hold his gaze, but he could see her cheeks color even from across the room.

Suddenly, Travis had the irrational urge to cover his ears.

"I want to apologize about yesterday."

"Erin, don't—"

"No. I'll never be able to look at you again if I don't say this. I acted like a child, throwing myself in your arms. I shouldn't have done that, and I'm sorry—"

He never heard the rest of her apology. He crossed the room before she had a chance to finish, pulled her into his arms, and covered her lips with his own.

She uttered a small gasp and he pulled back, but then her arms curled up and around his neck.

So he ducked his head, and kissed her again—first gently, then thoroughly. Kissed her like he'd wanted to since he'd first learned there was no Mr. Jacobs. Some part of his mind suspected it would be their last kiss so he made it count.

He finally stopped when he felt the flutter of her heart against his own. Realizing she wasn't fully recovered, he forced himself to break the kiss, but he couldn't let her go— not yet.

Pressing his forehead to hers, he whispered, "Don't ever apologize for needing me. That's the one thing I can't deal with. Do you understand?"

"Yes. No." Her arms remained entwined around his neck, and Travis felt as if he'd melted into the couch, into Erin.

He cradled her in his arms, pulled the afghan around her shoulders, and vowed to himself he would enjoy this one moment, then come to his senses.

Like the morning before, she fit next to him perfectly. "You smell like heaven," he murmured.

"That's just your mother's shampoo."

"Never smelled that way on my mother."

Erin sighed and snuggled deeper into him.

He kissed the top of her head, ran his fingers through her hair, down her arm. Felt her shiver, and delighted in the knowledge his touch had as much an effect on her as she did on him.

Her hand reached up, touched his face, his lips.

"I didn't think I could feel this way about anyone."

"Erin—"

"No. Let me say this." She slipped her hand back around his waist. "I saw the kind of relationship Jules and Nina had, and I was afraid I could never have anything as true, as special as what they shared. I was afraid to even try." Her voice tapered off to a whisper as she peered up at him in the dim light.

"Sweetheart." Travis ran a thumb down her face and prayed God would forgive him for what he was about to say. "I meant what I said earlier—you never have to apologize for needing me. I will always be there for you. Tell me you understand that."

She smiled up at him, completely trusting, and he wished it could be his own heart he was about to shred— which in one sense it was.

"Erin, we can't do this again. I initially asked to be transferred off your case, because I didn't feel I could be objective. My director refused the request." Confusion clouded Erin's face and she attempted to pull away, but he tugged her closer. "Listen. I care about you. I care about you like this, not like a caseworker should care about a client."

He kissed her again, briefly, softly—softer than the brush of a bird's wings in flight.

"Since I have to stay on as your caseworker, we need to put this away from us for a while."

"How long?"

"I don't know. Adoptions take a long time. You've seen

the process chart."

Erin stood, the afghan falling away, and stepped back from the couch. "What are you saying, Travis?"

He stood as well and clenched his hands at his side to keep from reaching out to her. "I'm saying we have to put Joshua first."

"But what about—"

"What about us? We're not as important, our needs aren't as important as his. You know that. You can't be that selfish."

Her hand flew to her mouth.

She turned and stumbled back toward the door. He stopped her. She looked down at his hand on her arm and pulled back from his touch.

"Wait, Erin."

"Why?"

"Don't. Don't go this way."

"Why did you kiss me? Why did you allow me to feel safe?" Her words found their mark in his chest.

"Because I wanted you to know you weren't imagining this attraction between us. Because I needed to know if you felt the same things I did. Because I'm not perfect, Erin."

She paused, slowed by his honesty.

"And I meant it when I said I will be there for you and Joshua. Whatever you need."

"But not this…" she stared at a spot past his shoulder.

"Erin, I can't."

She met his eyes for one brief moment, then turned and fled.

Twenty-Eight

Travis added an extra mile to his run the next morning.

It did nothing to alleviate the restlessness crawling on his skin.

Thirty minutes of Bible study with his coffee convinced him running from his problems—and mistakes—would only complicate them.

He called into the office and left Angela a message that he would be in after he made his first client call. Then he drove directly to his mother's. He pulled into the driveway at ten minutes until eight in time to see Erin loading her things into Shirley Smith's car.

"What are you doing?" He fought the urge to throw her over his shoulder and carry her back inside.

"I'm taking Joshua home."

"Don't you think it's a little soon? Two days ago you were in the hospital."

"I know where I was, Travis. I also know where we need to be right now—and it's at the ARK." She still hadn't looked at him, had busied herself fumbling with the keys and hauling the bag into the car's rear seat. "I'm much better. I have my strength back, and I need to start taking care of things again."

"You can barely manage your own overnight bag," he said tightly, pulling Joshua's bag from her hand and setting it in the back seat of Shirley's car. "Why didn't you call me? If you decided you had to leave, I would have taken you home."

"Shirley was more than happy to help." Erin moved the bag from the seat to the floorboard. She paused beside the car and cocked her head, finally meeting his gaze. "I'm re-establishing my social network, Travis. I thought you'd be pleased."

He searched his mind for a reply, but he couldn't think straight with her standing so close. She'd done something different with her hair, pulling the curls back in clips. It made her look schoolgirl fresh—and all too beautiful. He wanted to pull the clips from her hair and run his fingers through her auburn curls, loosen them and feel their silkiness like he had the night before.

He slammed the car door shut and scowled at her instead.

"Glad to see you slept well," he muttered. "You are better, Erin, but if you do too much too soon, you'll be in the same condition I found you."

Her smile slid from her face for a fraction of a second. She stepped toward him, her eyes filled with battle.

His adrenaline surged like when a fast ball came his way and he pulled the bat in tight, knowing he could knock it out of the park.

But then the front door opened. Erin stepped back and turned toward his parents. He wiped his sweaty palms on his pants, forcing his heart rate to slow.

"Travis, I didn't hear you pull up." His dad carried the last of Erin's bags out ahead of the women.

The next five minutes would have looked to any stranger like an ordinary confusion of good-byes. His mother made a fuss over Joshua as Erin tucked him safely into his car seat. His dad clumsily hugged her and exacted a promise that she would return for dinner before Joshua forgot who they were. No one would have believed they had met less than forty-eight hours ago.

Travis pretended to check Joshua's car seat. It had been two days since he'd held the boy. He wouldn't have thought it possible he could miss a child so much. At this point all Josh did was drink a bottle and poop.

Plugging the baby pacifier into Josh's mouth, he was certain the kid smiled at him. It eased the ball of tension inside his stomach, and he found himself smiling back. Who could not have their mood elevated around Joshua? The kid was like a bit of God's sunshine wrapped in an infant's playsuit.

The good-byes were grinding to an end, so Travis snagged Shirley's arm.

"I haven't seen you at any of our church outings lately, Travis."

"Yeah. Saturdays have been crazy."

"Still working on weekends?" She smiled up at him as he walked her to the driver's side of the car.

"Guilty. Hey, I'd be glad to take them home." He held the car door open for her, trying not to stare at her protruding belly.

"It's no problem. I'm already here, and it'll give us time to chat." With her hand on her stomach, she sat in the driver's seat sideways, then turned and slid in awkwardly behind the wheel.

"When's the baby due?" he asked.

"Six weeks, and I won't argue if he comes early."

"Another boy?"

"Yes, baby will make three little guys and one big one, at which point I call a stop to the team building." She smiled and waved as he shut the door.

Travis was used to being around adoptive parents, foster parents, or parents who for some reason were having difficulties with their families. Seeing Shirley's obvious delight, even as she struggled with a simple thing like fitting behind a steering wheel, tore at his heart like the too bright day.

It struck him that he was glimpsing something intimate, but then he realized he was only seeing a slice of normal life.

Perhaps he was working too much.

He stayed at the curb, watching Shirley start the car, then remembered he hadn't told Erin about tonight. He jogged over to her side, motioned for her to roll the window down, and prepared for the argument sure to follow.

"James and I will be out around six." She looked at him blankly, but didn't attack, so he kept going. "To take care of the animals."

"There's no need. I'm sure I can handle—"

"He's out of the office all day, and his cell's busted. I couldn't possibly catch him and cancel. Six."

He tapped the car's roof twice, stepped back, and he

might have laughed at the adorable look of irritation on Erin's face—except underneath it all was the heartache he'd brought on by kissing her the night before.

He felt it, and he knew she did too. It was something they'd need to talk about, set straight. Maybe they'd have a chance after James left.

Travis only hoped he'd find a way to make it right.

—

Shirley raised her eyebrows, but kept her gaze fixed on the road. Erin knew her friend would give her a minute, maybe two, to spill.

Chances of distracting her from asking questions about that parting scene were nil.

Somehow the thought didn't bother her so much. A week ago it would have struck her as intrusive. Reconnecting with Shirley felt like coming home from college and taking her dog, Jasper, for a walk again. It was as if they'd never missed a day in between.

"The grin isn't necessary." Erin slouched down in her seat and folded her arms across her chest, determined to throw her friend off the trail.

"Are you sure? Because it *feels* necessary."

"Oh, well, if you enjoy rescuing me from my caseworker's parents' house before eight in the morning, and," Erin waved her hand in the air, trying to make it up as she went, "all that, fine. Smile away."

"Uh-huh. So you're telling me there's nothing between you and Travis Williams."

Closing her eyes, Erin counted to five, then decided another five count would buy her time to come up with an alibi.

"I know you're not sleeping. Your foot is tapping. Your foot always did tap when you were agitated." Shirley's voice continued to ring with good humor.

Erin opened one eye to scowl at her. "You wouldn't find this so amusing if you knew the details."

"I'm sorry, sweetie." Shirley reached over, gave her hand a squeeze, then grinned. "Give me the details and I'll try to stop being amused. It's so nice seeing you... how do I put this... involved. You're a beautiful person, and Travis has been alone for much too long. Since—"

Shirley stopped abruptly, her eyes wide as she made a turn on to the loop.

Erin sat up straighter, cornered herself in the sedan, and studied her friend. "Since what? You were about to say something about Travis's past. What? I don't really know anything about him."

"Oh, it's really no secret. Travis doesn't have any lurid past that I know of, and in this town you couldn't hide something deep and dark." She rested her left hand on top of her bulging stomach and studied the houses as they left the main section of Livingston behind them. "I guess I've known him all my life, though he was in the grade above mine. That's probably why you don't remember him."

"I don't."

"He was a jock, of course. You can tell that by the way he's built." The smile spread back across her face. "Your sister and I didn't exactly hang with the athletic group."

Erin snorted, and the tension began to ease off her shoulders. "I don't recall you and Dana hanging anywhere, except at the theater every time a new movie came out."

"We'd have to watch it twice." Shirley nodded, a softness filling her voice. "As far as Travis, we see each other occasionally now. We attend the same church you know."

She tossed a glance Erin's way, then tucked her red hair behind her ear.

"So why is he alone? Is there something wrong with him? It does seem odd that a man his age wouldn't be married yet."

"Travis was engaged once a few years ago. It didn't work out."

Erin fiddled with a nail and studied Shirley.

"What happened?"

"I don't know. I don't think anything happened. Melissa wanted to live in Dallas. Travis didn't. They're still friends as far as I know."

"A nice-looking man like him, and all you can tell me about is one engagement? He's nearly thirty!"

"That's not ancient."

"Nowadays it is."

"It's good to hear you find him nice looking."

Erin squinted her eyes and re-crossed her arms. "That slipped, and you know what I mean. It's suspicious."

"Maybe God has been saving him for the right person."

Erin shifted in her seat and pulled on the seatbelt, trying to find a comfortable position. "I am not the right person. We barely even know each other. Besides, after last night…"

Erin stared out at the forest as they drove toward the ARK. It was an isolated stretch of road. She'd always liked the seclusion of where she lived. She wondered if the day would ever come where she'd find living there lonely.

"He knows all about my past. It's part of his job—to investigate me. Not that there's much to learn." Erin played with a frayed seam of her blue jeans. "I don't really know anything about him—personally I mean."

"You could ask him," Shirley suggested.

Erin nodded. "Last night he declared we needed to keep it professional."

"Sounds like something Travis would say. He takes his job very seriously—one reason he's good at it."

Erin felt the anger rise in her again, an unbidden thing she had no control over. "He says this *after* he kisses me. *After* he takes me in his arms and makes me imagine things that now he tells me can't be."

"So you do care about him." Shirley's voice rang triumphant, and she again reached over and squeezed Erin's hand, this time holding on tight.

"I don't know how I feel—confused, angry, excited when I remember how his arms feel around me, then angry all over again when I think of his speech and his rules. Men are infuriating."

"Don't I know it." Shirley laughed as she pulled into the ARK's long drive.

"You can laugh. Your future seems pretty safe."

"Yours is, too, Erin. Yours, Josh's, even Travis's. Your future is with God. And if He wants you and Travis together, you will be—regardless of Travis's rules."

Twenty-Nine

Josh was sound asleep by the time Erin carried him up the steps and into his room.

Why did it feel as if she'd been gone a week?

She didn't argue when Shirley began unloading bowls of casseroles and fresh fruit into the fridge. Most she recognized as being from Barbara. When Shirley hugged her and said, "Folks wanted to help," Erin believed her. Kindness was something she could grow used to given time.

Somehow she managed to drag herself around the animal pens, but dragging was all she did. Travis and James had done a good job of taking care of her menagerie of animals. A few items were set in different places, but she didn't care enough to move them.

She only cared enough to be sure the animals were fine—and they were. So she trudged back to the house, climbed the steps, checked on Josh one final time, and collapsed into her bed. Two hours later, Josh's crying woke her out of a deep sleep.

For the first time since she'd found him on the hunter's porch, she didn't panic.

She padded into his room, looked down into his crib, and smiled.

"Hey, Baby Josh. We're home."

He smiled back at her and blew a bubble.

That pretty much made for a perfect afternoon.

Her hair was a mess, she'd napped in her clothes, and by the slant of the sun coming in, she could tell she was late doing chores, but that was all right. Her body didn't ache. In fact, she felt refreshed after her long nap.

After changing Josh, she picked him up, held him close and buried her face in his curls. Inhaling deeply, she wondered if there was any better smell than a sleepy baby— warm, sweet, and full of love.

Erin normally moved quickly, efficiently, but something prodded her to stand there and watch the sun move toward the horizon. She didn't even want to hurry. Maybe she was done with rushing from one task to another.

"Thank you, Lord. Thank you for this baby and for this sunset. And thank you for taking care of us." The prayer came from somewhere deep inside of her, and it flew out on wings.

Josh gurgled.

"Was that an *'Amen'* or an *'I'm hungry?'*" Moving toward the kitchen, she plopped him into his highchair and hummed as she fixed his bottle, pausing to heat herself a cup of tea in the microwave. "We'll be late, but Kizmit will understand."

Twenty minutes later, she walked toward the barn with Josh in his pouch, feeling better than she had in a long time. Not just physically better. A peace had settled into her soul along with the rest and the friendship of the past few days.

Along with God's grace.

"Grace too," she whispered to Kizmit. "Especially grace."

"Talking to cows again?"

Her head whipped around, and she nearly tripped over the stool she'd set beside the dairy cow.

"Travis, what are you doing here?"

"I said we'd be by after work." He rolled up the sleeves of his flannel shirt but didn't move from where he stood in the doorway of the barn.

The last rays of afternoon sun silhouetted all six plus feet of him, and Erin felt her pulse pick up speed like a schoolgirl spotting a boy at the high school football game. He looked so normal in worn blue jeans and work boots.

She tried to remember why she'd been so irritated with him earlier, but all she could think of was how the blue in his shirt perfectly matched the color in his eyes—and both made her think of last night, his arms around her, his lips on hers.

His lips on hers.

"I can do this," she snapped, heat flaming her face as she suddenly remembered his lecture from the night before.

"You've got Kizmit?" A shorter, younger man with a crew cut stepped around Travis. "I'll take Bells then."

"Erin, this is James. He works with me and has some experience on a farm. He helped me out last night."

"Nice to meet you." James stepped forward, shook hands with her, then turned his attention to Joshua whom she'd placed in an extra baby carrier that she now kept in the barn. "And this must be Joshua. He's a beautiful baby, exactly like Travis described."

Erin met Travis's gaze, and some of her anger evaporated like the last of the day's heat. He'd said Joshua was beautiful?

Yes, she could read the truth of it in his eyes.

He cared for Josh like she did. How could he not? He was trying to be objective—about Josh, about her.

He was trying to do his job.

The sudden clarity pierced her, causing her to pull her arm tight across her ribs.

Travis was at her side in an instant. "Are you okay?"

"I'm fine. I've got this." She turned away, sat down on the stool, and began milking Kizmit, but Travis's scent lingered long after he walked away and began mucking out the stall.

One part of her wanted to struggle against their help—make a scene and prove to them she was strong enough to do it on her own. Instead, she took her time with the milking, luxuriated in the sound of fresh hay being shoveled into stalls, picked up Josh, and rocked him while the sound of male bantering played in the background.

Forty minutes later she walked both men back outside and was surprised to see not one but two trucks there.

"Same time tomorrow night?" James asked, running his hand over the top of his crew.

Erin held up her hand, palm out. "I do appreciate your help, but I think I've got it from here."

"You sure? Bells and I sort of have a routine going, not to mention at this rate I'll be able to drop my gym membership and save some bucks." His smile was so genuine, Erin couldn't help laughing at his eagerness.

She noticed Travis held back, let her make the decision, and she appreciated him all the more for it.

"I'll let Travis know if it's more than I can handle, but I plan on doing a little at a time tomorrow."

"All right. See you around town then." He turned to Travis and slapped him on the back as if they'd just shared a game of racquetball. "I'll see you in the cube."

———

Travis watched James pull away in his new Dodge truck, and he wondered why he didn't jump into his own Blazer and follow him. The last thing he needed to do was be alone with Erin again.

But he knew he couldn't leave until he had righted what he'd done last night. He couldn't spend another sleepless night knowing he'd hurt her. She meant too much to him. The thought literally pulled his breath from him. He felt like the fish he snagged from Lake Livingston—out of his element and gasping for air.

Grateful that it was dark, he turned to her. "I'll hold Josh if you want me to while you close up the barn."

"Okay. Thanks." Her hand brushing against his as she passed the baby to him sent his mind reeling into places he didn't need it to go—how sweet her lips had tasted, the softness of her hair, the way she'd curled into his embrace as if she belonged there.

Joshua began to fuss, so he laid him on his shoulder like he'd seen Erin do. Rubbing his back in tiny circles, he was surprised to see the baby turning his head back and forth, trying to catch glimpses of Erin in the dark.

When she returned to his side, he nodded toward the house. "Let me walk you back. I wanted to talk to you a minute."

"Okay."

He couldn't read her expression, but was grateful she seemed willing to listen. Something had calmed her down since this morning. Maybe his prayers hadn't been in vain, but then had they ever been?

"He was watching you." Travis shortened his stride to match hers.

"Who?" Her head jerked up and her voice rose a notch.

"This guy." Travis switched him to the other shoulder. "When you walked back to the barn, he kept moving his head around, trying to catch a glimpse. I didn't realize he was doing that already."

"Seems like he does something new every day. It's amazing. When you work with animals you get used to small miracles, but children? To me children are like a miracle a minute. I don't know what to make of it." Erin climbed the back steps and paused at the door. "I need to change Josh and feed him. What—"

"This will take a few minutes. Can I help you with dinner?"

She cocked her head in that gesture he'd seen the first night. What was she considering? Finally, she pointed down at his dirty work boots. "If you leave *those* on the porch."

Slipping her own off, she set them by the door, then took Joshua and disappeared inside.

Travis stood looking through the screen door.

He needed to go inside, needed to make things right.

But he couldn't afford to give in to what he was feeling again, not like he did last night. It wouldn't be fair to Erin, and he wasn't sure his own heart could handle the jolt.

Go inside, feed her, set things straight.

He could be home in time to catch a game on FoxSports.

Thirty

Travis stepped into the kitchen in his stocking feet. It felt odd—strangely intimate. He shook the notion from his mind and crossed over to the refrigerator.

"Shirley left a casserole in there." Erin smiled up from where she was settling Josh into his high chair, and Travis's heart slammed against his rib cage.

"Casserole."

"You can put some on two plates. Then either nuke them or set them directly in the oven on 350."

"You can put plates in the oven?"

"Those you can." She turned back to Joshua, buckled him in, and slipped the tray in place. The little guy was rubbing his fists into his eyes, but the minute he spied the baby bottle he actually began pushing against the restraint and crying.

"He knows he's about to eat?" Travis asked, his hand still on the fridge door.

"Oh yeah, and he'll fight you for this bottle." Erin stepped inside the curve of his arm, tugged open the fridge, and pulled out a flowery casserole dish. "Chicken casserole. I prefer it heated in the oven."

Suddenly, the farm-sized kitchen was too small. Travis took one step backward and felt the counter press into the small of his back. Trapped!

Erin smiled, and he realized she had a smudge of dirt on her forehead. He wanted to reach out and wipe it off, but he knew if he touched her... well, if he touched her again, they'd be right back where they were last night.

He shook his head.

"No? Okay. Microwave is to your left." She poured some powdered formula into the bottle, mixed in warm water, and began shaking it. "This will take me a few minutes. I think there's some precut salad fixings in the bottom drawer."

The pitch and timber of Josh's cries had grown. "Are you positive he's okay?"

"Proves he has healthy lungs like when a calf bawls." Erin laughed. "You're a strong boy, aren't you, Joshie?"

Travis knew when the bottle went in; a peaceful silence filled the air. He set to work on the dinner and tried to pull his thoughts back into order.

"Don't stop feeding that kid. I think he's starving."

"I'm betting you gave your mom just as much trouble when you were hungry."

"Not a chance. I couldn't possibly have screamed that loud. Josh is going to win the county yodeling competition, or singing competition if he learns to lasso his voice."

"There's strength behind it. God did give him that." Erin continued to talk with the boy as she fed him, but Travis noticed she didn't baby-talk like some moms did. He'd have to ask her about that later. There were a lot of things he needed to ask her if she was still speaking to him after tonight.

Scooping two helpings of the casserole onto separate plates, he popped them into the oven, something he would have never done at home. Two minutes microwaved did it for him. Why would anyone re-bake something already cooked? Shrugging, he dumped the premade salad into bowls and searched in the cabinet for bread.

Not finding any, he turned to ask Erin and realized she and Josh were gone. Following the sounds of splashing, he found them in the bathroom. Once there, he could only stop and stare.

Less than an inch of water was in the tub, but you would have thought a water park had sprouted from the very tiles if you accounted for all the toys she had laid out. For one two-month-old?

Josh sat in some type of bath carrier, grinning at a duck mobile that dangled from the arm of the carrier.

Erin laughed and said, "Good boy, Joshie. What does the duck say? Remember, sweetie? The duck says *quack*."

She bathed him with a cloth as she knelt by the tub. The warmth from the water had flushed her face and curled her hair even more.

Travis had a sudden urge to either join her beside the tub, or step back, leave the house, and drive away as quickly as the law would allow. Before he could force his feet to make a decision, she looked up with her radiant smile.

"You've entered the quack zone."

Travis vowed he wouldn't take a step closer. "How does a grown-up take a bath in here?"

"A grown-up could clean up the toys, but would be wiser to use the other bathroom. Could you hand me the yellow towel?"

He hesitated, then stepped into the hot zone. Instantly, baby smells surrounded him. He'd picked up the towel—with ducks—off the side of the wash basin when she pulled Josh out of the tub. The kid was trailing enough water to fill a horse trough.

Moving forward, he wrapped the towel around the baby.

"The hooded part goes on his head."

He focused on ignoring how damp her hair was, the way her sleeves were rolled up past her elbows, the flush in her cheeks.

"I don't see a hood."

"The triangle—it goes over Josh's head to keep him warm."

She held the baby between them as he continued to fumble with the towel. Finally managing to work out the contraption, he moved forward to place it over Josh's head.

Erin took a step back.

And they nearly all went down in the land of the ducks.

Travis grabbed them both just in time. His arms securely around her, Josh warm and wet between them, he stared down into her gorgeous brown eyes—eyes he could look into until he was a very old man.

"Are you okay?"

"I'm fine?"

"Josh?"

"Looks fine. Joshie, you okay?"

Josh rubbed his fists into his eyes, then curled into Travis's chest. Something loosened, unfurled within him, and he wasn't sure how he would ever get it back into the place he'd kept it locked.

"I'll take him," Erin whispered.

"No. It's okay. I can—"

Together they changed him and readied him for bed.

The evening wasn't going at all as Travis had envisioned it. Standing beside Josh's changing table, handing Erin items, and watching her hands as she diapered and dressed him for sleep, he realized firsthand how much care went into the daily tending of a person. It was evident in her every touch.

"If you'll rock him a minute, I'll go and check on our dinner."

He raised an eyebrow at the rocker.

"It held my foster father. It'll hold you."

He nodded, accepted the boy, and sat down gingerly. The old oak rocker didn't even groan.

Five minutes later Josh was out like the lights on Wrigley Field, and Travis could have been, too, if it weren't for the knots in his stomach over the conversation he needed to have.

He walked back into the kitchen and refocused on the reason he had come to the ARK tonight.

———

"I appreciate you coming over, Travis. I thought I could handle things on my own, and I probably could have."

Erin had put the finishing touches on the table before Travis walked in—the salad she'd added croutons and cherry tomatoes to, their plates set on cloth placemats, the toasted bread she'd found, and various condiments to spice things up, along with real napkins and silverware.

"But I would have been exhausted. Doc said he'd come by tomorrow to look over the deer and check on a few of the other animals. He also said he'd loan me one of his interns, and I think I should take him up on that—at least a few hours a day."

"Good idea."

She waited for him to sit down at the table with her. He was still standing in the doorway with his hands in his pockets. She felt the smile tugging at her face. She'd tried to stay angry with him, tried to focus on her hurt from the night before, but being with him felt too right. He gave her that boyish smile and her heart melted every time.

"Something wrong?" she asked.

"No. Nothing. Dinner looks great."

"I feel really awkward asking this." His head snapped up, and she wondered what he thought she was about to say. "I just wondered if you'd bless the food."

"Sure. Of course." He reached for her hand, then drew back—but not before she noticed.

Laughing, she entwined her fingers with his. The contact of his skin caused all thoughts in her mind to meld nicely together, much like the foods' aroma in front of them.

"Um, Father, thank you for this food. Thank you for the hands that prepared it, brought it to Erin and myself and Josh. Thank you for community and friends. Thank you for Josh and his great-grandmother, and thank you for providing Erin to care for him. Help us both to know his needs. Amen."

When she opened her eyes, he was staring at her. She felt the corner of her heart give another tug and remembered again that he had called Josh beautiful—the way he had looked holding him in the rocker. She glanced down at their fingers, still entwined, and felt the heat rise in her cheeks.

He pulled his hand away, picked up his napkin, and fiddled with his silverware. "Chicken spaghetti, huh?"

"Yeah. I don't even remember who brought it."

"Probably Miss Geitner. I've had this before." Travis shoveled a forkful in and closed his eyes as the mixture of pasta, cheese, and spices found their spot. He looked for all the world like a man who'd had his cares taken away.

"Are you having a moment there, Williams?" Erin sat back and studied him, waving her fork in the air. "Do you two want to be alone?"

"Didn't taste like this at my place when I broke my leg last fall."

"Let me guess, you nuked it."

"Guilty. Probably haven't turned my oven on in almost a year since I baked a turkey for the charity pantry last Thanksgiving."

Erin shook her head. "How did you break your leg?"

"Baseball, men's church league. Thought I could slide into home like I did in high school. Try this, Erin. It's amazing."

"I'm not very hungry." She took a tentative first bite and froze, her fork still between her lips.

"Uh-huh. Who's having a moment now?"

Erin laughed and took a second bite. "I'm surprised I like it. The words chicken and spaghetti don't really mix for me."

"You're a tomato spaghetti woman."

"Yes, I am."

The conversation came easily. They talked of food and family recipes, the things they did in high school, even sports. She didn't understand half of what he said, but it was obvious he was passionate about anything involving sweat, a ball, and a team.

He leaned back in his chair, pushed away from the table, and his voice took on the timbre of a storyteller. She felt as if she were sitting in the stands, ready to cheer for the home team.

When she reluctantly stood to clear off the dishes, he was out of his seat in a second.

"I'll help you with those."

"You've done enough tonight. Don't you need to get home?"

"Not a lot I have to do in an apartment. No yard work, not much laundry, no goat to feed."

She bumped him with her shoulder, and he stopped, blocking her way to the sink. There was no way around him, and she couldn't go through him.

"You're feeling much better, aren't you?" His eyes searched hers, dared her.

"Yeah, I am." She was holding their plates in both hands. She wanted to fidget, push her hair back behind her ears, but all she could do was look up at him and nod.

"But it's more than the meds and getting over the flu you had, more even than finally taking the time for some much needed rest."

She nodded again, a lump rising in her throat for the first time since he'd arrived.

"I'll wash, and you can tell me about it. If you want to."

And suddenly she did want to tell him. She wanted to know if what she was feeling was normal, and if it would last.

As he filled the sink with soapy water and slipped the dishes in, she picked up a dish towel and thought about the last twenty-four hours. "I suppose I was really angry at God when Jules and Nina died. If you'd asked me, I wouldn't have admitted that, but they were all I had—except for Dana."

"Your sister?"

"Right. And she's so far away."

"Where does she live?"

"New Mexico." She accepted the first plate, dried it, and set it on the shelf. The simple task made talking easier. "You'd like Dana."

"I would if she's like you."

Erin's hands froze on the next plate. She stared at Travis, her color again mounting. When he only grinned, she began to giggle. "Dana's nothing like me, but you'd like her anyway."

She dried the plate, and he didn't rush her. Instead, he washed slowly, allowing her time to find her words. "Dana wanted me to move with her to Taos, but I needed to stay here—"

"With the ARK."

"Yes, and maybe with the memory of my foster parents. I guess my bitterness had grown. I'm not sure. I wouldn't have said I was an angry person, but I had definitely shut everyone out. I didn't want to…" She stopped, wrapping the towel around her hand. "I didn't want to care about someone if there was a chance they'd be ripped away."

Travis took the towel from her, dried his own hands, then cupped her face. "Look at me, Erin. It must have been a frightening thing to find Josh. To start caring again."

She nodded and fought to ignore the shivers running up and down her spine from his touch. "I think I loved him the moment I laid eyes on him."

"God has a plan and a purpose for you two."

"Jeremiah 29:11. Evelyn and Doc shared that verse with me."

His hand trailed down her arm until he clasped her hand. "Want to go and sit in the living room?"

Erin nodded, though her stomach was doing flips. What was it about this man that caused such a reaction in her? Certainly he was physically attractive, but there was something more. His manner, the way he looked at her, the feelings he stirred up inside her. Travis Williams was more than she had bargained for, and he had been walking through her town all the years she had lived here. The thought confused her, as did her feelings.

Life had taken a strange turn, and she wasn't sure what she wanted to do about it. So she followed him to the couch and continued to pour out her heart.

Thirty-One

Travis needed to get this evening back on solid ground. One part of his mind recognized that.

The other part of his mind enjoyed holding Erin's hand—wanted to prolong the moment a little longer.

Something had happened earlier when he and James had first arrived at the barn. One moment she'd been prickly and guarded. The next all of her defenses had fallen. Why?

Fixing dinner, helping with Josh, then sharing the simple meal—through each part of the evening he'd reminded himself he needed to step back, to explain to her what had happened the night before, and why it couldn't happen again.

Instead, he was sitting on her couch, her small hand entwined in his.

"Faith isn't new to me," Erin said softly.

When she didn't continue, Travis rubbed his thumb slowly across the back of her hand, trying to give her courage.

"I don't think I ever stopped believing in God. I did stop trusting in His plans for me. They didn't seem to be something I could bear."

"Erin—"

She finally looked up, and he saw the tears sliding down her cheeks. Her vulnerability physically hurt him—felt like the times he'd taken a risk and slid into home base, pebbles cutting into his palms, the ground tearing at his legs. It had been worth it every time, but he'd always paid the price the next day.

"Nina and Jules took me to church every Sunday. I knew my Old Testament, knew God often teaches us by taking away what we love most."

"But He doesn't—"

"He did with Job, and I thought He had with me. I didn't want to have anything to do with that sort of God."

"Erin, that's before the covenant of grace. God isn't the reason Jules and Nina died in a car accident."

"I realize that—now. At least I think I'm beginning to trust that somehow God can use what happened. I don't fully know how." Her lip trembled, and she drew it in between near perfect teeth and bit down gently. "But he didn't cause their death. He couldn't have. Could He?"

"No, sweetie. God loved Nina and Jules."

She nodded, tucked her hair behind her ear with her one free hand, and clutched his hand more fiercely with her other. "Someone who chose to drink and drive is responsible for their deaths, and that person couldn't destroy God's plan for me. I don't really know what His plan is yet, but I'm ready to believe He has one. I'm ready to believe those words in Jeremiah—for Josh and for myself."

She smiled, and the incongruity of her smile and the tears still wet on her cheeks tore at his heart. He reached out and brushed them away.

"When I became so sick, I was frightened—terrified really. Lying there I began to appreciate the friends who have helped me since Josh came into my life—friends who haven't forgotten me. Part of the reason I learned that was because of you, because you pushed me out of my cocoon."

He shifted uncomfortably beside her on the couch. "I was doing my job."

"I know, but it made a difference in my life, and in Josh's. By taking me to your parents—"

"About last night…"

Travis looked down at their hands, cleared his throat, and wished he had brought in his glass of tea. He needed something to wet his throat, something to help the next words come.

"I remember what you said last night, Travis. And I'm confused about that. I'll admit it upset me after, well, after you kissed me, but I realized earlier tonight how much you care for Josh." She moved her hand up his arm, sending sparks all the way to his shoulder. "You do care about him, don't you?"

Travis shot off the couch like a bullet and pushed his hands into the pockets of his jeans. "Of course I care about him. It's my job to care about the cases assigned to me. Josh is important, and I want to oversee his welfare."

Erin angled her head and studied him, but didn't speak.

"Look, Erin. Do you mind if I go get a drink?"

"No. Of course not."

Travis escaped to the kitchen, calmed himself by retrieving ice from the freezer, then pouring tea into a glass. By the time he returned to the living room, he'd convinced himself to be honest with her—to be mercifully blunt.

He downed the entire glass and set it on the coaster.

"Erin, I've broken almost every rule between a caseworker and a client, and that isn't like me." He sat down in the chair opposite the couch, then stood back up again. "Of course, I care about Josh."

She crossed her arms around her waist, but still she remained silent.

"And you, I care about you, but I am your caseworker. I wouldn't want to jeopardize the status of Josh's placement or my job by becoming involved with you personally. That's why I said those things last night."

"And why did you kiss me?"

"That was a mistake." Her eyes widened, and he wanted to take her face in his hands, hold it, kiss her again. Instead he sat back down. "It wasn't a mistake in the way you might think. If you weren't my client, it wouldn't have been a mistake at all. But given our—"

"Situation?"

"Yes! Given our situation, it was a mistake. I shouldn't have done that." He sighed, relieved she was finally understanding his point of view.

"I didn't mind." She smiled at him, and he wanted to groan, wanted to pull her into his arms.

"Erin, you're making me crazy." He ran his hands over his face and tried to think of how to make her see the seriousness of their situation. "This was easier when you were mad at me."

"Excuse me?"

"Last night you were angry, and I knew how to respond to that. Tonight you're—" He searched for the right word, but came up empty.

"Reasonable?"

"Maybe. I don't know. My thoughts are all tangled right now."

He began to pace again.

"Travis, look at me. I understand now that you do truly care about Josh, and I think maybe you care about me."

"I do." The words felt like barbs as they escaped from his throat.

"This must be difficult for you. My feelings were hurt last night, because I thought I'd misread…" Her face turned crimson and her hands came out, then dropped in her lap.

"You didn't."

"So what do we do now? I don't want this to be hard for you. I appreciate all you've done, all you're doing. If God has a plan for me and Josh, and if it includes you, it will work out."

"Erin—"

"What I'm saying is, tell me what you want me to do." Her voice was gentle, patient.

He jerked his head up and studied her. "Seriously?"

"Yes."

"And you would do it?"

"Within reason, and provided I believe it's in Josh's best interest."

"Spoken like a true mom." He stood, paced the room twice more, and wondered if he'd lost his mind. Finally, he stopped in front of her. "All right, but hear me out. You're not going to like it."

—

Erin was almost relieved when Travis's cell phone interrupted their conversation. She needed time to process what he'd proposed.

As the night had progressed, her uncertainties had dropped away like a winter coat—left behind and forgotten as the days grew warmer. It seemed childish to question whether Travis cared for her.

He blushed whenever she touched him.

Stuttered when she stepped into his zone.

Lost his train of thought when she maintained eye contact.

Erin had never learned to flirt, and she certainly didn't consider what she'd done tonight to be anything that manipulative. It was more like a deer drawn to a stream.

She needed to touch him.

Wanted to step closer.

Longed to look into his eyes.

And so they'd danced around each other all night. She could no more deny the effect she had on him than she could reject the way her own heart fluttered when he was in the room.

Now to deal with his *proposal.*

She would laugh at the word if it didn't wring her heart with its irony.

When Travis stepped back into the room, one look at his face told her they had new problems.

"That was Methodist DeBakey Hospital—Mrs. DeLoach passed away earlier this evening."

Erin stood and hugged her arms around her middle.

"Sit down, sweetheart. You've lost all your color."

"No, I'm fine." She heard herself speak as if from some faraway place.

"I'm going to get you some water. Sit here until I come back."

The glass was cold in her hands. The water soothing on her throat. "It seems odd not to cry," she murmured.

"You've been through a lot recently, Erin."

"She was such a sweet old thing."

"Yes, she was."

"Josh and I visited her—a few days after you and I went."

Travis stared at her in surprise, but didn't interrupt.

"She told me then she was ready—ready to go." Erin drank more of the water. "She missed Mr. DeLoach and her daughter and Tara."

"I received two calls. One was the hospital, telling me of Mrs. DeLoach's passing. The other was from Mrs. DeLoach's lawyer."

Erin tucked her hair behind her ear, leaned forward, and placed the glass of water on the table. "I don't understand."

"There will not be a memorial, since there is no surviving family—except for Joshua."

Erin felt her face freeze at the words.

"I was going to tell you, and then with everything else… Well, I did receive the genetic testing results today. It's official—she was Joshua's great-grandmother. The lawyer has asked for you, Joshua, and a representative from Child

Welfare to be present for a meeting. As soon as we can set it up."

Erin felt her pulse thundering in her ears. She stared at Travis's face, trying to read something there beyond his words, but he didn't seem to be holding anything back.

"Why?"

"He didn't say."

"Did she instruct her lawyers to fight Joshua's placement?"

"I honestly don't know. They didn't give me any details."

"Okay. All right." She didn't realize she was clenching her hand into a fist until Travis leaned forward, pulled her hand into his lap, and gently pried open her hand and massaged the palm.

"Faith," he whispered.

Erin nodded, because she knew it was expected, but suddenly, she felt very lost again. Just when she thought she'd found some measure of peace, a bit of direction, another lightning bolt came out of the clear blue sky.

After saying good-bye and walking Travis to the door, she stared out into the darkness and tried to believe everything would work out for Joshua's good. She even threw up a short prayer. The darkness gave nothing back though, so she turned and walked into her home.

Thirty-Two

Derrick Pitcher stared at the newspaper clippings spread across the motel coffee table and struggled to ignore the hangover pounding at the back of his head. He gulped more coffee.

He was not a stupid man, and his instincts told him the stories in front of him could be turned to his advantage.

If his head would clear.

He slowed his pulse, forced his mind away from the money, and considered each article individually.

He'd at least found the cognitive brilliance to lay them out in chronological order. He never would have known the old biddy had died if his buddy at the bar hadn't slapped him on the back and declared, "You're buying, Derrick. The witch is dead."

Through the haze of a very nice buzz, he'd looked over the bar top to see the face of his ex-wife's grandmother splayed across the television set. That might not have sobered him, but the net value of her estate certainly did—in excess of 120 million dollars.

Asking the barkeep for a glass of water and moving closer to the television, he'd caught the picture of a woman and a baby as the piece ended. An hour later the spot replayed. By then he'd been closer to sober—close enough to realize the baby was his son, or so Tara had claimed.

At eight the next morning he'd arrived on the doorsteps of the Houston Public Library. The fiftyish woman had been more than eager to show him how to use the computer and printer. Now he stared down at three... count them *three*... news articles that could and would change his life.

Article one was dated several weeks earlier and published in a tiny paper called *The Livingston Daily:*

> *Local animal rescuer finds baby. Erin Jacobs has been surprised time and again while serving the residents of Livingston, Texas, but she's never been as shocked as she was the night she looked down into a washtub and found a two-month-old baby named Joshua. While Ms. Jacobs declined to comment until after adoption procedures are final, she has petitioned Judge Boultinghouse for permanent custody of the child. Caseworker Travis Williams will be overseeing the baby's placement.*

Pitcher stared at the picture of the woman. She was a looker all right. As far as the kid, he certainly bore no resemblance to him. Knowing Tara, she'd gone to one of those fertility banks when he'd said he didn't want children. If that was the case, no one had to know.

Article two was dated several days later:

Philanthropist's daughter declared dead. Authorities have called off a search for Tara DeLoach, the granddaughter of philanthropist and Austin resident, Dorothy DeLoach. According to authorities, Tara DeLoach was traveling aboard a forty-foot yacht with former husband, Derrick Pitcher, early Wednesday morning when she fell overboard. Pitcher immediately alerted authorities, but her body was never recovered. Detective Carmichael states the husband is not a suspect.

Pitcher reached for his coffee, but his hand shook too badly to pick up the mug. Wiping his palms on his jeans, he stood, walked to the window, and stared out at the parking lot.

It had been an accident.

They'd argued. Tara had insisted he take her back. The next thing he knew she'd fallen overboard. He'd run for the life ring, but by the time he reached the side with it, she'd disappeared under the water.

That was all he remembered, and he'd told the detective most of it. He hadn't mentioned the argument, or that it was about money. Of course she'd refused him—again. Tara acted as if she owed him nothing, as if giving her five years of his life wasn't worth something.

They'd dredged for her body for three days, and when they'd asked about the baby, he'd said she'd put it up for adoption. Or so she'd told him. Seemed like a plausible answer at the time.

The third and last article was dated yesterday. For this one, he needed coffee. Though his hands still shook, he reached for the mug, downed the now cold beverage, and wiped the back of his hand across his mouth. Then he leaned forward and read carefully.

Lawyers for philanthropist, Dorothy DeLoach, reveal contents of multi-million dollar will. Sources close to the estate have confirmed Mrs. DeLoach left virtually all of her estate—more than 120 million dollars to her great-grandson, Joshua, who was found by animal rescuer, Erin Jacobs. Miss Jacobs found the child at a hunter's cabin earlier this month. Not realizing he had any living family, Miss Jacobs had petitioned the court for legal and permanent custody. In a bizarre turn of events, the child's mother was lost at sea shortly after he was found abandoned in the woods. The detective assigned to the case, Leon Carmichael, states no charges have been filed in Miss DeLoach's death. At this point it is being ruled an accident. No other details regarding the will have been released, nor is there any information on whether the DeLoach estate will fight Miss Jacobs petition for the child.

Pritchett's fingers started at the top and retraced the print through each line. Stopped when they reached the word *great-grandson*. Of course the money was being left to the kid. All he had to do was gain custody, which should be easy enough. He was married to Tara at the time she became pregnant. Wasn't he?

Sure, sure. He remembered clearly the lawyer the old lady had sent to his place. She was so eager for him to sign the papers—what were they called? Something relinquishing his parental rights. Anyway, a nice fat check had arrived with the courier. He hadn't even hesitated. He'd never wanted kids anyway, and he'd told Tara as much.

Well a man could change his mind, especially when he'd been bribed.

With a 120 million dollars he could hire a nanny. He could probably hire the Jacobs woman if she was so attached to the kid.

He stood and began throwing his few clothes into the one battered suitcase he owned.

Livingston wasn't far, but he needed to sell his yacht first. Lawyers weren't cheap.

Thirty-Three

Erin walked into the children's wing of the church and fought the urge to turn around and run back to her truck. A promise was a promise though. Travis had certainly been right when he'd said she wouldn't like it.

Surely, she could survive anything for a year.

It wasn't as if she wouldn't see him.

He'd stopped by with James yesterday to help her with the animals. She needed to talk to him about that. Somehow she had a feeling it was his way of spending time with her, which was cheating per the terms of their agreement.

"So this is Joshua." Mrs. Harrington beamed as Erin stopped at the half-door leading into the nursery. "I've heard about you, young man."

"And I told Josh all about you, Mrs. Harrington. Told him you took good care of me, and he'd be in great hands for the evening."

"You were an easy baby, Erin." The elderly woman held out still strong arms and accepted Josh into them. She seemed timeless to Erin, as if she had reached some golden number and stopped aging. Her hair was pulled into a bun at the nape of her neck, exactly like Erin remembered. Blue eyes twinkled out of soft skin folded into a hundred layers. "I happen to have an open rocker, and Joshua looks sleepy."

"There's an extra bottle in his bag if he needs it, but he ate before we came."

"Good deal. You all have fun. What is it tonight, putt-putt?"

Erin rolled her eyes and tried to ignore the somersaults in her stomach. "I hope not. The last time I held any sort of putting club I was asked to relinquish it for the safety of those around me."

Why had she agreed with Shirley to attend the Friday night social? Shirley wouldn't even be there since she was now five weeks away from her due day and already her feet were swelling. She claimed that by nightfall she didn't want to do anything but prop them on the couch.

Erin probably wouldn't know a soul.

"Erin?"

Turning, she nearly fell over when she saw Mitzi and Elaine walk up to the door across the hall. The first woman was short and dark haired, the second was tall and blonde.

Mitzi was holding the hand of a toddler.

"I didn't know you were back in town, Mitzi. I thought you were…" Her words trailed off as she swallowed her embarrassment.

Mitzi and Elaine exchanged glances.

"Go on in, honey." Kissing her daughter with the same dark hair, she handed over a nursery bag covered in dancing vegetables.

Walking over to Erin, Mitzi embraced her in a hug and murmured, "We can talk on the way out."

Once they were outside the church building, Mitzi looped her arm through Erin's while Elaine went to collect a schedule of the night's festivities from their group leader.

"Antonio was killed in Iraq a year ago."

"I'm so sorry. I hadn't heard." Erin paused then wrapped her arms around the woman she hadn't seen since their high school graduation. "I was so surprised to see you. I shouldn't have said anything."

"It's all right. Molly knows, but I'm not sure how much she understands. I moved back to Livingston six months ago."

"Took a lot of coaxing from me and her parents." Elaine returned with three pieces of paper. "We're glad she's home now. We can look out for her."

"I'm sorry about Jules and Nina." Mitzi pulled her into a hug. "I tried to call a few times, but no one ever answered at the house."

"I haven't been the most sociable person or I would have bought an answering machine." Both Erin and Mitzi swiped at their tears while Elaine studied them with a smile.

"How are you, Elaine?" Erin said.

"I'm good. You look… better than the last time I saw you."

Erin squinted her eyes, trying to remember.

"Three snakes? Long. Made a rattling sound."

Erin started laughing, the day coming back to her like a pile of photos dropped in her lap. "That's right. I was covered in mud. I'd caught two of the diamondbacks—"

"And one was still in the library foyer."

"Which I managed to track a good amount of dirt through."

"I didn't care a bit as long as you took that reptile out of our building. Still gives me shivers every time I unlock in the morning."

Mitzi glanced from one to the other. "I love being home. Things are never dull around here like they were in El Paso."

Erin cinched her purse over her shoulder, suddenly glad she'd come for the evening.

"If you two are finished playing catch-up, we can go show the rest of this group how to play some putt-putt."

Mitzi and Erin both groaned.

"What else is on the agenda?" Mitzi asked.

"Putt-putt, dinner at the Mexican food place, followed by laser tag and dessert at *The Diner*."

"Sounds like plans for a whole weekend. Why did I agree to this?" Erin sagged against the side of her truck.

"Who tricked you into it?" Mitzi asked.

"My caseworker."

Mitzi and Elaine exchanged looks. "They can do that?"

"If you only knew." Erin climbed into her truck. "All right, ladies, who's leading this night of fun?"

———

The night turned out better than she had imagined and helped her forget the pressure of the news reporters and, of course, the money. She had blocked out all details of that meeting. It seemed as though it had happened to another person.

There were another twelve adults at the putt-putt course when they arrived. Erin was still terrible with a putter, but who cared when giant dinosaurs loomed over you as you tried to hit the little ball up and down the slopes?

She was hitting her fifth stroke on a par three when one of the men decided she could benefit from a little instruction.

"Would you like some help?"

"My score just passed a hundred. I'm beyond help."

"I'm Russ. Russell Lawson." He was barely taller than her, with short dark hair and a muscular build, all topped with a warm smile and a deep tan.

"Glad to meet you, Russ. I'm Erin." They shook hands under the tyrannosaurus, and she stepped back toward her ball. She nodded at the group of preteens waiting impatiently behind her. "They're betting this will take me three more swings."

"Ahh. My first suggestion would be to stop gripping your putter like a baseball bat." He showed her the proper grip, which of course entailed putting his arms around her. Erin couldn't help noticing his light aftershave and comparing it to Travis's. Something in her heart yelped like a puppy being stepped on, but she firmly shut the door and focused on the ball.

"Eye on the ball, line up the shot, and tap."

The ball rolled and went into the hole. Behind her were groans, and coins exchanged hands.

"Thanks."

"No problem. I'm sorry I waited until the last hole."

As they walked toward the counter to turn in her putter, she learned he worked at a golf course in Huntsville and was also a physical trainer two days a week at the hospital in Livingston—both of which explained the biceps.

"You're a busy guy."

"I like it. I'd get antsy if I had to sit behind a desk. What do you do?"

Mitzi and Elaine joined them as they walked to the parking lot.

"She definitely does not sit behind a desk," Elaine teased.

"Unless there's something *in* the desk that doesn't belong there," Mitzi added.

Russ sent a confused look from one woman to the other. "I get it. This is like fifty questions."

Erin rolled her eyes, refusing to actually take part, but enjoying the fun everyone was having at her expense.

By the time they reached the restaurant, Russ stepped out of his Jeep, met them at the door, and offered, "Detective."

Elaine and Mitzi laughed, then walked on through to the table where the rest of their group was already seated.

"I'd be happy to tell you what I do for a living."

"No way." Russ shook his head and managed to look offended. "I love a good puzzle. I didn't really think you were a detective. She threw me with the desk thing. Do I get another clue?"

He held out Erin's chair as they sat down at the last two places.

"Why are you getting clues, Russ?"

Homer, a big bull of a man, ordered sweet tea, then leaned forward to hear what Russ was saying. Most of the people at the table were aware of Erin's profession, but five had somehow managed to not need her services.

Throughout the dinner—in between fajitas, tacos, chalupas and enchiladas—those who didn't know would shout out questions that could only be answered with a yes or no.

"Does it require a license?

"Yes."

"Is it dangerous?"

A resounding "yes" circled the table, and Erin nearly choked on her taco salad.

The conversation would fade back to the latest movie or who was building a new house, then someone would call out, "Have you been in the paper?"

More "yes" answers crossed the table, followed by muffled laughter.

Someone tried to Google her on their phone, but they were caught and shamed for cheating.

As everyone pushed back from the table, Russ focused his eyes on her like a laser.

"You answered *yes* to the question, 'Do you work with animals?'"

"Correct."

"But you answered *no* to, 'Are you a veterinarian?'"

"I'm not old enough to be a vet." Erin grinned over her tea. "Vets are at least twenty-six. They attend eight years of school."

"No wonder it costs so much to get Shadow's shots." Russ fell into step with her as they all filed toward their cars and a round of late-night laser tag. "Vet tech?"

"Nope."

"But I'm close?"

"Yes."

"You make house calls?"

"Yes."

Russ held open the restaurant door, and Erin thought of how his manners mirrored Travis's. Was she destined to compare every man to Travis?

He snapped his fingers as they walked toward their cars. "You rescue animals."

The smile spread across her face of its own accord as it did every time she thought of what she did. "Correct."

"Wow." The admiration in his voice was genuine. "There was a special on the national news not long ago covering animal rescue people and what happened during Hurricane Katrina. It's a gutsy job, Erin."

"I'll take that as a compliment, so thank you. Most of what I do isn't nearly as dangerous as what happens during or after a hurricane though."

"I'll bet you have some stories to tell." He stopped by her truck and waited while she unlocked the cab.

She felt torn. It was nice to have someone express a genuine interest in her and in her work. Someone who wasn't judging her for doing something too dangerous for a woman. And Russ seemed like a generally pleasant guy. She peered at him in the darkness and held in a sigh.

Is this what Travis wanted? For her to give someone else a try? A fist squeezed around her heart, and she struggled to ignore the sensation, to maintain the light mood they'd shared all evening.

"I want to hear some of those stories, but if we don't hurry, everyone else is going to be through round one of laser tag—a game I usually win." His grin in the reflection of her dome light magnified his youthful appearance. How old was he? Twenty-two? Twenty-three? Practically a child.

Then she caught her own reflection in the driver's window and realized *she* was twenty-two. Why did she feel so much older? She didn't realize she was shaking her head until Russ placed his hand on her arm.

"Don't worry. If you've never aimed a rifle, I can help you. It's pretty simple."

The competitor in Erin raised its head. "Oh, I've aimed a rifle. I own a Pneu-Dart 178 Air Activated Rifle, among other things."

"Ever use one with a night scope?"

"Of course. I get called on night rescues."

Russ threw his hand up in a high five, and she couldn't help responding, even though it made her feel like a teenager again. As she followed him out into the small line of cars, she realized maybe that wasn't such a bad thing. Perhaps it was okay to leave behind her grown-up responsibilities for a few hours.

And it definitely would be okay to win some rounds of laser tag. Finally, a game she would be good at playing.

Thirty-Four

The problem was not the rifle.

The problem was the garb.

"Are they serious?" She held the vest in one hand, the helmet in another.

"Afraid so, sweetie. Boys will be boys." Mitzi pulled the vest around her considerable bosom and tightened the cords as though she'd done it a hundred times.

"Or in this case, men will be boys." Elaine plopped the helmet over her hair, flipped up the visor, and grinned. "It is kind of a rush. I always wanted to be on a SWAT team."

"Why do you two know how to do this?"

"They hang out here." Russ walked over, already suited out. "I've seen them on Saturday nights, taking down the high school crowd."

"That is not true. Tony loved laser tag though." Mitzi flipped her visor shut, but not before Erin saw the wetness in her eyes. "Fair warning—I'm good at this."

Turning, she marched off to her team's huddle.

"She's not lying," Elaine said. "She'd beat her husband every time he came home on leave. It made him crazy."

Russ had been demonstrating how to adjust Erin's vest straps, but he froze at Elaine's words. "Is this too, uh, emotional for her? We could do something else."

"No way. If I know Mitz, it will help release some of her tension. I'd stay out of her line of fire though. You two are on the opposing team." Elaine saluted and jogged to catch up with her best friend.

"I'm never going to get these strap things adjusted in time, Russ. Go on without me."

"It's not that hard once you get the hang of it. Pull up on the black catches here and pull down on the straps here. See?"

"I see the catches on yours, but mine don't seem to be in the same place."

"They should have given you a teen vest. This one's too big. Do you want me to exchange it?"

"No."

"I think it will work if you'd just pull the straps tighter."

"Do it for me." Erin looked over at their team. Homer was waving at them wildly to hurry and join them.

"Okay. Hold your arms out." He moved closer, pulled the straps tight, and she felt the vest snug to her body.

Just as Russ looked down and into her eyes, pulling the last strap tight, Erin felt someone else watching her. Arms still out, she turned so Russ could check her straps one last time.

That was when she saw him.

Travis was standing on the sidelines, and his eyes locked with hers.

For a moment she felt as if all the wind had been squeezed out of her body, then she realized it had.

"Too tight," she gasped.

"Huh? Oh right. Sorry."

He eased up the strap around her chest and she drew in a deep breath. It did nothing to help the ache in her heart, but it did help clear her head.

"Am I ready?" She turned her attention back to Russ.

"Yeah, except for the helmet. You definitely look ready." He was staring at her curiously.

"What's wrong?"

"An attack look suddenly came over your face. I'm glad I'm on your team."

"Yeah. You should be." She pushed her helmet on, flipped the visor down and marched over to her group, wondering if Travis would receive an electrical charge if she happened to open fire.

What gave him the right to show up and spy on her? Is that what he was doing? It would be different if he was participating, but he wasn't. He was standing there watching, making her nervous. She'd finally begun to relax, to enjoy the evening, and then he shows up and...

Her anger evaporated as she realized how much she missed him. Missed his laughter, the feel of his hands in her hair, his lips on hers, his voice in her ear.

Why couldn't he at least be a part of the group?

Why couldn't he make this easier for her?

The rawness of her pain was too much.

As Homer directed her toward a three-foot wall and the lights went out, she suddenly needed to clean her body of the frustration that had built up over the last week.

The laser rifle was a handy tool.

She threw herself into the fight with all the concentration and energy she could muster. Played as if the Enemies of Morgon were chasing her, and any capture would result in Joshua living an orphaned, penniless life. She didn't know who the Enemies of Morgon were, but she'd heard one of Shirley's older boys discussing a video game, and they served as a good enough visual.

She didn't waste a single shot. Her aim was true, and her instincts primed by Travis's intrusion. When she felt someone closing in on her position, she threw herself behind a barrier without regard to the bruises she would have the next day.

Jerking her head around at the last moment, she caught Mitzi's form silhouetted by a laser shot meant for someone else.

She saw Mitzi raise her weapon and knew there was only one way to escape the kill. Throwing herself over the two-foot barricade, she landed squarely on top of Russ.

"Don't shoot me," he muttered.

"You okay?"

"I'll live if you point that laser gun the other direction."

Erin quickly assumed a defensive position. "There's at least one, maybe two hostiles on the other side."

"Bless my mother, we've unleashed a fighter."

"Put your back to mine, Russ. This is no time to play around. We have them hurting, but Mitzi wants this. They'll attack our position any minute."

The hail of laser fire began the second she stopped talking. One part of her mind realized it was a game, but the other part had too much invested.

Russ pressed his back against hers, turned his head so she could hear him, and offered a plan. It wasn't a good plan, but the giant wall clock said they had one minute, twenty-two seconds left.

"On my mark?" he asked.

"Absolutely."

"Three, two, one…"

Both stood and fired into the darkness, in opposite directions, semi-circular patterns.

Erin felt the slightest twinge in the shoulder of her vest as it immediately lit up. She pulled her trigger another three times before she accepted she'd been hit and her rifle would no longer work.

She was lowering her weapon in defeat, when Russ's shout of victory rang out.

"Yes! We did it!"

The lights were coming on, and Erin blinked against their brightness to read the time on the game display clock. Eighteen seconds?

"We won?"

"We won. We did it!"

Then Homer, Justin, Kayli, and two others Erin couldn't remember the names of were gathered around, chanting and celebrating, laughing and raising their laser rifles in victory.

Erin looked over at Mitzi and Elaine. They were huddled in their group, also whooping it up and celebrating their total hits for the game. Apparently, it had been very close.

Erin started toward Mitzi at the same time Mitzi turned toward her.

"Great game," Mitzi said.

"You too."

"Yeah. It helps work out some of my frustrations." Mitzi sat on top of the three-foot wall and swung her foot. "I forget everything for a little while."

Erin looked over to where Travis had been standing.

"I know what you mean," she said softly. "Maybe you and I could meet back here for a mid-week rematch."

Mitzi flipped off her helmet, and red hair spilled loose from underneath it. When she looked back up at Erin, a mischievous grin had spread across her face. "Maybe next time, you and I will be on the same team. Then they won't have a chance."

She placed her hand in the air in the universal invitation to high five. As Erin made contact, then pulled her into a hug, suddenly something from the night was salvaged. She hadn't solved any of her own problems, but she had helped to lighten the load of a friend, even if only for a minute.

For now it was enough.

They walked shoulder to shoulder back toward the rest of the group amid whistles and mock bows of honor.

"You can all put your money where your mouth is," Mitzi said, tossing her rifle to Elaine.

Homer tried to back toward the edge of the group without being noticed, something difficult for a former college defensive back.

"Homer, I think you bet I couldn't finish ahead of you in the rankings."

"Didn't realize we'd have a new Rambo on the set," Homer muttered.

"That's no excuse. *Conozca a su enemigo.*"

"I didn't realize Erin was my enemy, but I'll pay up."

"*Bueno.* I'd like the old greenhouse fixed up before the first frost." Mitzi's grin was unrestrained as they turned to walk toward their cars.

"What did he bet you?" Erin asked as she fell into step beside her.

"That he would see about weatherproofing an old greenhouse I have behind my place. The roof leaks a little and the windows are drafty. I'd love to be able to continue to grow vegetables and my herbs in there during the winter."

"And Homer didn't think you could win tonight?"

"Homer didn't think she could even finish in the top three." Russ's voice next to her sounded amused. "Of course, he hadn't counted on you either. You were great in there, Erin."

"Yeah. I had a little built-up tension to release."

"You don't say." Russ studied her as she unlocked her truck. "Whatever the reason, it was a lot of fun."

Erin shifted in the dim light of the parking lot. She thought of what Shirley had said about trusting her instincts, and her instincts were telling her right now that Russ was looking at her with a familiar light in his eyes—the same way she looked at Travis.

"You're coming for dessert, right?"

"I can't."

"It's just dessert, and it's only nine-thirty."

"Yes, but I need to pick up Josh."

"That's your little boy—the one you found?"

She nodded, unable to explain what he meant to her. Suddenly though, she needed to be with him, needed to cradle him in her arms.

Russ held the door as she climbed into the truck. "I'm glad you came tonight."

"I'm glad I came too, but—"

"You don't have to say anything, Erin."

Her head snapped around, and she searched his eyes.

"We're friends here. We back each other up. Try to get out and have some fun for a few hours a couple times a month. It's all good."

"I feel like I'm in a different place though." She searched for a way to explain all the conflicting thoughts and feelings percolating inside of her.

"We're all in different places. Drive safe." He shut the truck door gently, stepped back, and waved.

———

Travis walked into the diner and stopped short at the front counter.

"Table for one?" The waitress had a short gray bob and looked at him skeptically over wire-rim glasses.

"No. Thank you. I'm meeting some friends." Travis nodded toward the group in the corner, then moved slowly toward them, feeling trapped. He'd scanned the table twice, but hadn't spotted Erin's auburn curls. If she wasn't there, he had no desire to stay, but with the waitress shepherding him toward the only vacant chair, he didn't feel as if he had much choice.

"Look who decided to grace us with his presence." Homer's smile knocked the sarcasm out of his welcome, much as his bear of a handshake temporarily knocked Travis's worries out of his mind.

Searching for a way to distract the big guy, Travis looked over the table. "Cherry cobbler?"

"That would be mine." Homer released his hand and sat back down. "Should have made it here sooner Williams. You might have scored a piece. Should have made it to the laser game, too, though I doubt you would have scored there. I would have had you on the mat in the first thirty seconds."

"Travis was at the laser game." Elaine leaned back in her chair and blew on her steaming mug of coffee.

Eleven pairs of eyes turned to stare at him.

"Actually, I was." Travis waved away the menu the waitress offered, but eagerly accepted the cup of coffee. He shouldn't. His shoulders already felt like knotted rope, but the caffeine kick would help him attack the bulging bag of paperwork in his car.

"So what gives, man? The game look too tough for you?" Homer scooped up another piece of cherry cobbler, dipped it into the ice cream waiting on the side, and popped it into his mouth.

Travis wondered if the homemade dessert had him grinning like a fool, or if the big guy really was that arrogant. "Come on, Homer. I've beat you at everything this group has played."

"Ha! And you're scared you'll lose at laser tag. That's it, isn't it?"

Choruses of "he looks scared" lapped the table. Travis took the ribbing good-naturedly. If it distracted the group from his real reasons for stopping by now and why he'd left earlier, it was worth the misunderstanding.

Ten minutes later, he'd finished his cup of coffee. He stood, stretched, and deliberately looked at his watch. "I'm afraid I have a few hours of paperwork, boys and girls."

People waved and said good-bye. A few threw a "see you Sunday" his way. Elaine nodded, smiled, then turned to talk to her friend, Mitzi. What made him think they were talking about him?

He needed sleep. Why had he drunk the coffee?

Heading out of the diner's door, he nearly jumped off the curb when he felt a hand on his shoulder.

"Sorry, Travis. Didn't mean to startle you." Russ Lawson smiled back at him in the curbside lamplight.

"Hey, Russ. I'm a little edgy, that's all. Shouldn't have had the coffee."

"I know what you mean. We'll all be up late now, what with the caffeine and the sugar. Could I talk to you a minute?"

"Sure. Like I said, I was heading out to get some work done." Travis stuffed his hands in his pockets and tried to look overburdened with work, which he was.

"This won't take long. We've always been straight with each other."

Travis searched his mind for where Russ could be heading, but came up blank, so he simply nodded.

"I saw you come in during the laser game too. Seemed to me like you were watching over Erin, maybe checking on her."

"No. Absolutely not." Travis felt his face redden and tried to stop himself from over-protesting. "I mean she's one of my clients…"

The lie died on his lips. He had no idea how to end it.

"So you'd have no problem with me asking her out on a date? Because the thing is I felt a real connection with her tonight. I don't know if it's mutual, but I think it might be."

Travis stared at Russ, then realized the man was waiting for an answer to something.

He backtracked in his mind and replayed Russ's words.

"You don't need my permission to date Erin Jacobs." The obvious came out in a growl.

"And I wasn't asking for it." Russ studied him a minute longer, then held out his hand. "Just making sure I wasn't stepping into your space. As long as the path is clear—"

Travis shook his hand and resisted the urge to break it, which would have been juvenile and pointless no matter how good it might have felt. Then he walked back to his truck and sat there, wondering how things had reached this point.

He watched Russ walk to the parking lot and unlock a hot-rod Mustang—a Mustang! Is that what he thought he would take Erin out in? The image was the last straw.

He stepped out in front of Russ pulling on to the street and held up his hand in a stop symbol.

Russ rolled down his window, lowering the music that had been cranked to an ear-splitting decibel. "Forget something?"

"Who Erin dates is her business, but you do realize she is taking care of an infant?"

"Sure. We talked about Joshua. I'm cool with that."

Travis cringed at the slang, told himself not to judge, and tried to think over the muffler's roar.

"What I'm saying is you might want to take some time to think about this before you start anything." When Russ looked at him blankly, he rushed on, trying to find the right combination of logic and advice. "She's a woman with responsibilities, not some girl from high school."

"Bro, I haven't been in high school in four years, and Erin is definitely no girl."

The pain radiating up Travis's jaw was a testament to his self-control. He nodded curtly and stepped back from the car. As he watched the Mustang pull away, he felt older than he had in a long time.

He wanted to pull Russ Lawson out of the car and give him a good thrashing. Why? He'd done nothing more than act like a boy.

Or was it because he'd seen himself in comparison to a twenty-two year old?

Perhaps it was because he'd realized Erin was Russ's age and not his own.

Walking back to his Blazer, he told himself Erin was nothing like Russ. She probably wouldn't even be interested in dating him.

If she was, he had no one to blame but himself.

Thirty-Five

Travis stepped out of the Blazer, stood watching Erin brush the paint horse, and considered his best approach. From the way she studiously refused to meet his eyes or offer any greeting, he suspected his one chance of success would be a direct attack.

Wincing at the choice of words in his mind, he walked toward her.

"Afternoon."

"Since we didn't have a scheduled visit today, I'm assuming this is a surprise one. Josh is in the house with a sitter. You're welcome to go and check." She moved around the big horse, conveniently turning her back toward him.

Though he had no one to blame for the cold shoulder but himself, he couldn't help bristling over her abrupt manner. At the same time he had to admire the view. She wore a work shirt the color of the yellow flowers growing near the fence, tucked into well-fitted jeans, which in turn were stuffed into a pair of scuffed work boots.

In other words, she looked like everything he wanted.

Something tightened in his chest, and he fought to find a way past it. He hadn't seen her since Sunday, and it had taken all the reserve he could muster. He was not going to let her sassy attitude get the best of him.

"Actually, this isn't an official visit. I had another stop on this side of town and thought I'd drop by."

She turned then, looked him straight in the eye, and challenged the lie. "I'm past the end of town, and you should have called first."

He stepped closer and caught the scent of baby shampoo. Putting his hand on the head of the horse, he considered and rejected a few more reasons he could offer up for the visit. Finally, he settled for the truth. "I miss you."

Her brown eyes softened, and her hand stilled on the brush. For a moment he thought his honesty would be enough. Then she tossed her head as if to shake off her feelings and moved around the paint, putting the animal between them.

"You don't play fair." She brushed the horse vigorously, each stroke brisk as she ticked off her points. "You lay out your plan, convince me it's the best way—"

"You agreed."

"Yes. I did agree." She pointed the brush up at him, and he took a step back. "I'm not finished though. I agreed with you that we shouldn't *see* each other except on a professional basis, that we wouldn't *call* each other, and that I should reengage in whatever passes for a *social* life in this town."

She punctuated each word with quick brush strokes.

The paint flicked its tail, and Travis couldn't help feeling pity for the animal at the same time he envied it. At least she had her hands on the horse, her eyes intensely studying it. Yes, he would readily trade places.

"I followed your rules to a T." She stopped brushing and finally looked up at him, a frown on her face.

He met her eyes. "Yes. You did."

"But you show up every time I turn around. Do you know what that feels like?" She dropped her gaze to the brush and began to curry the horse again. "When you walk into a room, it's as if all the oxygen is suddenly sucked out, and I don't know why. I turn around, and there you are. I see you, and I forget why we're doing this." Her hand stilled on the brush as tears filled her eyes.

Travis watched her, waited for her to recover, and felt his own pulse accelerate.

Told himself he shouldn't have come, should have stuck to the plan.

Told himself to walk away.

Instead, he walked around the horse, took the brush out of her trembling hand, and pulled her into his arms.

"I'm sorry. I keep doing this wrong. I'm sorry."

The moment she slipped into his arms, the ache in his chest stopped. He could finally draw a deep breath for the first time in two weeks. It didn't matter anymore that he'd broken their rules, or that they'd have to start all over.

All that mattered was she was in his arms.

She didn't sob and didn't protest.

She only buried her face in his shirt.

He ran his hands through her curls, rubbed her back, and when he couldn't resist any longer he eased her back, framed her face with his thumbs, and kissed her.

Gently, softly, trying to convey all he'd locked inside since the last time he'd held her.

When she pulled away, she was half laughing and swiping at the unshed tears in her eyes. "If you think you're forgiven, I'm still undecided."

"I can live with that."

"Come on, Jacks. Let's put you to bed."

He followed her to the horse stall. Helped her close up the barn for the night. By now the chores felt like second nature.

As she turned to walk from the barn, he pulled her back into its cover and tried to wrap his arms around her again. She pulled away, stepping out into the dying light.

"What's wrong?" he asked.

She walked to the fence and put her hands against it as if for support. When he started to follow her, she turned, holding up her hands. "Stay there, Travis. Please."

"Talk to me."

She pulled in her bottom lip and hugged her arms around herself. Seeing her that way, in what little light remained, he was reminded again of how vulnerable she was and how strong she was. Erin Jacobs was a lesson in contradictions, part of the reason his mind and heart were constantly spinning.

Just as he knew that he was supposed to stay away, but he needed to be with her.

"I'm glad you came by. I needed to know I wasn't imagining what I'm feeling—"

"What *we're* feeling." It came out with more of a rumble than he intended, but something in her tone didn't sit well with him. How did he know he didn't like where this was headed?

"Okay. Right." She tucked some curls behind her ear, and he wanted to offer to do that for her. Then she re-crossed her arms, not in a defensive posture like women sometimes did, but tighter—clutching her ribs—as if she needed to hold herself together.

"It helps to know that." She smiled, and it was one of the saddest things he'd ever seen.

He closed the distance between them in three steps. When he reached out and touched her arm, she began to shake.

"Erin, don't—"

"Let me finish. I need to do this. You made the rules. You said this charade of our only knowing each other professionally was important so I can take care of Joshua, so his adoption would be approved, and you would appear impartial."

"Do I look impartial?" The words tore from his throat.

"But you're going to try, and you've explained everything to Director Moring. You have done that, correct?"

He managed to nod.

"We're being honest, and we're trying to do what's right and keep the number one thing number one. Joshua has to stay number one. Especially now with the complication of Mrs. DeLoach's estate." She shook her head, refusing to let him interrupt. "You know how much I love him, how much he matters to me?"

He nodded again and stuffed his hands in his pockets in the hope she'd calm down.

"I care about him too."

"I believe your feelings for Josh are as trustworthy as your feelings for me, and that's why I know you'll do what I ask." She took in a deep breath, finally pulling her eyes from the horizon and looking deeply into his. A shock went through him like lightning, all the way to the marrow of his bones. Before he could process what he was seeing in the depths of her eyes, she continued. "I don't want you to come here again, not alone."

"Erin—"

"If you need to do a site visit, let me be sure my sitter is here—actually here with us—or Doc's wife."

"That's not necessary."

"It *is* necessary." Her voice ripped away what was left of any lies he'd told himself. "I can't do this. Don't you see I can't do this? I have to watch you drive away and then wonder if it's going to be another week or ten days. Maybe it'll be a month this time. That's not fair, Travis."

"Erin—" He searched frantically for a way to change her mind, but the panic and the emotion was leaving her voice as her jaw took on a firm set.

"I can't talk to you on the phone, or e-mail you. Do you know how lonely that is? It's the worst kind of separation, knowing you're a few miles away. Knowing you might appear at any time. No." She stepped back, bumped into the fence, and moved sideways along it. "I agreed to your rules, now it's time for you to agree to mine. Until the adoption is final. Until Joshua is safely placed."

He reached for her, but she continued to slowly step away, her feet making soft sounds in the night, leaving permanent imprints on his heart. "I don't understand. Earlier, you seemed... you seemed okay."

"When you kissed me?" She shook her head, auburn curls bouncing. "Don't you think I wanted that as much as you? Don't you think I'm as weak as you are? But then..." she waved toward where he was parked. "Then it's time for you to go, and I realize, I have to start all over again. Not knowing and wondering."

The back porch door at the house banged shut, and Erin's head snapped around. "I have to go. It's a school night for my sitter."

She turned and walked toward the house.

He watched her go and wondered how things could have gone from bad to wonderful to worse in the space of an hour.

"Erin."

She stopped, hesitated, and finally turned around.

"Are you sure?"

"No."

He couldn't make out her expression in the darkness.

"I'm not, but sometimes you have to go on instinct and faith. Both tell me this is the only way."

He watched her complete the slow walk in the near darkness, then climb the porch steps and enter the old farmhouse. More than anything he wanted to follow her, join her in the kitchen, hold Josh. Instead, he climbed into his Blazer and headed back down the lane. It felt like a bitter sacrifice, and something told him it wouldn't be the last.

—

Erin waited until the sitter was gone.

Waited until Joshua was freshly bathed, sung and prayed over, and tucked into bed.

She waited until the dishes were done and the kitchen cleaned.

She even went back outside and scraped off her work boots, trying to figure out what she would say. Of course, she had the luxury of the time change, but finally she knew she could put it off no longer. Dana had been gone for six weeks—and what a six weeks it had been. While her sister was honeymooning in Europe and the Caribbean, she'd become a mother.

Her child had been declared a millionaire.

And she'd fallen in love.

Some of those things she'd communicated through e-mail. Some she hadn't. Twice more Dana had insisted she and Ben would fly home early, but Erin had talked her out of it. Today they arrived back in Taos, and Erin wanted to give them time to settle in, but she needed to talk to her—tonight.

Thinking back over the last week made her heart ache, so much that she actually put the work boot down, reached up, and rubbed at her chest.

On Sunday morning she had attended worship services for the first time since Nina and Jules died. She had been expecting a painfully emotional hour, but actually it was merely pleasant. She'd smiled at the children's sermon and tried to picture Joshua toddling toward the front of the sanctuary.

It would be many months—maybe a year or more— before he'd be old enough to make his way down the aisle and toward the treasure chest filled with stickers.

She wouldn't think about Joshua growing that quickly. If she did, she'd need to run into the house and watch him sleep.

Silly.

She brushed the thought away as she finger combed her hair back from her forehead.

She needed to talk to her sister. But what would she say? How could she explain the situation she'd stumbled into?

Sunday's sermon had been about God's perfect timing. She'd wondered if Pastor Perry had been preaching specifically to her, which hardly seemed possible. He barely knew her. Any uneasiness she'd felt had been washed away with the final music, a contemporary version of a song she remembered hearing Nina hum as she cooked.

Yes, Sunday morning had been almost perfect. Until she'd picked up Josh. The single hour away from him had suddenly seemed like a dozen. Gathering him into her arms, she'd felt a touch on her shoulder and she'd hoped—no she'd actually closed her eyes and prayed—it might be Travis.

Even sitting on the back step in the darkness, she blushed to think how she must have looked when she turned and saw Russ Lawson's face. He'd known. She could tell by the way the smile on his face had frozen, but he'd recovered quickly and asked her to lunch. She'd begged off, claiming work with the animals, which wasn't a lie.

To make matters worse, as she was leaving, her eyes were drawn across the foyer, and there he was, standing with his parents. Her feet had frozen to the floor, absolutely unable to move, his eyes locked on hers.

Then Josh had started to cry, and Shirley asked if she needed help. When she looked back across the foyer, Travis was gone.

All week had been like that.

Every time the phone rang.

Every time a car drove up.

Every time she checked her e-mail.

Her heart lurched every single time, but it had never been him.

Until tonight.

She pressed her palms against her eyes and forced her mind to forget the memory of his lips against hers. She shouldn't dwell on what she couldn't have. She needed to get through tonight and tomorrow.

She needed to call Dana.

She had waited too long. She should have paid the international charges and called her weeks ago.

Standing up, she found the strength to walk back into the house, pull her cell phone from her purse, and walk into the living room.

Then she pressed and held the number 2 on her phone. She didn't have many speed dial pre-sets entered, but there was one person she could count on in an emergency.

Thirty-Six

B en answered the phone. "Baby sister. We were about to come down with a hostage rescue team and bring you up to the mountains. Haven't you heard Taos is beautiful in the fall?"

Erin snuggled into her recliner and smiled. How was it she'd known Ben Marshall for less than a year, but he could make her feel like it was Christmas morning? Maybe because she'd never had a brother.

"By the way, I have a present for you and baby Joshua," he teased.

"No kidding? It's a while until either of us has a birthday, so I hope it keeps."

"Oh, this won't go bad. Let me tell you about it." There was the sound of tussling, followed by laughter. "Dana's driving me crazy—"

Finally her sister came on the phone, breathless and murmuring, "Shoo. This call is for me. Go finish the dishes. We need gab time."

"Hey, Sis." Erin closed her eyes and took her first deep breath of the day.

"Hey, yourself. I was about to call."

Erin didn't answer, couldn't speak for the tears clogging her throat.

"Is Josh okay?" Concern crackled through the line.

Why had she waited to call? She'd always shared everything with Dana. Somehow this situation had grown unwieldy—something bigger than her, something she couldn't hold in her arms or grasp firmly in her hands.

"Josh is fine. Growing like a puppy. I had no idea kids changed so much in such a short time."

"Tell me everything."

"He's started reaching for his bottle, at least that's what I think he's doing. Mrs. Harrington said he turned his head when he heard my voice."

"Ben, book me a flight. Get your cell phone out, seriously. I need to go to Texas."

"Oh, Dana. You can't imagine how good it feels to talk to you."

"I should be there. I haven't even met my nephew. He sounds like a child genius."

"You should wait." Erin gripped her cell phone. "Wait until the hearing. I'll need you more then."

"I have quite a bit of vacation time saved up you know."

"And you just took off for six weeks. I imagine your staff would like to see you. Not to mention you hate being away from that office, which is why you have so much saved."

Dana laughed again, and Erin was struck by how different her sister sounded, how much lighter. Is that how love was supposed to make you feel?

Silence stretched between them as she tried to think of how to broach the subject of her troubled heart.

"What's wrong? It's not Josh—"

"No." Erin walked out on the front porch and sat with her back against the house. A little of the day's warmth remained, and it comforted her in some way, knowing the sun had been faithful to shine on her home, and it would do so again tomorrow. Even if she didn't understand the path her life was taking.

"Front porch or back?" Dana asked.

"Front." Erin smiled, placing her palm flat against the porch floor's oak boards.

"Screen door still squeaks."

"I keep meaning to oil it."

"Screen doors are supposed to squeak a little. You always did think better outside."

"Maybe I should try camping then."

"Or you could sleep in the barn."

"Josh likes his crib." She smiled and loosened her grip on the phone.

"I can take the red-eye out of here." Dana's voice settled somewhere between big sis and director of the local Homeland Security office. It was one thing Erin loved about her—the ability to be loving *and* in charge. "We'll work this out, whatever *this* is. Spoil my nephew a bit, then go down to Stella's for some world-class pie."

"I think I needed to hear your confidence. I feel as if my life has become a labyrinth, with no exit and a very confusing pattern."

"If your life is a labyrinth, it's a holy one designed by God. You can bet there's purpose and loving care designed in every step."

Erin reached over to a pot of orange chrysanthemums sitting by the front door and began to pluck off dead blooms as they talked. "I forgot you'd found religion."

"Nope. I found the Lord." Dana snorted. "Not that He was lost. I'd just been ignoring him for quite a few years."

"Yeah, I've been fairly good at that myself. Did I tell you I went to church on Sunday?"

"You did not! Ben will be so excited. We've been praying for you."

Erin didn't know what to say, so she turned the plant and continued tending to it by the light of the living room window.

"Was church your social worker's idea?"

"Travis. Yes and no. Maybe it was. Actually, when I was staying at his parents' home there was this mosaic on the wall—did I tell you about it?"

"No. You told me you were ill and stayed with them two nights."

Erin spilled it all, from the moment she'd awakened in Barbara's house, feeling grace splash over her like a refreshing shower, to this evening's parting. When she was done she felt spent, but immeasurably better.

"You're dealing with a lot right now, Erin."

"I thought perhaps I was being childish, overreacting."

"Not at all. A girl wants love to be simple, beautiful—flowers that show up on your doorstep inexplicably and a walk on Saturday afternoon." A screen door shut, and Erin knew Dana was walking out on her own back porch, looking out over the mountains surrounding Taos.

"Doesn't work that way." Erin's voice was a whisper.

"No. At least not for the Jacobs women."

"It wasn't easy for you and Ben either, not at the beginning."

"I didn't think it would be possible, so I pushed down my feelings for him. I didn't believe I deserved someone as kind as Ben, as loving." Dana paused and seemed to stumble over the memories of the past year. "I almost threw away the love God intended for me. I wouldn't want to see you make the same mistake."

"How do I know though? I do love Travis, but this hurts, Dana. I don't think it's supposed to be this way. Are relationships supposed to make your heart ache?"

"Maybe not, but some things worth having are worth waiting for. I think you were right to set some boundaries because you need them to make it through this time. Now trust that God will be faithful to have a perfect plan for your life. And believe Travis will do his part."

"I don't know how to have that kind of faith."

"Pray, and get up each day believing God cares for you. He does. He cares for you as much as he cares for Joshua. As much as I care for you both."

Erin laughed, but it felt ragged like the rough edges of a board where the paint had worn away. "It's hard to believe God has time to care in such a personal way. I know what happened at Barbara's was real, but what you and I share... what family has... that's different.

"It's not."

"It is." She searched in her mind for proof, but shied away from the obvious memory they both avoided. "You ate my broccoli for me."

"True. I had selfish reasons though. I didn't want you to have to sit at the dinner table all night."

"Nina finally caught on to the fact I'd eat it raw." The memory of her foster mother no longer hurt, and that was a blessing.

"The thing is, and I'm new at this, too, but I think God is willing to eat our broccoli for us. I think He cares that much. So you can trust him with tomorrow."

Erin studied the potted flower, noticing the places where new blooms were waiting for the sun to touch them.

"Kiss Ben for me."

"You know I will. You're going to love this present he brought you from the Caribbean. It's—"

"Don't tell me. I could use a surprise to look forward to."

"All right, but remember I tried to warn you."

They said their good-byes and promised to call again soon.

Erin walked inside, tidied the house, and peeked in on Josh.

Standing over his crib, she thought of all that had happened in the five weeks since her phone rang, sending her on a mission into the forest.

She had so many questions. Why had his mother abandoned him? Why did Tara DeLoach call the ARK?

She reached out and touched his face puckered in sleep. He was a precious child. She couldn't imagine a thing in the world that would cause her to walk away from him—no threat, no enticement, no love.

Her heart could break, then break again, but she was a grown woman. She would never put her needs before his.

This was a child like she had been that dark night nearly twenty years ago. Dana didn't think she could remember. She said two years old was too young to have memories, especially of something so traumatic.

But she did remember.

Dana picking her up. Dropping her tattered bear. Dana running with her into the forest. The smell of her father. The smell of fear.

Wanting her mother and crying.

Perhaps she remembered that most of all.

She had seen her father looming in the darkness before Dana had. Had seen him as Dana had sat her beside the old pine tree and told her to wait quietly.

She still remembered the look on his face, the threats, and the way Dana had stood up to him to protect her baby sister.

The dreams had stopped when she was twelve. She'd found the place in the forest, taken the bear there, and left it. Dana had thought she'd lost the stuffed animal, and she let her sister believe that. What she'd left there was any hope her life would knit itself back together.

From that moment she'd never looked back. She'd accepted Nina and Jules were her parents, her mother was dead, and her father was never coming back—to harm her or to love her. She'd moved on with her life.

She'd been back to the forest many times since—maybe not their particular road, though she knew where it was. The place held no power over her, because the child she had been no longer existed.

Erin reached down and tucked the light blanket around Joshua.

It seemed now as if the child she had been and the adult she had become had somehow come together into a whole person, but the seams ached a bit.

And where did Travis Williams fit into the picture?

Driving to the hunter's cabin had moved her life in an unexpected direction, and she was thankful for it because the turn had brought her Joshua. It had also brought her Travis. Her life had been simpler before, but plain—black and white.

What would happen next?

Dana was right. She'd have to trust God had planned that turn and the next. Trust it was for her best and for Joshua's.

And maybe she could even find the faith to believe what they were caught up in was the best thing for Travis Williams, which didn't mean the weeks and months they had in front of them would be any easier to endure.

Thirty-Seven

Travis sat on the deck of his Yamaha Skeeter, rubbing a cloth along the already clean seats. Everything about the ski boat gleamed in the afternoon light, from the bright-blue leather seats to the metallic-blue and gray fiberglass hull. The tank was topped off with thirty gallons of fuel, and the two hundred horsepower engine sparkled. Even the small fridge was stocked with bottled water and sodas.

Yes, his vessel was in top condition. Actually, it looked better than the day he'd bought it—probably because he'd spent the last three hours cleaning it instead of taking it out on the waters of Lake Livingston.

And that was a mystery he admitted to himself as he sat back in the captain's chair and studied the cove. Still plenty of daylight left, and plenty warm enough for the second Saturday in November. They were having an Indian summer of sorts, and he wouldn't complain about it.

He should take her for a spin and burn off some of this restlessness.

Then his eye caught on the leaves of a Texas Red Oak turned a deep red by the autumn sun, a red the exact color of Erin's hair.

He stared at the tree and thought of pulling out his cell and calling her. What stopped him was the memory of the look in her eyes that night. He'd kept his distance since then as she'd asked—as she'd wanted—although it was killing him.

For two weeks he'd given her the wide berth she'd asked of him.

Grabbing a bottle of water from the fridge, he popped the seal open and began to down it. The cold liquid did nothing to soothe the dull pain in his throat though.

Disgusted, he picked up his rag and again rubbed the already polished railing. That's when he heard a familiar footfall on the dock.

"Dad. How are you?" Travis dropped the rag and met his dad on the ramp to the boat.

Shaking his hand, then pulling him into a hug, his dad held up a brown sack larger than your typical lunch bag. "Your mother worries. She sent this over."

"Lunch?"

"Sandwiches, tea, some homemade lemon pie, sugar free of course."

"Enough for two?"

"Absolutely."

They sat in the back seats, spread the food out between them, and talked about football, his nephews, the approaching holidays—anything but what was burdening his heart.

"Sorry I haven't been by. Things have been crazy at the office."

"Figured as much. Man has to earn a living."

Travis stared out over the water, watching a Great Blue Heron take off. "Truth is I'm struggling with some personal things, so it helps to spend more time on the job and think about it less."

"How's that working out for you?"

Laughing at the directness of his dad's question, he ran his hand over the crick in his neck. "Not so well. Not so very well."

His dad reached over and kneaded the muscle on his shoulder and neck. Travis suddenly remembered when he'd come home from baseball, hyped up, jazzed. Then the muscles in his shoulders and neck would begin to cool, start to lock up, and his dad would rub the soreness out like he was now. The memory made him smile, and the smile lifted a bit of his heaviness.

"Want to talk about it?"

"I don't know, Dad. I'm not sure it would do any good."

"Fair enough."

The sun moved toward the horizon, bringing with it the usual restlessness that plagued him this time of evening. When had he stopped enjoying evenings on his boat? Seven weeks ago by his best calculation. Now the thought of calling the guys, getting together a fishing trip, held absolutely no appeal.

He looked at his dad, thought of what his parents had shared for so long, and couldn't help envying them.

"Times were simpler when you met Mom."

His dad moved a toothpick from one side of his mouth to the other, seemed to consider the question seriously, and finally nodded in agreement. "Pretty much. Nixon was ordering troops to cross into Cambodia. That sparked the marches that led to the Kent State riots. Terrible tragedy, but simple I suppose."

"All right. I didn't mean it was a perfect time. I know my history and 1970 was a bad year." Travis sat forward and ran his hand through his hair. "I meant what you had with her—*that* was simple."

"I was shipped stateside because of a bullet I took in the leg—wouldn't heal no matter what they tried. I didn't want to come home. Didn't want to leave my unit even though Nam was a terrible place, worse than what you read about it. But those men had become my family."

Travis watched the memories overtake his dad and wondered if he'd drop the subject as he so often did or continue.

"I tried to talk Sarge out of sending me back, but there was no changing his mind when a doctor said go." His dad laughed, the effort crinkling the skin around his blue eyes. "That's how I met your mother though. Guess God used an enemy's bullet for good."

He took out the toothpick and pointed it at Travis. "She was volunteering at the hospital over in Houston. Prettiest thing I'd seen in two years. You can bet your baseball cards on that."

"And you knew. The minute you met her."

"Well, I knew. Your mother now, she took some convincing."

"You were too ugly I imagine."

Dad laughed again. "She'd seen too many army grunts. One more wasn't going to turn her head. No, I had to work on her real gentle like. Took some persistence."

He reached out and slapped Travis on the knee. "We Williams men know about persistence though. It's what makes us good at so many things."

Travis shrugged. "I'm not sure I'm following."

His dad pointed at the bow of the boat. "Remember what condition this boat was in when you bought her? Had to have her towed to the dock. Look at her now. You could probably get top dollar."

"Wouldn't take it though."

"Exactly my point. You had the patience to restore her, and now she's a part of you. Same thing with a relationship."

Travis ran his hand along the seats and considered what his dad was trying to tell him. Finally, he shook his head. "Women are more complicated than boats."

"I agree with you there, but they're considerably more valuable too." His dad stood and stuffed his hands in the pockets of his khaki pants.

The move caught Travis off guard. It was like looking in a mirror. For a moment, he thought about how much his dad acted like him, then he realized it was the other way around. He had the disorienting feeling of looking through binoculars the wrong way. It made what his dad was saying all the harder to digest.

"I'm going to make a leap here and assume we're talking about Erin."

Travis stood, stuffed his own hands in his pockets, then feeling self-conscious yanked them back out and crossed them over his chest. "Yeah, I guess. Maybe."

"She's a beautiful woman. If you have feelings for her, tell her so."

"Not that simple." Travis began picking up their lunch debris and stuffed it all back into the sack. "I'm Erin's caseworker. It's a breach of my code of conduct to be personally involved with her."

"I see. Yet God put Erin in your path for a reason and gave you these feelings for a reason. We know things happen by design, not accident. Have you talked to your boss?"

Travis felt the sandwich churn in his stomach as the memory of the lie he'd told Erin mixed with the chicken salad. "I told Erin I had. I tried to—twice—but Director Moring brushed me off both times."

When his dad didn't comment, Travis blurted out the rest of his fears. "I've compromised myself professionally, lied to Erin, and now I may have pushed her away."

"That's a lot of guilt to carry. No wonder you're staying on your boat." His father's voice was gentle.

When Travis finally met his gaze, all he saw was compassion in his dad's eyes.

"I shouldn't have lied to Erin. Should have admitted I couldn't get Director Moring to hear me out, but I don't think Erin realizes what a conflict this could be."

"Erin seems fairly intelligent."

"Yes, she is."

"So she probably would understand the situation if you explained it to her."

"Dad, I—" Travis walked to the edge of the boat and peered out over the water. "When I'm around her, I can't control my emotions very well. That's not like me. I know how I should act, but then I do things I would normally never do. I tell myself I'm going to stay away from her, then I make up reasons to visit. I'm acting like a seventeen-year-old kid instead of a grown adult."

For the first time since he'd blurted out his confession, his dad grinned, and that eased even more of the knot tied around Travis's heart. "You sound to me like a man in love."

"Because I do stupid things?"

"Love sometimes causes us to do *different* things than we would normally do. After I was released from the hospital in Houston, I was supposed to move to Ft. Worth. Had a good job waiting there for me. Called them the day I was supposed to show up and told them I wasn't coming. Had no job, no place to stay. Just my VA check coming, which wasn't much."

His dad took the bag of trash and stepped over to the dock. "There was a young lady I needed to see, working at a certain hospital in Houston, so I figured I would find some work there, and eventually I convinced her to move back here to Livingston with me. Didn't make much sense, but then sometimes what your heart tells you to do doesn't make a lot of sense."

Travis stayed on the boat, looking up at his dad.

"You're telling me to follow my heart and ignore my mind." He shook his head. "Goes against all my training."

"I'm telling you to talk to your director. You've decided you can't do both—your job and have a relationship with Erin. Might be true, might not be."

His dad looked toward his car, then back. "But son, jobs will come and go. I'm not sure how many opportunities you'll get to meet the love of your life. If I had moved to Ft. Worth, would God have had a different plan for me? Couldn't say. I like the way this life turned out."

He waved once, then turned and walked away.

Travis was left with a decision to make, but at least he had it out in the open now. He was no longer merely chasing nightmares around in his own head. Accepting Erin had been right to draw a line also helped to ease some of his unrest. As he buttoned the boat down for the night, he realized he didn't have all the answers—but he had more than when he'd stepped on board.

He considered that to be progress.

—

On Monday morning, he skipped his morning run and arrived at the office before Moring. By the time she walked off the elevator and around the corner at 6:45, he was waiting outside her door.

"Williams. I don't hold meetings before eight." She sailed through the door of her office, turning on lamps and punching the *on* button to her private coffeemaker.

"And I've tried two other times, so I'm going to need you to make an exception this once."

Her eyebrows moved up slightly as she turned and studied him. "All right. You have five minutes."

He laid it out for her in the most succinct, business-like language he could manage—not glossing over the reality he'd broken more than a few protocols.

"You tried to tell me this the Friday before I went into the budget meeting." Moring walked to the coffeemaker, poured the hot, brown liquid into her cup, and offered one to Travis, which he waved away. The last thing he needed at the moment was more acid on his stomach.

"Yes and before that on Wednesday. I realize that's no excuse. I've felt this way about Erin since the flood, maybe since the day I met her." He dropped the file he'd meticulously combed through after church the day before on her desk. "Everything's up to date, and I transcribed all my notes myself. I figured you would want to pass this off to someone else as soon as possible. James is at least familiar with the case—"

"Are you presuming to do my job now?" Moring sat but didn't pick up the file. "Travis, I don't need to look in that file. I've supervised your work for six months, and the director before me highly recommended you. Have your personal feelings for Ms. Jacobs caused you to forget how to complete your job?"

"Well, no—"

"Have you represented the child's interests to the best of your abilities?"

"Yes, of course. Joshua is very important to me."

"I'm sure he is." Moring set her coffee aside, steepled her fingers, and though he wanted to interrupt her and explain some more, he knew better than to say anything while she studied him in that way.

Finally, she pushed the folder back across the large mahogany desk and picked up her cup. "Take it. I have no patience for someone trying to dump their cases on their coworkers."

"Maybe you didn't understand what I said." Travis fought to control his anger and lost. He bolted out of the chair and paced back and forth in front of the window that looked out over downtown Livingston where cars were beginning to wind their way down the street.

He remembered his father's words—about only having so many chances. Erin was out there somewhere, and so was Joshua. Suddenly, all he wanted was to be with them.

"I can't handle this case. I don't even want to try anymore." He turned on Moring. "I'm going to marry Erin if she'll have me. That's more important than my job."

"Short engagement or long?"

"What?" Travis sat down in the chair before his legs gave out completely.

"I assume you and Erin would want a short engagement given the situation with Joshua, so we'll fast-track this case. I'll speak with the judge myself this morning." She made a notation on her calendar, then beamed at him. "I'll expect an invitation. Now you've used more than your five minutes. Was there anything else?"

"But… how am I supposed to do this?"

Moring sighed, closed her eyes temporarily, and he saw for the first time a bit of her age. When she opened her eyes, she stood and walked around the desk. Picking up the file, she placed it in his hands.

"Travis, the guidelines we have in place are just that— guidelines to protect the interests of the people we help. If you hadn't come and talked to me, I might have been worried you couldn't be objective in this case. The fact you have indicates to me you will continue to go out of your way to do so, as I'm sure this file indicates."

She walked across the room and paused with her hand on the doorknob. "I'll make the judge aware of the situation. All you need to do is maintain a degree of public decorum until we pass this through the court system, which I imagine will be very quickly."

"How quickly?" he asked, his head spinning at the idea he was still employed and hopefully soon to be engaged.

"We could be assigned a date within a month."

Travis nodded, walked out of the office, and to the elevator. It wasn't until he was back in his Blazer that he remembered he was supposed to be in his cubicle, working.

Thirty-Eight

Derrick Pitcher set ten thousand dollars in cash on his attorney's table. The weasel's finger actually twitched, but he had to give him credit—the man didn't count it.

Instead, he pushed a button on his phone and called in his secretary. The woman could have been a model, but no doubt she earned more bringing William Hammett coffee each morning.

"Mr. Pitcher needs a receipt, Jessica."

"Sure thing, Mr. Hammett." Jessica counted out the hundred-dollar bills, then wrote out the requisite receipt.

As soon as the door had closed behind her, Derrick launched his attack. "Why haven't you filed any motions?"

"I told you I'd file my first one when I received my retainer."

"It's been four weeks! What if they've already awarded the Jacobs woman custody?"

"If you were in a hurry, you should have put your affairs in order more quickly."

"Do you know how hard it is to sell a yacht?"

"Not my problem, Mr. Pitcher. Time is not a concern in this matter. Child Welfare does not move quickly. I've been watching the case and little has been done. Director Moring requested the case be fast-tracked on Monday."

"What?" Pitcher's blood pressure soared so high he heard the sound of the surf in his ear drums. He'd handed this idiot one-third of the money he'd received for his yacht, and for what? To learn about these things after they happened?

"Judge Boultinghouse approved the motion today." Hammett leaned back in his chair. "We'll file our motion at four o'clock."

"Four—"

"Four o'clock, Mr. Pitcher." Hammett picked up his coffee and sipped it. "By the time the judge receives it and notifies the Child Welfare office, everyone will be gone. By Monday morning, you will show up looking presentable, as you do today, with your considerable sum of money and your very understandable explanation of why you didn't appear earlier."

Pitcher stopped gripping the chair and squinted at the man across from him. "My cover story, you mean."

"Call it what you like, but limit yourself to the details we agreed upon."

Suddenly, it occurred to him he'd rather not play poker with this man, but then he didn't need to. If he won the custody case, he'd pay him his exorbitant fee, hire a nanny for the kid, and live the life he'd always deserved.

Walking out to his rusted Jeep, he felt optimistic for the first time since Tara had stepped onto his yacht. Maybe this could work to his advantage after all.

———

Erin stared at Shirley's protruding stomach, amazed her friend could still waddle at all.

"You look miserable."

"I am, but it'll be worth it in a few days." She put one arm back against her couch and half fell into a sitting position. "This one's actually been the easiest of the three."

"How do you figure?" Erin peered down at her feet, which were barefoot in spite of the fact that the temperature outside had dropped below fifty for the first time.

Shirley wiggled her toes. "Do they look bad? Be honest. I haven't seen them in two weeks."

"Yes, and no. Your toes look great since I painted them, but your ankles, they look painful."

"Actually, I can't feel them too much. I cut out the salt like Doc Mason said, but the only difference I can tell is my food tastes bland."

Erin gawked when Shirley's shirt printed with a fall leaf pattern began to move. Tiny fall leaves slid left to right.

A smile spread across both their faces.

"He hasn't moved much lately," Shirley whispered. "Hey, Daniel. Whatcha doing in there?"

Grabbing Erin's hand, she placed it on top of her belly. "I thought things were too crowded." Shirley pressed her hand against the side where the leaves had heaped up in a pile. "Feel that? I think it's a foot. I hope it's a foot. Otherwise, we're coming out upside down, but Doc assures me Danny's feet are firmly placed at the top now."

Erin wondered again what it would be like to have life inside of you—growing there within your being. There had been a time when she'd actually hoped another child might be in her future, a sibling for Josh. But lately she'd given up on that dream. It didn't seem like God meant it for her, at least not anytime soon.

With her hands on Shirley's tummy though, it felt as if she were holding the entire world. In that moment she felt so much happiness for all she had added to her life and so much sadness for all she had lost. The incongruity gripped her, squeezed her heart so that she suddenly had trouble breathing.

A natural bodily function, and she simply forgot to do it.

"Erin!" Shirley slapped her on the back and pounded between her shoulder blades. "Are you okay? Take a breath."

"I'm… I'm fine." She took deep breaths, like a diver coming up from the dark recesses of the ocean. Stupid. It was stupid to go under. It had happened twice before, and she swore it wouldn't happen again.

"What happened?" Shirley pulled her red hair back with one hand, but kept the other placed firmly on Erin's back. "You looked like you'd choked on something. Your faced turned white as a new moon."

"It's nothing." Erin rubbed her chest and took a few more steadying breaths. "I'm going to get a glass of water. Do you want something?"

"Sure. Bring two bottles of water from the fridge and the plate of homemade apple-raisin cookies on the counter. Barbara Williams brought them over yesterday, and I do not need to eat them all."

Erin's steps froze at Barbara's name, but she somehow kick-started herself and walked to the kitchen, where she retrieved the cookies and water. By the time she returned to the living room, Shirley was looking at her like Nancy Drew who'd just solved the latest mystery.

"It's Travis, isn't it? I've been wanting to ask you, but I didn't know if I should bring it up or not."

Setting the plate of cookies on the table, Erin shrugged. "I don't think talking will help, but then I can't feel any worse about it either."

"He still hasn't called?"

Erin shook her head, picked up a cookie, and nibbled around the edge.

"How long has it been?"

"Nearly four weeks."

"Have you seen him at all?"

"Once. Josh and I had a visit at the office. He made sure James was present—pretended he needed someone to take interview notes."

Shirley sighed, picked up the plate of cookies, and balanced it on her belly. "It *is* what you asked him to do, so at least he's honoring your request. Shows he respects you."

"Doesn't make me feel better."

"I don't know, honey. It's a difficult situation. What did you want to happen?"

Erin felt the bands around her heart tighten and fought to keep her tone light. "Maybe he'd decide he couldn't live without seeing us. It's amazing how much Josh has changed in even four weeks. He's starting to grab hold of things, and if you lay him on his tummy he raises up his head. He smiles at me all the time."

Tears rolled down her cheeks, but she brushed them away. She was through with crying. "I know Travis's job is important to him, and I respect that. I suppose I'd hoped he'd find a way to make it work where he could be involved in our lives… if he wanted to." Her voice grew smaller. "Maybe he doesn't want to."

Shirley wiggled forward, set the plate on the table, and pulled her into a clumsy hug. "I'll keep praying. You are a wonderful person, Erin Jacobs, and I'm pretty sure Travis knows it as well as I do."

"I feel like I'm in limbo, and I don't know how to handle that or how long it will take. Am I supposed to wait around?" Erin brushed her tears away with her palms and knew she'd have to reapply some makeup before picking up Joshua.

"Nope. Live your life, and let God handle the details. He's pretty trustworthy. Speaking of details, where is Joshua?"

Erin laughed, her heart lightening at the thought of her little man. "He's with Evelyn. I had a call while I was with Doc, and she insisted on keeping him."

"What was the emergency this time?"

"A boa constrictor escaped in a second-grade classroom. A little boy brought him for show-and-tell, but forgot to check with the teacher before bringing him to school. Then when he went to show Lanky to the class, there was a small panic."

"Oh my. Tell me you found him."

"Found, recaptured, and safely returned home."

"Your job is not boring."

"No, it is not."

"Does anyone pay you for those calls?"

"The child's mother made a nice donation."

Erin left Shirley's home feeling somehow cleansed. She'd carried Travis's absence around in her heart for too long. Sharing it with her friend helped to ease the pain. Her natural inclination was to stay home and nurse her wounds. She'd made a promise though—to Travis, to herself, and most importantly to Joshua.

She was going to make good on her vow to become a part of this community. So she headed back to Evelyn's and picked up Josh. She had an ARK to get in order. After all it was Friday night, and Friday night was adult's night out. Tonight's calendar included a movie and a game arcade.

Neither was her favorite thing to do, but it probably beat flipping through TV channels.

On the other hand, she hadn't quite figured out how to handle Russ and Homer. The thought of those two brought an involuntary smile to her lips. They were like two giant Labradors, vying for her attention.

Attention was one thing every girl could find a way to handle, especially from such good-natured guys. Too bad her heart was firmly entrenched across town in the hands of one very silent social worker.

—

Travis stared at the church calendar and frowned. He hadn't been to a movie in a very long time. Most of what Hollywood put out did not appeal to him, and this one didn't promise to be much better—an adventure flick with a twenty-four-hour timeframe, ticking bomb, professor-type hero, and the obligatory beautiful woman. If only life were so easy.

All followed by an hour at the local arcade?

He'd rather spend the night going through his new case files.

Throwing the calendar on his countertop, he looked over at James and scowled. "I'm not sure this is a good idea."

"At my church we get together for board games—everything from Monopoly to hearts." When Travis raised a skeptical eyebrow, he helped himself to another fistful of chips. "You should suggest it. Better than... what was it? An hour at the arcade. How do you get rid of the teenagers?"

"A guy at our church owns the place. He cordons off one room for private parties."

"Who plays arcades anymore? Now if he had game systems..."

"I'm really not interested in either."

Travis collapsed into his leather recliner and flipped through the lengthy array of sports channels. He had splurged on very little in his life—his boat being one, and his plasma television and leather couch and recliners the other. Of course, he was nearing thirty with no family. The thought brought on another twinge of pain.

It was his own fault he had no family. He'd made work his priority for much too long, and tonight was his chance to fix that mistake.

"Great game of racquetball." James grabbed his keys off the counter. "I might have to move into these apartments so I can beat you more often."

"Their athletic facilities are a perk, but even if you lived here, beating me would always be a rare event."

"Dude, the last score was 15-2."

Travis dropped the remote, then stood and stretched. "I was distracted."

"I'll say. Nervous?"

"A little. I haven't seen her, except in the office, in four weeks."

"For what it's worth, I think you're doing the right thing. You received Moring's clearance on Monday."

"I was waiting for the judge's go-ahead."

"Which you received today."

"Right."

"Man, you need to keep your head in the game."

Travis froze midway to the door and felt all his muscles stiffen and automatically tense up. "Erin isn't a game."

"No, but all women like to be wooed, even the ones who are in love. She hasn't been living alone on a real ARK you know. You stepped out of the game, and now you're stepping back into it. Sort of missed a quarter."

Still scowling, Travis opened his door and stared out at the storm coming in with the darkness.

"I'm saying go in easy. Assess what you've missed and where she's at right now."

"I don't exactly have free rein. Moring told me to 'maintain a degree of public decorum'. How I can do that and let Erin know things have changed at the same time?"

"You'll find a way." James grinned, shook his hand, and slapped him on the back, then walked through the door. Turning at the edge of his upstairs balcony, he grinned back. "I've got it. You can let her beat you at Donkey Kong. I remember that is a clear signal you're cool about a girl."

Travis waved his friend away and studied the incoming clouds. He felt a storm brewing of an entirely different kind. Or maybe his nerves were talking. Either way it was time to find out what Erin's reaction to him would be.

James might have been on to one thing though. He had been out of the picture, and he'd completely forgotten about Russ Lawson. The conversation with the guy came back to him, suddenly, like the rain falling upon the pavement below.

He was a kid, barely twenty-two if that. But then Erin was twenty-two. The thought twisted his stomach and was immediately followed by more just like it—how much the two had in common, how many Friday nights they'd spent together, how Russ really *was* a nice guy, how Erin might have needed help over the last few weeks and he hadn't been there.

Looking down at his hand, he saw he was holding his razor. Like the worker driving into the office who didn't recall the route he'd taken, he didn't remember walking back into the apartment and entering the bathroom.

James was right. He needed to get his head in the game.

He couldn't afford to lose tonight like he'd lost this afternoon at racquetball. There was more at stake with Erin. This was their future, and he'd already bungled it once.

Thirty-Nine

Erin settled into the movie seat, grateful to be off her feet no matter what the flick was they were about to watch.

Her new donkey had decided to escape his pen and had been in no mood to return. It had taken her so long to corral him, she'd barely had time to finish the rest of her chores, bathe Joshua, and make it to the church in time to drop him off with Mrs. Harrington.

She sank back into the chair and relished the knowledge no one would need feeding or changing for the next three hours.

"Is this seat taken?"

She opened one eye and found Russ grinning down at her.

"Uh, no. But most of the guys are—"

"Great. I'll take it then."

Erin bit back a grin and closed both eyes, determined to enjoy her few moments of reprieve. Mitzi and Elaine's conversation to her right focused on shoes and holiday plans.

Behind her Homer was discussing a steer he'd taken in to see Doc England. She relaxed in the sensation of being comfortable with this group—not needing to say a thing if she wanted to simply be with them.

It was a novel feeling for her.

"You look pretty tonight, Erin." Russ settled beside her, and she was again reminded of a Labrador waiting for attention.

"Thank you, Russ."

"Busy week?"

"It was, actually."

"Heard about that snake situation. I have a nephew in the same class. Apparently, you made a real impression on the kids. Miss Hancock has been plagued with requests for books about animal rescuers and vet techs."

Erin smiled, but refused to open her eyes. "Glad to be of help."

She thought he might have turned his attention to someone else in the group when he cleared his voice and started again. "We have a couple of minutes until the movie starts. Could I bring you something from the snack bar?"

Opening one eye, she offered him a smile. "Actually, at the moment, I'm pretty content."

Unfortunately, her stomach chose that instant to growl.

"Ah-ha! You might be content, but your stomach is craving popcorn and a soda."

"Erin wants popcorn?" Homer leaned forward, stuck his ball cap, along with his head, in between them. "Buttered or plain?"

"I'm buying." Russ leapt to his feet. "Buttered or plain?"

"I never eat butter—"

"Plain it is." Before he reached the end of the aisle, he pivoted back toward her. "RC, right?"

Erin couldn't have stopped the smile if a week's donations were riding on it. Russ was such a nice guy, even if he wasn't the right guy. "RC would be great, Russ. A small one though. Kid's size."

"Sure thing."

He bounded down the stairs, and she sank back into her seat, allowing her eyes to drift shut again.

"I've never seen a man so happy to buy popcorn." Mitzi elbowed her arm off the armrest between their chairs.

"I thought you were talking shoes."

"Doesn't mean I can't watch the drama going on beside me."

"Uh-huh."

"Puppy eyes. That boy has puppy eyes." Mitzi turned back to Elaine, who was declaring the merits of snakeskin boots over leather.

Erin allowed herself to sink back into that restful place. Soon the movie would start, Russ would return, and the evening's activities would begin. It was an effort for her to keep her spirits up. She'd rather let her mind wander to the way things could be, even though she knew it was a dangerous daydream to indulge.

It wasn't unusual for her fantasies to become full blown—include even the scent of him. Like a dream she refused to wake from, she reached for the memory, sought the familiar even when she felt the seat beside her jostle.

How had Russ possibly sprinted back so quickly?

Before she could work her eyes open, his voice sent shivers down her spine. Her pulse kicked into a double rhythm as she turned and met his gaze.

"This seat taken?"

Blue eyes slammed into hers, and Erin knew she wasn't dreaming. She couldn't have dreamed up that smile if she'd tried, because she'd never seen Travis smile quite that way before.

He plopped into the seat beside her, looking as if he'd hit a home run.

"Actually that's my seat, Williams. Find another one." Russ had made his way down the aisle and stood waiting, his arms filled with snacks.

"Oh, sorry." Travis answered Russ, but continued to grin at Erin—and he showed no indication of moving.

Erin searched her mind for an intelligent reply, but there was a light swooshing sound in her head. She could actually hear it, like the whisper of the wind through the pines at night. All she could think of was that he was here, and he'd actually spoken to her—in public—as if she were a real person.

Mitzi came to their rescue. "I can move down, Travis."

"But—" Erin licked her lips, gripped the arm seat between them. Holding on was probably a good idea at this point.

"It's no problem at all." Mitzi patted her hand and whispered in her ear, "This will be more fun to watch than the movie."

She had scooted down a seat before Erin regained her equilibrium.

Travis finally stood, shuffled in front of her, and dropped on the other side, greeting the rest of the gang behind them as he moved.

Russ proceeded to dump snacks in her lap, far more food than she remembered ordering.

"They were running a special," he explained when she began to protest. "And women like chocolate, at least I thought…"

"I love chocolate, Lawson. I'll take those if Erin doesn't want them." Travis reached across and plucked the chocolate candy off the snack pack tray on her lap.

Russ was quick though and snatched them back. "I bought those for Erin."

"She doesn't look hungry. I hate to see good food go to waste."

"She was plenty hungry until you sat down. Maybe she lost her appetite looking at your ugly mug."

"Is that true, Erin? Did I take away your appetite?" Travis grinned down at her, and Erin wondered if she'd fallen asleep and possibly dreamed the entire absurd situation.

Then Homer popped his head in, and she knew it had to be real. She couldn't dream up anyone as comical and endearing as Homer. "I'll take those if they're going to be a problem. Or maybe I should come sit between the three of you."

"I think you all should quiet down." Elaine leaned across and gave them a motherly scowl. "The previews are starting, and I love previews."

"No one loves previews," Russ grumbled. "Previews are like commercials."

"Wrong. Previews are like mini-movies, and you get to see them for free."

Erin glanced Travis's way in the midst of the bantering. The lights had dimmed, but she hoped to catch his profile. Perhaps find a clue as to why he was here—what had changed.

He turned the minute she looked at him though, a scene on the screen flickered with light, and she was again drowning in those blue eyes she'd dreamed of every night since she'd last seen him.

—

Travis thought the movie would never end.

Every moment was agony. Sitting next to Erin was like sitting in front of the tree on Christmas morning, waiting for his parents to wake up. He'd always been the first to crawl out of bed, and he'd have to wait, staring at the gift he knew held what he'd dreamed of for months.

So close, but not able to hold it in his hands yet.

That's what the 124-minute feature felt like—heaven and agony combined.

He wouldn't have missed it for anything.

He did feel a small slice of guilt that Russ had invested a good ten bucks in trying to impress Erin. Apparently, he was warming up to make his move. Which served to bring home the fact Travis had almost waited too long—not that she would have fallen for the kid, but Erin Jacobs was a beautiful woman.

Seeing her as he'd walked up the steps of the theater he'd felt like he'd taken a baseball to the side of his head. She'd pulled her auburn hair back with little clips, but as usual small curls had escaped. The result was a look that had his heart racing as if he'd climbed a mountain instead of a few steps. He barely noticed the blue sweater she was wearing, except that it highlighted her light, creamy skin.

He could have stood in the aisle and soaked in the sight of her for the entire movie, but he'd seen Russ come in the door and start up the stairs. There'd been no doubt in his mind where the kid was headed.

Now the credits were rolling and they were headed out to dinner and an arcade? Good grief. He needed to talk to whoever planned these events—maybe offer a bribe.

Erin had only glanced at him once after the lights went out, but it was enough. He could tell from the brief look how she felt. What had his dad said? It was just a matter of convincing her, persuading her.

He thought of the time he'd spent on his boat, the gentle way he'd restored her, and smiled. He might not understand women, but he understood boats. He'd need to use the same gentleness.

Following Erin into the lobby, their group formed a small knot as people made suggestions on where to go for dinner.

Travis was about to recommend a restaurant in the next town, so they wouldn't make it back before the arcade closed, when Erin reached into her bag and pulled out her cell phone.

She studied the screen, looked up at him in alarm, and stared back down at the phone.

"What is it?" He stepped closer, looked over her shoulder to read the text, then reached for his own phone as it buzzed.

Several other phones went off at the same moment.

"Oh my," Mitzi said. "It's Shirley."

Travis placed his hand at the small of Erin's back and pocketed his phone as a smile spread across his face.

"I don't know about the rest of you, but Erin and I are headed to the hospital."

"I'll swing by the burger joint and pick up some sandwiches," Homer offered.

"And I'll drive to the house and find some cards and dominoes," Elaine suggested. "If I remember correctly, her last baby took about twelve hours. Could be a long night."

"I'll have to pick up Joshua," Erin murmured.

"You still have a few hours. Let's see what happens." Travis held the door open for her.

"I can pick Joshua up and bring him to the hospital," Russ offered.

"Or one of us can take him to Evelyn's." Travis walked her to the truck and waited as she unlocked the door.

"Thank you," she whispered.

"You're welcome." He didn't offer any apologies or explanation for the weeks that had passed. He realized now wasn't the time. Now was the time to be there for her, to let her enjoy this moment with her best friend. So instead he shut her door and jogged to his Blazer.

A brand new baby born on the night he'd taken the first step to turning his life around.

Seemed like a sign—a very good one.

Forty

Travis paced up and down the small waiting room. How could people play dominoes when a new life was about to begin?

The door to the nurses' station opened, and he nearly dropped his coffee. An elderly lady wearing a volunteer uniform moved past them at an unhurried pace, pushing a cart filled with flowers and baby balloons.

Travis sighed and collapsed back into the plaid-upholstered chair.

"You act as if you have a baby being born," Erin noted.

She hadn't spoken to him directly in the last hour. He had given her space, thinking she was worried about Shirley.

A raucous cheer broke out at the domino table, and he jerked his thumb toward Russ and the others. "How can they play games? I don't think I could count the dots. And yes, I feel like it's my child being born."

When she tilted her head and waited, he leaned forward and rubbed his hands through his hair roughly as if it would unjumble his thoughts. "I've never actually waited on a baby to make an appearance."

"What about your nephews?"

"I was still in school then, except for the last one—and I was out of town. Missed the entire thing." He felt self-conscious revealing his weaknesses. Then he thought again of his boat—the amount of care and patience he had put into it and how relationships had to be built one small act at a time—and he punted.

"It's all pretty frightening. The morning Shirley picked you up from my parents, I was so concerned about you I didn't really stop to think about this life inside of her." He stopped, searching for the right words, peeling through the layers. "I was so caught up in my own drama, I didn't take the time to take an interest in her life."

"She's a special person to me."

Travis slid out of the chair and sat on the floor in front of her so he could see into her eyes—speak directly to her without being overheard. "I can tell that, and I know…"

He stumbled, forced himself to continue. "I know she's been there for you when I haven't. All my inadequacies pale beside this, beside what's happening back there. It's a miracle, isn't it?"

Erin's eyes widened, and a small smile tugged at the corners of her mouth. More than any other moment tonight— and there had been many—it made him want to pull her into his arms and kiss her.

He stayed where he was though, forcing himself to be patient.

"Yes, it is a miracle. It's going to be a boy, you know."

"She did say something about the team building stops with this one."

"They originally thought it was a girl, but the last ultrasound confirmed he's definitely a boy."

"Another boy?" Travis jumped up, unable to sit still a moment longer. "They're sure?"

Erin laughed. "His name is Daniel. Daniel Scott."

Travis stopped mid-stride, turned, and walked to the domino table. "Did you hear that? The baby's name is Daniel Scott."

"Welcome to the group, Williams. If you showed up a little more often, you'd know these details." Homer laughed and slugged him in the arm. "By the way, I'm surprised you even received the text message. How did you get on the list?"

"He's still a part of the group, even if he's usually too good to go out with us." Elaine picked up the ribbing as she dealt the next hand of dominoes.

Travis waved them off and returned to the windows. Another boy! Shirley and Jess with another boy. He looked over at Erin and caught her watching him. Was there any chance God had such a plan for him, for them?

The idea shot his adrenaline through the roof, causing sweat to trickle down his back.

"I think I need another soda."

"You've probably had enough caffeine." Mitzi looked up from her magazine. "The last doctor who walked through here looked ready to sedate you."

"Yeah. All right. I'll grab a bottle of water." He smiled weakly at Erin.

Suddenly, he could picture her pregnant, carrying his child. The thought had the coffee in his stomach tumbling. It also had him wanting to run out and buy a ring before Russ could snatch her up.

He might be nervous, but he had no doubts anymore.

Erin Jacobs was the woman he intended to marry, the woman he wanted to have his children. All he had to do was wait until after her court date to propose.

—

Erin watched Travis walk out of the waiting room. She could not fathom what had precipitated the change in him, but there had been a change. She could read it in his eyes, sense it in the honest way he responded around her.

A baby cried somewhere and all of her group glanced up—*her* group. Even as the phrase entered her mind it brought a smile to her lips. Soon they'd have a new member, albeit a very small one. She glanced at her watch—still at least an hour before she needed to decide about picking up Josh.

Unable to sit in the chair a moment longer, she stood and walked to the large, plate glass window. The rain had finally started in earnest. It had threatened all day—pressure building in the air, thunder rumbling across the sky, an occasional spatter. All afternoon she had expected to be drenched, but the big showers had held off.

Now the rain fell in sheets. She could only see out the window by pressing her nose against it. The heaviness that had plagued the area had eased though, and perhaps that was why Daniel had chosen to make his appearance a week early.

She didn't mind enduring a storm if it brought Daniel into their midst.

"Why the smile?" Russ asked.

She turned, studied his short hair, open face, and kind eyes. He reminded her of the younger brother she'd never had. "I didn't hear you walk up. Lose the game?"

"Not likely. Girls wanted a stretch break." He slipped his hand into the back pocket of his jeans. "It's good to see you smile. I was worried about you at the movies. You seemed tired."

"I was," she admitted. "My animals were stirred up this afternoon. Probably because of this storm."

He stared out the window for a minute, obviously not looking at anything beyond the pane of glass. "I need to say something, Erin. It might not be the right time, but I'd feel better putting it out there."

He glanced around the waiting room, then turned back to her. "I can see how things are with you and Williams."

"Russ—"

"A guy can tell, and it's okay. I might give him a hard time, but Travis is all right. If he wasn't, I wouldn't do what I'm doing right now."

"What are you doing?"

"I'm telling you I understand, and your friendship is important to me. I haven't known you long, but you're a special lady. Any blockhead can see that. So don't feel awkward around me, and don't avoid me."

"Of course, I won't." Erin had an overwhelming desire to reach out and rub the top of his crew cut.

"Good." He held out a hand for her to shake, but then laughed and pulled her into a hug.

Travis found them that way. He had just walked up when the nurse stepped into the waiting room.

"Anyone here with the Smith party?"

Eleven people said "yes" at once.

The nurse blinked, consulted her clip board, then announced, "Mom and baby are doing fine. We have a healthy, eight-pound boy."

The rest of what she said was lost in the sea of cheers. Erin wouldn't have heard it anyway. She was too busy trying to fathom the look of pure joy on Travis's face and the way his eyes sought hers.

There was something there, something he was trying to tell her, and it wasn't about the Smith baby.

Forty-One

Monday afternoon Erin stood beside Travis and stared up at Judge Boultinghouse. Her terror was so great she was sure her legs would not support her.

"Steady," Travis whispered.

The judge's gavel sent a dread through her bones equal to what she'd felt when she'd received Travis's phone call that morning.

How could things have gone so wrong so quickly?

Glancing over at the table for opposing counsel, she suppressed a shudder. Her worst nightmare couldn't have conjured up the pair.

"Mr. Hammett, I have your motion here filed on behalf of Mr. Pitcher."

"Yes, Your Honor."

"Several things about this motion bother me, Mr. Hammett."

"Certainly not our intent, Your Honor."

"First and foremost, I'd like to know why your client has not attempted to contact this child since his birth, most especially since the death of Tara DeLoach—"

"I can explain." Derrick Pitcher attempted to step forward around the table, but his lawyer put out a restraining arm and stopped him.

Pitcher was dressed in khaki pants, a button-down shirt, and matching tie. The new clothes accentuated his bronzed skin, as did his recent haircut, which left a good half inch of paler skin between his tanned face and blond curls, curls that had Erin's stomach turning flips.

"I haven't asked you to explain yet, Mr. Pitcher." Judge Boultinghouse peered over her glasses at him. Her face was set in a grim line, her expression one of the few things offering Erin any measure of peace this afternoon.

The judge was no happier than Erin with this turn of events.

"One might expect a concerned father to immediately seek out his child after the death of said child's mother. We know Mr. Pitcher was aware of Tara DeLoach's death since you have conveniently provided us with the police report stating Mr. Pitcher was present at the time."

Out of the corner of her eye, Erin saw Pitcher flinch. She began to fervently pray Joshua would not spend any time with this man.

He might not live with me, Lord. But please, do not let him go with this man.

"Secondly, I would like to know why now, eight weeks after Joshua's mother was declared deceased, your client has decided to show up and petition this court for custody rights, something he relinquished over eight months ago—another document you kindly supplied to this court."

The judge removed her glasses and sat back in her chair. "Well, go ahead. Explain why you'd expect to have any rights before this court."

"Yes, Your Honor—" Mr. Hammett straightened his tie, but stopped speaking when he noticed the judge shaking her head.

"Not you." She pointed with her glasses at Pitcher. "You."

The man bobbed his head like a kid listening to rock music. "Good questions, and I'm glad you asked them. About Tara, now that was an accident, Judge. The detective said so. I felt real bad about what happened, but we'd been divorced for some time. I was surprised she even came by to see me that day."

Pitcher glanced at his attorney as if to see how he was doing. The attorney refused to meet his gaze and busied himself studying the folder on the table in front of him. "And I would have come to check on the kid—er, little Joshua—but Tara told me she'd adopted him out. I didn't know he was still in the state until I saw it on the television."

"You mean until you heard about the money."

Pitcher reddened, but he didn't rise to the bait. "Then I did try to get here as fast as I could, but I had to put my affairs in order. I wanted to be able to stay in Livingston as long as this takes."

He offered no more explanation.

As Judge Boultinghouse studied him, Erin listened to the seconds tick on the large clock at the back of the room.

Listened to her and Josh's life hang in the balance.

Finally, the judge put her glasses back on and sat up straighter in her chair.

Erin felt Travis stiffen beside her.

"I am not approving your motion to postpone the ruling on Joshua's placement. We will go ahead with the hearing date two weeks from Wednesday. Between now and then I'm authorizing supervised visits once a week with Mr. Williams."

Erin heard the words and felt them slice through her like a knife.

Travis's hand closed around her arm and somehow she remained standing.

"As to your parental claims, I'll review those during the intervening time. Mr. Williams, I'll need this strange turn of events to be reflected in your final report."

"Of course, Judge."

"That's all."

The gavel sounded again, but Erin barely heard it this time. She needed to be at Evelyn's, to hold Joshua this minute and every minute she could.

How many minutes were there in two weeks?

Turning to leave, her eyes caught the gaze of Derrick Pitcher and a shiver danced down her spine. A smile split his face, and he nodded her way.

Didn't he realize he was tearing her world apart?

Somehow she made it out the door, down the steps, and across the street. Travis pulled her into the diner at the corner. After the waitress poured two cups of coffee, he shoved one into her hands.

—

"Give us two pieces of chocolate pie, Sally."

When the waitress had left, he reached across the table and covered Erin's hands with his own. They were ice cold.

"Drink the coffee, Erin."

She raised her eyes to his, those beautiful brown eyes, swimming in tears.

"Sweetheart, it's going to be okay."

"How do you know?"

"I have faith."

Erin's reply was so quiet, he had to lean forward. "I do too."

They sat without talking until the waitress returned with two large pieces of chocolate pie and an expression that said she knew who Erin was.

"I know you have faith, and I can assure you the judge was not happy with those two. I can promise you that." Travis leaned back and studied his pie. "I've been in Boultinghouse's court for five years. When she takes that look and tone, watch out."

Picking up her fork, Erin stabbed at her pie, but didn't eat it. "Travis, she said he could see Joshua."

"With me. You trust me, don't you?"

"Yes, but—"

"Erin, this is like a seventh-inning stretch."

She looked up at him, confusion clouding her expression. It was an improvement over the tears.

"Sometimes, in the seventh inning, strange things happen. Things you'd never expect at the beginning of a game. You keep your head in the game, stay focused, and trust your coach."

Erin smacked him with her fork.

"Ouch!"

"This isn't a baseball game. We're talking about Joshua." She took a bite of pie, then washed it down with a gulp of coffee. "Pitcher does not deserve that child. He abandoned his own baby—*if* Joshua is his baby. And who knows how Tara really died."

Each phrase was punctuated with another stab into the pie, which somehow disappeared as she laid out her argument.

"Tara DeLoach was terrified when she called me. Of course, Pitcher knew she was coming to see him. There was a reason she didn't take Joshua with her—a reason she kept that sweet baby away from that despicable man. And now he wants custody? After all this time and after Mrs. DeLoach has left the bulk of her estate to Josh? Ha! Some coincidence."

Travis sat back in the booth. Could God have given him a more beautiful woman?

"*What* are you smiling about?"

"I was just thinking that with Judge Boultinghouse being an intelligent woman—like you—she'll probably come to the same conclusion."

Forty-Two

Erin drove steadily toward the ARK, barely seeing the road out of Livingston. As so often happened over the last two weeks, her mind wandered past what she was seeing. This time she was back in the hospital, back to the night when Daniel had been born.

She still didn't know what Travis had wanted to say to her. The evening had turned into a crazy blend of celebration, prayer, and mad dashes to the gift shop to purchase balloons, flowers, and teddy bears.

Looking out her windshield, she barely saw the passing trees. Instead, she saw Travis standing at the nursery window, a look of wonder blanketing his face.

Travis searching for her, a promise in his eyes.

Travis.

Everywhere she looked these days she saw Travis.

He'd been in the courtroom that terrible Monday afternoon.

Twice he'd picked up Joshua and taken him to Pitcher, taking a slice of her heart with him.

Both times he'd safely brought Joshua back to her.

He'd been at each Sunday morning worship service, and, of course, her final home visit.

Each time he'd been open, pleasant, careful to stand or sit near her, and acted for all the world like a man on the verge of something big.

What though? He treated her as if she were made of precious glass, but he didn't call except to confirm the hearing date was this coming Wednesday.

She released the wheel and wiped her hands against her jeans.

Each time she picked up Joshua, held him close, she was reminded that his future rested in someone else's hands.

Correction, his future rested in God's hands. The truth hit with the strength of a kick from the mare she'd owned as a teen.

Joshua's future rested in God's hands.

Her future rested in God's hands.

And she could trust in God's grace.

She relaxed her hands on the wheel, forcing deep breaths into her lungs. Reached for the radio to turn up the music. She'd be back at the ARK in fifteen minutes. Joshua had been with her teenage sitter all afternoon, and she was ready to spend some time with him. Maybe she could get there in time to play with him in the backyard before complete darkness fell.

Looking out the side window to judge whether she could beat the sunset, she noticed a glow in the eastern sky and thought for a moment she'd managed to turn herself around.

But no, she hadn't.

The glow came from Cameron's farm.

Her heart tripped into an adrenaline fueled rhythm even as she pushed the old truck to its top speed, which wasn't so terribly fast. Hopefully, it would be fast enough.

Cameron owned a horse stable.

Had anyone taken the animals out?

She pulled her bag across the cab seat, fished her phone from it, and dialed the emergency number.

"Livingston Police Department. State the nature of your emergency, please."

"Alice, this is Erin. I'm on County Road 351, and I'm seeing fire to the east. Looks like it's coming from Cameron's place."

"Roger that, Erin. We have fire and rescue dispatched to the scene."

"Has he released his horses?"

"Cameron didn't call it in. My log shows a neighbor noticed the flames."

"My ETA is four minutes. Would you tell whoever's on scene that I want access to those corrals?"

"I'll pass it on."

"Thank you."

Erin was about to disconnect when she realized Alice was still talking. "Be careful, Erin. The chatter is that fire is especially hot. Lots of fertilizer stored in the barn."

"Got it."

She disconnected. Tossed the phone into her bag and rounded the corner to Cameron's place.

The scene that greeted her was straight out of hell.

Erin thought of Joshua and all he meant to her. She also knew this was what she'd been trained to do. She slammed the truck into park, grabbed the bag behind her seat, and ran toward the burning structures.

—

Travis was returning from Huntsville when he received the call from James.

"I just heard this from Angela, who caught it on the police scanner she watches on her computer."

"It's against protocol to—"

"Listen! There's a fire at Cameron Stoke's place out on 351. Angela heard the fire department dispatched out there twenty minutes ago."

"Why—"

"Then five minutes ago she heard Erin call in and ask if anyone had rescued the horses."

Travis felt his heart stop, literally stop beating in his chest. It was a curious sensation. He counted—one, two, three, four seconds—and then he felt it beat again. The car behind him honked and swerved since he'd forgotten to press the gas pedal.

He checked his rearview mirror and completed a U-turn in the middle of the county road.

"You're telling me Erin's out there?"

"I thought you'd want to know."

Travis disconnected the phone, floored the Blazer, and prayed.

It took him twelve minutes to reach the stables.

Twelve minutes, and by then the barn roofs had caved in. Three of Livingston's fire trucks were there, and plenty of cars were lined up with people gawking.

He searched for Erin's truck, spotted it with the door still open.

No auburn hair in the crowd.

No Erin standing on the sideline.

He pushed his way to the front and crossed over the tape they'd set up to keep everyone back.

Dan Baker looked up in surprise, a clipboard in one hand, a walkie-talkie in the other. "You need to stay behind—"

"Is Erin in there?"

"I need you to stay on the other side of that tape. This area is volatile."

A small explosion sounded from the southwest corner of the structure. Dan spoke into his handheld set and began to move away.

Travis reached out and grabbed him by the arm.

"Is she in there?"

Dan stopped and looked him in the eye.

"I tried to stop her, but there were horses trapped in the back."

"How long?"

"Fifteen minutes ago. I gave her a suit, tried to give her a walkie, but she took off—"

Travis began to run, but Dan tackled him.

"You can't go back there. No one else goes back there until these buildings are stabilized."

Travis looked at this man he'd known all his life, respected all his life, and knew he'd deck him if he had to in order to go after Erin. The realization hit him at the same moment a gasp rippled through the crowd.

They both turned and saw a slight figure walking through the smoke. She was leading a horse with each hand. Each horse had its head covered with a blanket.

Nothing could have stopped him.

He ran to her, took one of the reins, then wrapped his arms around her.

"I was so afraid." He spoke into her hair, which smelled of smoke and dirt, fear and exhaustion. "Are you okay?"

"I think so. Maybe a couple of scrapes." She began to cough, and he wouldn't, couldn't let her go. "Help me with these two?"

"Tell me what they need."

"Water, drops. I'll show you."

Together they doctored the animals first, and that shouldn't have surprised him. It was a good hour before he convinced her to see the paramedics.

"How many were there?"

"Six. I managed to get the other four out the back, but these two were too scared."

"So you covered them up and walked them out." He stared at her as the medic checked her vitals.

"It was all I could think of to do. Anyone know where Cameron is?"

"Out of town. Dan has managed to contact him. He'll be back tonight."

He wanted to rage.

Wanted to scream and holler that a horse wasn't a fraction as important as she was.

Wanted to tell her she'd stopped—literally stopped—his heart from beating. Instead, he waited until the medic nodded, but he couldn't wait until he left.

He pulled Erin into his arms, and he kissed her like he'd wanted to for what seemed like forever. When he was done he whispered those words that had been lodged in his throat for too long.

"I love you, Erin Jacobs."

He didn't know if her tears were from happiness or smoke inhalation, but he was going to hope for the former. Clasping her hand in his, he walked her to her truck.

Forty-Three

Erin accepted Daniel when Shirley handed her the infant. She couldn't resist the urge to pull his tiny hand from the blanket and lightly stroke his pink fingers. "He's so perfect. I can't believe he's two weeks old already."

"I know. Seems we were just rushing out of here."

"I wish you could have been in the waiting room. It was absolute pandemonium. Travis acted as if—" Erin smiled at the memory, but the aches of the past few weeks were too much. The smile felt stretched, sore. She allowed it to slip away and focused on the miracle in her lap instead and waited for the tears blurring her vision to clear.

Shirley handed Josh one of his toys from the diaper bag. He was lying on a quilt in the middle of the living room, as comfortable in Shirley's home as he was in his own. Banging the toy on the floor, he grinned.

Both women clapped and cheered.

"He reminds me of Bam Bam some days."

"Your sanity is about to end. He'll be crawling before

you know it, then the world is his."

"Our hearing is Wednesday," Erin said softly.

"I know it is. I've been praying. We've all been praying. You don't have any doubts about Travis's recommendation, do you?"

"No, but the ruling rests with the judge." Erin reached out and ran her fingertip softly over Daniel's fine red hair.

"And Pitcher?"

"Travis is picking up Joshua this afternoon for his final supervised visit."

Silence stretched between them as they both considered the ramifications of Joshua's father still being in town.

"What were you about to say before? How did Travis act when I was in labor?"

Erin laughed, but the sound hurt her throat. "As if he were waiting for his own child to be born. It was the first time he was," she searched for the word "*normal* with me in a long time."

"What happened between you two?"

Erin's head snapped up, and after a heartbeat she continued. "I'm not supposed to talk about it." Shaking her head, she tucked Daniel's hands back under the baby blanket.

"Humph. I don't like rules, especially ones that put walls between friends." Erin started to protest, but Shirley forged on. "I've liked having you back. I missed Dana when she moved away, and then you closed yourself up in the ARK."

She worked her fingers through her bright red hair, and Erin couldn't help smiling to think how much Daniel already looked like his mother with his little strands of red hair, couldn't help finding joy in spite of their conversation.

Her stomach was doing somersaults, but Shirley could

make her smile just by the way she worried over her. That, too, was something Travis had given her—her friends back. It was impossible for her to hold any anger against him.

"Sure, I had the rest of the group at the church," Shirley continued. "And other folks from our high school class, but I missed you. Now I see you're hurting—and yes, I know you try to hide it—but Erin, I don't know how to pray for you if you can't share with me."

Erin shifted Daniel to the crook of her arm and settled back into the corner of the couch. "It's not like a rule. It's more something we both agreed on when I was sick. And we didn't actually *say* we wouldn't talk to anyone, we only agreed it would be best kept between the two of us."

"For how long?"

"At least until after the hearing, but more likely until after the adoption is finalized. Probably a year."

Shirley stood, went into the kitchen, and came back with two mugs of warm tea. "That's a long time to carry something alone, especially when that something is the fact Travis Williams is in love with you."

This time Erin's mouth fell all the way open, and she didn't shut it.

"Put a cookie in your mouth. It'll help with the shock." Shirley sat back with her own mug and cookie and grinned at her. "You really think we didn't know?"

"Who is *we*?" The question pitched up at the end, the same way her world was somersaulting. She clung to Daniel, suddenly afraid she might drop him.

"I would think the entire town, but maybe I'm exaggerating." Shirley set her mug down and moved closer on the couch. "Relax, sweetie. There hasn't been a feature in the paper, but it seems so obvious. Someone would have to be blind to be around you two for five minutes and not notice."

"But…" Erin swallowed and tried to think what they had done wrong. "I've followed his rules."

"There you go with that word again." Shirley's eyebrows shot up to the top of her hair line. "I think I better take Daniel. You're looking a bit pale. Drink your tea. Rules? Seriously? You have never been one to follow anyone's rules very well, Erin Jacobs. You've always gone by your own playbook, to use a man's analogy, and don't look like you're going to argue with me. The ARK is a perfect example. Anyone else would have joined an established vet clinic like Doc asked you to do when you came back to town."

"It hasn't been easy," Erin admitted.

"Why don't you start at the beginning?"

Erin thought back to that night in her home, the night he'd come to help her with the animals, the night after she'd stayed with his parents.

"I knew I was falling in love with him," she began, picking up her mug but not drinking. The warmth seeping through the ceramic emboldened her. She looked up at Shirley, smiled, but the memories she'd tried to bury were stirring deep within her. "When I was so sick with the flu, Travis took me to his parents' home."

"I remember. I wish you had called me."

"You had your hands full. Plus I did call you to take me home."

"I remember how upset he was that morning." Shirley sat back, slipped Daniel to her shoulder, and rubbed his back in slow, gentle circles. "He tried to talk me out of taking you back to the ARK."

Erin sipped the tea and let the sweet taste bring back the memories of those days. "Something happened while I was sick."

"It helps when a man drives up in a monster truck, wades through flood waters, and rescues you." Shirley reached for another cookie, but chose a strawberry off the tray instead. "Did he kiss you?"

"Oh, yeah." Erin felt the blush in her face rising. "Why do I feel like I'm in high school?"

"Because we're acting like we're in high school. Keep talking."

"While I was at Barbara's, I had—I guess you'd call it a spiritual experience. Sounds odd, but I don't know how else to explain it. I suddenly understood I'd been running from God."

"I knew something had happened. That's why you started coming back to church."

"It's part of the reason." Erin set the mug down, picked up the throw pillow instead, and hugged it to her chest. "The first time Travis kissed me was at his parents, and I think it frightened both of us."

"Why, Erin? You make such a wonderful couple."

"It's complicated though. Travis is my caseworker." She paused and allowed the full implications of that to sink in and knew when they had by the shift in expressions on Shirley's face.

"Couldn't they switch your case to someone else?"

"He asked, but his director denied his request. So after you took me back home, Travis came by to help and stayed for dinner. I told him I realized God had a plan for my life, for Joshua's life, and it might include him."

"Holy cow. Did he run out the front door?"

Erin laughed for the first time since she'd walked in, and it helped to put some perspective on the scene she'd kept buried in her heart for so long. "He did act as if I'd branded him with a hot iron, now that you mention it."

"Did you ask him to marry you?" Shirley's grin had turned mischievous.

"Are you crazy?"

Joshua let out a hoot at just that moment, and both women started laughing.

"Anyway, after he paced a trail in my living room, he told me how much he cared about me, but he didn't say he loved me."

"It's so obvious."

Erin stopped and stared at her dubiously.

"Erin, I wish I had a video of every time you two are in the same room. It's as if he's a moon gravitating around you."

"He's so formal around me!" Erin's voice grew as her frustration vented itself. Baby Daniel squirmed in his mother's arms, and Erin lowered her voice. "If he shows up at the ARK, he makes sure there's someone else there so we won't be caught alone."

"Which you asked him to do."

"True, but he acts as if he's afraid I'm contagious."

"Honey, the way that man looks at you, he is saying it all with his eyes. I bet you know the second he arrives in a room, even with a dozen people there."

"Yeah, I do. It's very strange."

"Um-hmm. He doesn't have to *talk* to you to focus all

his attention on you."

"Well, I don't understand. I mean I've felt some of what you're describing, but I don't know. Some days I think I've imagined the entire thing, including the way Travis might feel about me." The tears pricked her eyes again as she shared her biggest fear. "Then the afternoon of Cameron's fire he kissed me in front of the medic."

"I bet he was terrified you'd been hurt."

"And he told me he loved me—but maybe he meant he loved me, you know, like a sister."

"Did he kiss you like a sister?"

Erin shook her head, lost in the memory.

Shirley adjusted Daniel in her arms and stroked his cheek with her fingertip. "Every woman has trouble learning to trust her intuition. I think God gives it to us for a reason though, maybe for times like this. You know how Travis feels about you, even if he can't show it right now, and you're definitely not imagining it."

"That night at my house he gave me a second round of lectures about his job, and I felt so bad for the guy. He looked like he was struggling with the responsibility of a dozen men, carrying more than the responsibility of Noah's ARK." Erin smiled as she shared the image that had crossed her mind so often in the last weeks—Travis carrying the burden of Noah's ARK, of her ARK on his shoulders.

"So his great plan was…"

"His plan was for us to see each other only in a professional capacity so that we not jeopardize Joshua's adoption in any way."

"Sensible."

"Exactly. And I was to continue re-establishing my

social network by involving myself in the community or church groups."

"He asked you to date?" Shirley's voice rose in the "I'll-take-you-on" tone Erin recognized from her debate team wins in high school.

"I don't remember him putting it that way."

Shirley stood and moved Daniel to his bassinet between the living room and the kitchen. When she turned to face her, Erin felt like a fox caught in a trap. "He asked you to date! He told you something like you needed to be sure of your feelings, and if they were real you'd still care about him when this six-month period or year or whatever timeframe he set expired."

Erin could only stare at her friend. Finally, Shirley plopped down beside her on the couch, reached out, and tucked some of the curls behind her ear. "Sweetie, it doesn't take a genius to figure out the mind of Travis Williams."

"Are you sure you don't have my living room bugged?"

"Hardly. Now I know why you've broken two hearts in our group."

"Not true and you know it." Erin scrunched down into the couch, enjoying the feel of Shirley's hand on the top of her head. She'd missed the physical contact of friends. She didn't want to go back to being alone again. The thought hit her with the clarity of a well-placed arrow.

"They're all nice guys," Shirley murmured.

"But not the right guy."

"No." They sat that way for another moment. Finally, Shirley broke the silence. "So what are you going to do? Wait him out?"

"I honestly don't know. I was prepared to, but suddenly

I feel itchy, as if something is about to change."

"Like what?"

"I have no idea. I have a lot of questions. I wonder how he can stand to be apart when we're only a few miles away. Even when we're together he acts unerringly polite. Then when we're in a group, I can feel him watching me. It stirs up my emotions."

"That's a lot for a young mom to handle."

"Don't I know it. I've realized how hard it is being alone, running the ARK and taking care of Josh. Don't get me wrong. I wouldn't change anything for the world, but I understand the challenges I'm taking on, and it is lonely out there. I was never lonely before."

Shirley reached out and clasped her hand. "You know you can call me anytime."

"I know." Erin brushed away her tears. "That's not all though. I keep praying, and then last night I spoke with Dana and Ben again."

"They're coming for the hearing?"

Erin nodded and ran her hand over the seams of the pillow she still clutched. "They fly in tomorrow and want to talk to me about something, but Dana wouldn't say what. She wanted to discuss it in person."

Shirley sighed, then moved to collect the mugs and cookies as Erin picked up Josh's toys. "Whatever it is, we'll pray and trust that God already knows the problems and the solution."

"What do we pray for though?"

"Wisdom. Let's start by asking for wisdom, for you and Mr. Travis Williams."

Forty-Four

Travis gazed across the courtroom at Erin. Hard to believe it was the same woman he had nearly knocked off the porch three months ago. She was fussing with Joshua. He could see his chubby hands reach up to grab her earrings. Something in Travis's heart tightened at the sight of the two of them together.

He suddenly needed to speak with her, needed at least to catch her eye, but the hearing was about to begin. She didn't give any inclination she noticed his presence on the other side of the courtroom.

How could she not? For Travis it was as if the room centered around her instead of around the judge's bench.

She wore a trim fitting black dress, and her hair had been styled with some sort of gel women used to tame curls. It made her look sophisticated. The entire image had him squirming in his suit. He preferred the woman he had first met—the one in her ridiculous men's work clothes with hair askew.

He preferred her in his arms.

He pushed the thought away and looked down at his case notes. Everything appeared in order. He would, of course, recommend placement. The fact that Erin and Joshua would remain in Livingston was an added bonus. Annual follow-ups always made the court more comfortable about permanent placement.

Derrick Pitcher was nowhere in sight.

No doubt the man was back on his yacht—or whatever boat he could buy with the money he had left. Technically, Travis shouldn't have left the folder detailing Joshua's trust fund—clearly labeled and placed on top of his workbag—on the park bench where the man might have looked through it. When Pitcher steadfastly refused to change the child's dirty diaper, or even hold the boy, Travis had gone to the park's restroom to do it.

He'd suspected Pitcher would disappear once he'd read the details of Mrs. DeLoach's will—and the man did not disappoint. He'd even left the sheet on top detailing that none of the money would be released until Josh turned twenty-five.

His absence this morning proved Travis's suspicion about his greed was correct.

The doors to the courtroom opened, and Travis turned to see who had arrived. Erin's attorney already stood beside her table, and he certainly wasn't expecting any witnesses.

The couple at the back of the room only had eyes for Erin. The woman was striking—tall, beautiful, with a bearing and gaze that spoke of law enforcement. The hair gave her away. Shoulder length and straight, there was an amber cast to it perfectly matching Erin's. He swiveled his head from

Erin and back to the couple again, noticing the similarities in the women's profiles. More than that was the warmth in their gaze, the way they hurried toward each other.

Travis understood immediately. The taller woman was Dana, Erin's sister. Which meant the man with her was Ben. Suddenly, the man turned, and their gazes locked. Something passed between them, an understanding that startled him.

Then the bailiff proclaimed, "All rise," and he forced his attention to the front of the court.

"I'm happy to report Mr. Pitcher has withdrawn his petitions from this court. For what it's worth and any future bearing on this case, I want entered into the record that I found Mr. Pitcher has no paternal rights in the case of Baby Joshua, also known as Joshua DeLoach. Mr. Pitcher relinquished those rights legally before the child was born and that ruling stands. Now to move on with the original petition..."

Fifteen minutes later, he was on the stand, looking down at Erin who sat twenty feet away, and making his recommendation to the judge.

"I believe the best placement for Joshua is with Miss Jacobs."

"Thank you, Mr. Williams. Does counsel have any other questions or concerns?"

"Actually we do, Your Honor."

Travis glanced to the back of the room as the oak doors again opened and Director Moring stepped through and silently took a seat.

"My client was, of course, aware of Mr. Williams's recommendation before today, as was this court. However, her circumstances have changed in the last twenty-four hours and we would like to petition the court for permission to move with the child out of state after the initial ninety days, pending approval by this court of that initial assessment period."

Travis heard the discussion going on around him, tried to make sense of the conversation, but failed. All he could do was gaze at Erin's face, at her eyes which were now locked with his, at her expression which seemed to want to tell him something. Had her attorney said *out of state*?

"I don't see any problems with that, counsel. Mr. Williams has made it quite clear Ms. Jacobs has proven herself an acceptable guardian for Joshua. It's not in this court's purview to decide where a parent and child should reside. Mr. Williams, if you have nothing to add, I'll consider this matter closed."

Travis swallowed, tried to process what he'd heard, and swallowed again. He sat up straighter in the witness chair and pulled at his tie, which now seemed uncomfortably tight.

"Mr. Williams?"

"I'd like to request a brief recess to confer with Miss Jacobs, Your Honor."

"For what purpose?"

Erin's sister leaned forward from the second row, whispered something in her ear, but Erin shook her head and raised Joshua to her shoulder.

"For what purpose, Mr. Williams?"

"Your Honor, I wasn't aware of any request to move Joshua out of state."

"Understood. However, unless your opinion of Miss Jacobs has somehow changed in the last four minutes, I fail to see what bearing that has on your recommendation."

Travis squirmed again in his seat, tried to find any reason to justify a recess, and failed.

He turned and met the judge's inquisitive stare.

"Five minutes, Your Honor."

She removed her glasses before answering. "All right. This court is adjourned and will meet back in five minutes then."

The gavel fell heavily, leaving Travis with the feeling of a door closing—one he might not have the power to open again.

———

Erin passed Joshua to her sister as Travis walked toward her. She knew what was coming, understood she owed him an explanation, and though she would prefer to hide behind her son she had never considered herself a coward.

Given they had five minutes, Travis didn't introduce himself to Dana or Ben. He leaned down and whispered into Erin's ear, "We need to talk."

She didn't resist as he grasped her elbow and pulled her toward a door at the side of the courtroom.

When they'd entered the room, when the door had clicked shut, she couldn't bring herself to turn and look into the eyes of the man she loved. Instead, she walked to the window and stared out at the bright December morning.

It should have been overcast.

The weather ought to have known her heart was breaking.

Steeling herself for what lay ahead, she folded her arms across her waist and grasped her elbows as if she might be able to hold herself together for a few minutes.

Then she sensed him behind her.

"What are you doing, Erin?"

"Dana and Ben arrived last night." The words tumbled out of her mouth. The explanation she had rehearsed while she lay in bed convincing herself this was the best path for her and Joshua. "You were right, Travis. I can't do this alone. I need family. I need…"

Tears threatened to consume her. She clutched her arms more tightly and tried to still the shaking before it caused her to fly apart.

"I need someone, and I tried. I couldn't though. There wasn't…" The tears tracked down her cheeks, but she didn't dare wipe them away—couldn't release her hold on herself.

Travis was standing behind her now, so close she could feel his breath against her hair. "I'm moving to New Mexico to be with Dana and Ben. They'll help me with Josh. Be my support system. You said I needed support."

His hands on her arms, gentle as the breeze outside the window, stopped her. Erin closed her eyes and savored his touch even though it hurt like a knife slicing through her heart. This would be the last time she'd be alone with him. After today chances were slim she'd see him outside his office.

A tremor started deep inside, and then she didn't think she could stand.

He turned her in one fluid motion and framed her face with his hands. "Why?"

"I told you, Dana and Ben—"

"Why are you doing this, Erin?"

She looked at his tie, his shoulder, anywhere but in those eyes that meant the world to her.

"Look at me, sweetheart." He choked on the word, and her eyes flew to his. "It's because of me, isn't it? Because I've been too stupid to tell you how much I love you."

"You—"

"I should have listened to them, but I was worried about procedures and rules."

"Listened to—"

"And now you're going to leave and take Joshua. The two people I care about the most in this world are going to walk away in—" his gaze flew to the clock on the wall, "in one minute and I have only myself to blame."

She stared at him, too shocked to believe the words he'd uttered, too afraid to move.

Suddenly, the door to the room flew open and the bailiff stepped in. "The judge is ready to reconvene."

"Tell the judge I'm proposing. Ask for five more minutes."

The bailiff's eyebrows went to the top of his snow-white hair, but he recovered quickly. "That I can do, Mr. Williams."

"You're proposing?" Erin gasped.

Travis let go of her face, clasped her hand, and knelt down next to the client-attorney table. "Erin Jacobs, will you marry me? I realize I've been a fool, but I believe God intends for us to spend our lives together—all three of us. If you and Joshua will have me, I vow to do my best to love and cherish you."

Erin covered her mouth with her free hand, unsure if she was going to laugh hysterically or cry. She looked down into Travis's face and asked the question pinging around in her head. "What about your job?"

"I can find another job, but I'll never find another you. I realized that ten minutes ago when you told the judge you intended to move."

"But…"

"Do you love me, Erin?"

"Yes." The truth was something she'd accepted long ago.

"If you need to move to New Mexico, then we'll move. We can work all that out later, but right now, I think we better go talk to the judge." He touched his lips to her hand, stood, and kissed her lips gently, then more thoroughly.

Which was how the bailiff found them when he reentered the room.

Forty-Five

Travis watched Erin walk down the aisle of their church and realized dreams do come true.

He'd prayed many times that Erin would feel comfortable returning to God's house.

He hadn't realized it would be as his bride.

Ben smiled as he handed her over, and Travis stood a little taller remembering the talk they'd had the night before. Ben Marshall was more than Erin's brother-in-law. He also considered himself to be Erin's father in the absence of her own. He'd be watching to make sure Travis cared for Erin in the ways God expected.

He'd gone on to offer advice in case Travis needed anyone to talk with about the intricacies of being a new husband. Since Ben only had a six-month head start on him, Travis found that more than a little amusing, but the man's heart was in the right place.

The girls had cared for each other a long time, even from a distance. Though Travis and Erin had decided to stay in

Livingston for at least a year, he'd see to it Erin visited Dana in New Mexico as often as possible.

In what seemed like an impossibly short time, the minister was requesting the rings, and Travis was looking down into Erin's sweet face.

Finally, Reverend Perry said the words he'd been waiting for, and Travis lifted Erin's simple white veil. When he did, he used his thumbs to wipe away the tears glistening on her cheeks. The smile on her face told him they were tears of joy as did the quick glance at Joshua who waited on the front row in Dana's arms.

"I love you, Erin. I have since the first day I saw you." Then he was kissing her, lost in the promise of their lives together. He would have been happy to remain there, but a spattering of laughter brought them back.

"I forgot they were here," he growled softly as he pulled away.

In response, she reached up, pulled his head gently back down, and kissed him again.

The applause mingled with the flash of a few cameras. Then the minister said those words Travis never dared believe he'd hear. "I now present to you Mr. and Mrs. Travis Williams."

—

Erin looked out at the small gathering of people—small, but precious to her—and thanked God for the changes he'd brought into her life.

As she walked to the back of the church, Evelyn engulfed her in a hug as Doc pumped Travis's hand.

"Hard to believe this all started with one phone call," Evelyn sniffled. "I said I wouldn't cry."

"You always cry at weddings, honey. Here, use my handkerchief." Doc pulled the white linen square from his pocket as he hugged Erin close. "Your mother would be so proud."

"Thank you, Doc." Erin didn't even try to stop the tears.

"You ladies are going to have to share. I only brought one." Doc's eyes twinkled good- naturedly, but Ben came to the rescue.

Soon Erin felt herself being passed from one set of arms to another, including into the loving arms of her in-laws.

"I knew you and Joshua belonged in our family," George declared.

"He did tell me as much—months ago." Barbara beamed as she embraced the newest additions to her family.

For Erin, it was hard to dwell on who was missing when so many people had been added to her life.

The next hour passed too quickly and was a blur of cake, punch, and gifts, including a very strange piece of pottery from Barbados.

"It's a dog," Ben explained.

"I know what it is, Ben."

Dana stared at the four-foot piece of pottery, and Erin wondered what she would do with it.

"We can use it as a hat rack, honey." Travis circled his arm around her waist. "You can have the right ear. I can have the left."

"See? I knew you'd love it. I didn't know it would be a wedding present." Ben and Travis high-fived, as Erin crouched down and allowed Shirley to take her picture with the unique *gift.*

When she finally collapsed into a chair beside Dana and pulled Joshua onto her lap, she buried her face into his curly hair.

"You'll only be gone a week," Dana pointed out, tucking her straight hair behind her ear. "The Caribbean is beautiful, and you two need some private time."

"A week sounds like forever though. We could probably buy an extra airline ticket."

"Oh, no you don't. I want to spend some time with my nephew." Dana used her older sister voice, and they both started laughing, heads together, Joshua clasped between them.

"Six months ago, when I saw you and Ben married, I didn't think it would ever happen to me. I didn't think I deserved the kind of happiness you two had."

"God has a special plan for each of us, Erin. He promises us that—hope and a future." Dana reached out and touched her face.

"I know. I know that now, but I doubted it for a long time."

Dana nodded, and Erin smiled as Joshua reached for her veil.

Erin's gaze drifted to Travis and Director Moring.

"Who's Travis talking with now?"

"Director Moring. He was sure he'd have to resign after what happened in court that day."

"And because you were a case of his."

"Right." Erin smiled, a blush painting her cheeks. "Director Moring said it was a wonder it had taken him so long to figure it out and that he should have done something sooner."

"So he'll keep his job here?"

"Yes, and I'll keep working with the ARK. He wants me to go back to school, but with Joshua and the animals my life feels pretty satisfying right now."

"Not to mention your husband." Dana nudged her. "Speaking of which, he's looking for you. I think it's time for you to go."

Erin stood, holding on to Joshua, hugging him one last time. She turned to Dana to pass the baby to her, but before she could she felt her husband's strong arms around her.

"The two people I happened to be looking for."

She turned in his arms, smiled up at him, and he enclosed them in a circle of warmth and love.

Joshua laughed and reached up for Travis's tie, pulling and unloosening it. Travis kissed his hand, then kissed Erin's lips.

And she knew in that moment that trusting God's grace had been exactly the right thing to do.

The End

Discussion Questions

1. Erin tells Travis "When I give my word, I keep it. It matters to me that I honor my promises." Sometimes that's a difficult thing to do. What does the Bible say about honoring our commitments? Try reading Psalm 119. How does that scripture apply to this topic?

2. Doc reminds Erin to "Lay it down… You can't carry every burden, and you needn't worry about every outcome. Let the good Lord do that." Do you agree? Should we worry over problems in our lives? Why or why not? Back up your answer with a specific verse from the Bible.

3. Erin realizes that "Shirley would be there for her if she'd just let herself open up, but opening up was hard." Why is it so hard to let our guards down around people? What can we do to be more genuine—whether it's helping someone else or allowing others to help us?

4. Travis tells Erin that "every person needs a safety net of friends and family." Do you agree or disagree with this statement? Why or why not? How are we, as Christians, called to be that safety net for one another?

5. When Erin wakes even more sick than when she went to bed, she has the thought that "she hated her weakness." We are all weak, at one time or another. Matthew 11:28

says "Come to me, all you who are weary and burdened, and I will give you rest." How can God give us rest? In what ways can He ease our burdens?

6. The word *grace* is found in the Bible over 120 times. When Erin finally releases her burdens to God, she embraces that grace we are all offered. Find at least five verses with the word *grace* and discuss their meaning.

7. Erin finally gives God credit for the turns that her life has taken. We learn more about her past and see how it has affected her future. What about your life? Think of a turn that God has orchestrated and how it affected you and those you love. Share that turn with someone else.

8. Erin finally accepts that Joshua's future rests in God's hand, not man's. That's a difficult thing to do, especially in regard to our children. Read Isaiah 41:13. How does it relate to this idea of trusting those we love to our heavenly father?

Author's Note

This book is dedicated to those who serve in the Department of Family and Protective Services as well as those who dedicate their time and resources to animal shelters across our country. These individuals deserve our gratitude and support—both emotional, financial, and spiritual.

According to Hope International, 5,760 children become orphans each day worldwide. There are approximately 120,000 adoptions in the United States each year.

Over 13,000 community animal shelters nationwide place 27 million shelter animals in homes. We have our local animal shelter to thank for bringing our Labrador, Phoebe, into our family. She has given us much joy and is a blessing even when she wakes us at five a.m.

I'd like to thank the folks who have helped this project see the light of day. My pre-readers—Kristy Kreymer and Janet Murphy. A special thanks to Barbara Scott for editing this project and to Ken Raney for the cover. Cait Peterson did the formatting, and her help was invaluable. A special thanks to all of the readers who purchased copies of *Hidden* and clamored for more. I alsoowe much gratitude to my mom. She was a single mom living in Los Angeles, when she met a social worker who would change her life—my father. This story was inspired by their relationship and marriage of thirty-two years.

I have visited the area of Livingston, Texas; however, I have never held a job within the foster care system. Although my research was thorough, I have taken creative license for the purpose of my story. Any errors are my own.

And finally … *always giving thanks to God the Father for everything, in the name of our Lord Jesus Christ* (Ephesians 5:20).

Blessings,
Vannetta

Also by Vannetta Chapman

Jacobs Family Series
Hidden (Book 1)

Shisphewana Amish Mystery Series
Falling to Pieces (Book 1)
A Perfect Square (Book 2)
Material Witness (Book 3)

Amish Village Mystery Series
Murder Simply Brewed (Book 1)
Murder Tightly Knit (Book 2)

Pebble Creek Series
Home to Pebble Creek (free ebook short story)
A Promise for Miriam (Book 1)
A Home for Lydia (Book 2)
A Wedding for Julia (Book 3)
Christmas at Pebble Creek (free ebook short story)

Shorter Novels
A Simple Amish Christmas (Book 1)
The Christmas Quilt (Book 2)

Novellas
Where Healing Blooms, from the collection *An Amish Garden*
Unexpected Blessings, from the collection *An Amish Cradle*

Made in the USA
Monee, IL
20 March 2021

63392475R00213